RICHARD D ROSS

The Hybrid Enemy

A James Macrae Thriller – Book 1

First published by Steel Door Publishing, Toronto, Canada 2021

This novel is entirely a work of fiction. The names, characters and incidents portrayed in it are the work of the author's imagination. Any resemblance to actual persons, living or dead, events or localities is entirely coincidental.

Richard D Ross has no responsibility for the persistence or accuracy of URLs for external or third-party Internet Websites referred to in this publication and does not guarantee that any content on such Websites is, or will remain, accurate or appropriate.

Real world characters are used only in a purely fictional context.

Second edition

ISBN: 978-1-7778601-0-3

This book was professionally typeset on Reedsy.
Find out more at reedsy.com

'Hybrid methods of warfare, such as propaganda, deception, sabotage and other non-military tactics have long been used to destabilise adversaries. What is new about attacks seen in recent years is their speed, scale and intensity, facilitated by rapid techno-logical change and global intercon-nectivity.'

Jens Stoltenberg, NATO Secretary General

Contents

Preface

Characters

Macrae Shipping Company
Richard Macrae – Chairman.
Mary Macrae- Richard's wife
James Macrae – President.
Sarah Macrae – James's wife
Hal Spencer– Chief Financial Officer (CFO)
Rob Bisset – Director Operations
Lynda Ferreira – Director Human Resources
Jason Ferreira – Director Safety/Training
Chad Greening – Director of Sales and Marketing
Janet Rushton – Director IT
Martin Farley – Director Legal Affairs
Mateo Ariti – General Manager, Piraeus Terminal, Greece
Flavio Romano – General Manager, Genoa Terminal, Italy
Jusuf Kahya – General Manager, Istanbul Terminal, Turkey
Laura Wesley – Manager, Accounts

Euro-Asian Freight Services
Hugh Stanfield – Owner
Edmond Andreas – CFO
Dan Nash – Hydraulics Engineer

Blue Water Maritime Bureau of Shipping

Ben Mitchell – Chief Inspector

Sterling-Judge Marine Insurance

David Morris – Claims Assessor

Peter Owens – General Manager

Claybourne Cartage

Chris Claybourne – President

MI6

Jack Fox - Director MI6

Jeremy Hirons – MI6 Special Agent

Other characters

Sultan Dastagir – Indian deckhand

Jack Carter – Friend of Hugh Stanfield

Nabil Quraishi – Bedouin truck owner

General Shen – Chinese general

Acknowledgement

Times of India: Article: 'Mumbai Sewage' May 15,2017

'Back-to-Back' museum Birmingham

www.livescience.com/32087

Viking history

www.birmingham.gov.uk/info/50050

Birmingham canal system

Archive and library of Lloyd's Register Foundation.

LR Ships in Class – Lloyd's Register

Reader's Digest Article 'Scandal of the Rotting Tankers'

by Tom Mangold

'Fraud and sinking ships in marine insurance'

by Hugo Tiberg, professor Maritime Law .

Pacific Islands Legal Institute - Maritime Law

Fort Myers News Press, Tuesday March 22, 1994

Article 'Tanker explodes' News Press wire services.

www.npr.org/series/650482198/

Chinese Firms Hold Stakes In a Dozen European Ports

October 9, 2018 Joanna Kakkissis.

www.joc.com/maritime-news/container-lines/

Information on Chinese shipping companies

www.glassdoor.ca/Reviews/COSCO-Shipping

Information on Chinese shipping companies

www.futurelearn.com/courses/politics-of-economics

Nottingham University/China Capitalist or Communist

Country?

www.bbc.com/news/world-middle-east-14546763

Iraq profile – timeline – BBC News

www.kitimat.ca/en/index.aspx

Information on Kitimat

www.britannica.com

Marinetraffic.com

Satellite tracking of vessels worldwide.

www.justia.com/criminal/procedure/

Legal procedures multiple defendants involved

Epoch Times 10/11 Edition 2020 -China's Silent War

Bowen Xiao & Omid Ghoreishi (Intro Dana Cheng)

www.museumoflondon.org.uk › museum-london

Roman London History

https://www.britannica.com/topic/waterboarding

I

Part One

1

Chapter 1

September 1980

She had first seen him from a distance, striding up the valley following a rough track that the sheep had worn for themselves through the heather and moor-grass between the rocky outcrops on the hillside. As he got closer, she could see that he looked tall, extremely fit, tanned and quite handsome. It was a cool day with a slight breeze. The low early morning sun shining down the vale gave him a radiant glow. As he approached her at the peak, he was over six feet tall with a well-built muscular frame and close-cropped light brown hair. He looked a little intimidating, until he gave her a huge disarming smile. She still greeted him a little apprehensively.

'Good morning. You're way off the trails. Are you lost?'

'No, actually I'm not. Just following the Ordnance Survey map and compass and the route I've set for myself. I try to do about fifteen miles a day. I love this entire region of Wales. How about you?'

She smiled back. 'No. I'm not lost either. I'm a local and prefer to hike way off the well-beaten paths. Less people, better scenery and more challenging.' She studied him more closely and thought for a moment, rubbing her chin with her hand. 'You know, you look familiar.'

He looked directly back at her face, tilting his head slightly to one side. 'That's funny because I just had the same sort of feeling about you. I come this way on the odd weekend and camp behind the Vaynol Arms pub in the Llanberis pass. I do a lot of climbing around here as well.'

She thought for a moment. 'Perhaps that's it. Are you a member of the Beddgelert Climbing Club?'

'That's it,' he replied. 'That's where I've seen you. Yes, I think I met you and your partner once when Joe Brown gave a presentation at the town hall on his Himalayan conquests. In fact, I believe I sat next to you! He held out his hand and smiled warmly. 'James Macrae, great to see you again!'

As they shook hands, she laughed and said, 'Holy smoke! I remember that now as well. I'm Sarah. Good to see you again too! You haven't come to the club for a while, though?'

'I only come up here when I can get away. I work in my family's business back in Birmingham and there just seems to be less time to escape up here.'

'I live in Llanberis and work in Caernarfon, so I'm spoiled with the countryside here.'

'You can say that again! Do you want to walk together for a while?'

'Why not? I like to push myself as well. So, you camp in the field behind the Vaynol Arms?'

'Yes, I do. It's great to have dinner and drinks straight afterwards and then stagger back and collapse in the tent. And

I don't have to drive.'

They walked on together admiring the magnificent views in the Snowdonia National Park arriving back at the Vaynol Arms later that Saturday afternoon.

'Would you like to join me for drinks and dinner later?' James asked.

'Yes, I would like that, but first I need go back home to shower and change. My house is fairly close by.'

'Great!. Shall we say in about an hour?'

'Yes, that would be good. See you later.'

James washed himself using the old cast-iron hand water pump at the back of the pub and changed into fresh clothes. Being late autumn, there were fewer patrons in the pub. James waited for Sarah in the lounge and sat close to the log fire roaring away in the stone fireplace. Not long afterwards, the front door opened and in walked Sarah. James was taken aback. She wore a smart pair of black pants, white silk blouse and a loose short black coat draped around her shoulders. Her shoulder-length auburn hair, olive skin and attractive looks completed the picture in front of him. Sarah joined him in front of the fire. They were both relaxed and rejuvenated, their faces glowing warmly after pushing themselves to the limit that day.

Over dinner, Sarah asked, 'Can I ask you a question James?'

'Sure, go ahead.'

'You mentioned this afternoon that getting away was getting harder for you. I sensed that you would prefer to live here rather than Birmingham.'

James smiled back at her. 'You're very astute. Does it show that much?'

'Well, to me it does. I don't know about anyone else.'

James looked down for a few moments, seemingly to wrestle with his emotions. Looking back at her he said, 'You're right. I would prefer this way of life, but I feel obligated to my family. You see, I'm fourth generation in an established international shipping business and unless I take responsibility for the business, it will simply disappear. My father is getting older now and is starting to have some health problems.'

'Do you have any brothers or sisters who could help out?'

'Unfortunately, I don't. I did have an older sister, however she passed away five years ago with leukaemia.'

'I'm so sorry, James. It must be very hard on your parents and yourself.'

'It is. There's a void that can never be filled. I guess that's one of the reasons I come here when I can, to get away sometimes. So, let's talk about you.'

'Not much to tell, really. I was brought up in this part of Wales. My parents still live in Caernarfon. As a historical architect, I'm asked to consult on restoration projects around the country involving listed buildings. In fact, I restored my own cottage.'

'Seems to me that is a great career to have! Each job must be very different from the other?'

'Yes, it is. For me it's a labour of love but also a financial necessity as a single person.'

'I'm fascinated over how old historic buildings are in the UK. It's incredible that some of these structures are up to one thousand years old.'

'Tell you what. Why don't we go back to my place for coffee, and you can see some of the work I have done.'

'I'd love to!'

As they left the pub, Sarah walked over to a Land Rover in

the car park.

James stood back. 'You know, I would have thought you were a sportscar girl!'

'Me! Not really. I'm more of a practical person and I need a four-wheel drive sometimes on the building sites.'

'Um, that makes sense.'

They went back to her stone cottage a couple of miles down the road, in Llanberis village. They sat down in her lounge in front of a cosy woodstove, each with a glass of single malt scotch and coffee. It seemed the perfect thing to do after a good meal. 'So, tell me some more about your job, Sarah. You said you travel. Does that include overseas travel as well?'

'Sometimes, yes. Since Britain has a heritage of stone masonry, I'm often asked to visit different old buildings in Europe to ensure the historical authenticity of the renovations. I've worked in both France and Italy to oversee some of the projects that my company was involved in.'

'Sounds really interesting,' James replied as he stretched his legs out straight and relaxed back into the settee cushions.

'Well you must have done your fair share of visiting Europe with your job?'

'Actually, I have. My father sent me to work at every terminal in Europe, doing a six-month stint in each. My apprenticeship was doing every job there was in our business, including all the dirty jobs. He wanted me to know every aspect of the industry from the bottom end up and just how hard they are.'

Sarah thought for a moment. 'Wow, that must have been tough. Being the boss's son and having to do all that.'

James laughed, reminiscing. 'Oh, it sure was. I wasn't cut any slack! You can imagine what it was like working alongside stevedores as the boss's son. I got bullied a few times.'

7

'Bullied? But you were the boss's son!'

'Yes, that's right. A lot resented it, always throwing the silver spoon in your mouth comments at you. So yes, I was bullied badly in a couple of places. Still, I had two choices. Either I could go back to my father and complain about the guys, in other words hide behind him, or I could stand up to them. I stood my ground and won. You can push me only so far and that's when I fight back.' He paused and then added, almost as an afterthought, 'hard.'

'Remind me never to cross you, James Macrae!' Sarah laughed and lay back next to him. James leaned over and kissed her gently. Sarah responded and then took his hand and led him to her bedroom.

***

He lay there listening to what sounded like a mortally wounded lion. The sound was heavy and uneven, with intermittent bursts of air being exhausted, rather like a whale puncturing the surface of a placid sea and exhaling loudly through the blowhole at the top of its head. His mouth felt like the bottom of a birdcage that hadn't been cleaned for months. He tried to open his eyes, but the shock of light was just too much to bear, the eyelids feeling as though they had been glued together. Lying flat on his back, he tried to lift his head up. The pain increased exponentially, like a metal clamp tightening around his head.

'Oh god. What have I done?' he murmured to himself. He managed to turn his head slightly to the left and tried to open his eyes for a second time to focus on where he was. There was a mass of auburn hair and the bare back of someone. *Sarah, yes, Sarah.* Yes, that was it. He'd met her hiking that day, way off the beaten track in Snowdonia National Park in Wales. James peered over the bed sheets and checked the room around him. He appeared to be in an older stone house with a low ceiling and small paned windows.

James gingerly lowered his right leg onto the bedroom floor, padded to the bathroom and then scouted out the kitchen downstairs. He made a pot of coffee and found some aspirin in the cabinet. Half an hour later, or so, he felt human again. He took Sarah a coffee and went back to bed.

'Good morning Sarah! Welcome to the world,' and handed her a coffee.

'Oh, do I ever need that!' she muttered, yawning at the same time.

'How are you feeling?'

She stretched her arms up in the air, yawning. 'Never felt better! Did we get hit by a train last night?'

'It sure felt like it!'

Shortly afterwards, they ventured into the kitchen. Sarah barefoot, wore a short dressing gown. She looked more fantastic the morning after, with sparkling hazel eyes, long legs and hair strewn wild over her shoulders. James hugged her and they sat down together at the table.

'So, what's your plan for today?' James asked.

'Well, I was supposed to drive to Shrewsbury tomorrow and start a new restoration project on the cathedral, however it has been put back two weeks. I'll probably take a day off instead and reorganise my studio. How about you?'

'I thought I would go climbing on Llanberis pass crag, but I hadn't planned on last night. So, I'll just go back home sometime today. I have a busy week in front of me at work. I really enjoyed yesterday and last night, being with you.'

'You know, I did too. It was fun, wasn't it?'

9

'Sure was. I think I would like it to last a little longer,' James said, holding out his hand across the table.

2

Chapter 2

May 1994

James Macrae drew in an invigorating breath. He had completed his early morning run and felt ready to take on the world. His office was heavily carpeted with paintings of the Macrae fleet, including earlier sailing ships, adorning the walls. A computer screen sat behind him, quietly monitoring the daily fluctuations of the commodities market. Looking through a massive glass window, it was a beautiful sunny day. Gas Street Basin, the canal complex in central Birmingham, England, with its restored and inviting pubs and inns were decked in bright red geraniums hanging down from window boxes. A number of barges, resplendent in their colours were moored in the large canal basin. The reflection of the buildings and blue sky on the still water gave an impression of Venice.

Spinning round, he picked up the latest edition of *Mercantile News*.

At thirty-eight, James was now president of the family

shipping business, Macrae Shipping Company, with its head-quarters in Birmingham. It was a medium-size company within the global transportation industry, dwarfed by Maersk and Hapag-Lloyd.

Hearing a knock, he looked up from his magazine at his open office door. 'Good morning, Rob, come on in. How are you today?'

Rob Bisset, his director of operations, came forward and looked at James, swallowing hard. As he sat down in one of the chairs facing the desk, he rubbed at the left side of his neck. 'Not good, I'm afraid. Sorry, James, I don't have good news. The warranty claim for the engine of *Antares*. The manufacturer turned it down flat. They will not even pay a percentage of the costs.'

James shook his head. 'Not possible, Rob. How could they do that? The vessel was only launched one year ago. The hours on the engine would have been well inside the warranty limits. If I remember right, the blades in the turbines came loose and entered the engine, causing the failure? I know our losses were huge due to the late delivery of the cargo and the consequent repairs, but this is ridiculous!' He held out his hand across the desk. 'Let me see the letter.'

Rob handed it over and remained silent, tapping his foot on the carpet.

'There must be some mistake.'

'That's what I think too, James. I've asked the manufacturer for an urgent meeting. With all the business we have given them over the years, this is crap!'

'Bloody right! I want to be in there when you meet them.'

James got up from his desk as Rob left his office and went to grab coffee from the staff kitchen. His IT director was there.

'Hey, Janet. How are you?'

'Oh hi, James. Doing well, thank you. How about you?'

'I'm good too. Tell me, was your husband able to transfer from the London office to the Birmingham one yet?'

'Yes, he has. At least he won't have that commute every week now.'

'That's great news. Say hello to him from me, will you? How have the children settled in?'

'Aidan seemed to fit into his new class straight away, but Emma is taking a little longer. She is more resistant to change, but, then again, she's two years older.'

'Listen, I'm so glad you are on board with us, taking care of our IT. We've needed your expertise to bring us up to date for a while now, big time. It took a long time to find you and I'm really impressed with how efficiently you have turned our systems around. Thanks.'

'Thanks, James! I'm really glad I made the move.'

James returned to his office and studied last month's financial reports. He was immersed in the consolidated report when the phone rang.

James answered, then closed his eyes, taking in a deep breath. 'Get back to me when you have more information. Thanks, Mateo.' James put down the phone slowly. 'Fuck!'

He stood up, staring blankly through the floor-to-ceiling window. How had his day gone downhill so fast? *This doesn't make sense. Why are we having so many accidents? We've always had such a good safety record.*

In three of the four European ports they owned, there had been recent, serious accidents. One dock worker had died, and several others had been injured on the job. Some of the cranes, hoists and other machinery had failed annual insurance inspections and hydraulic leaks had increased. In Valencia, the port safety licence had been suspended for no apparent reason. Apart from the human tragedy, the accidents were starting to put the company under financial strain.

James also felt torn. Although he didn't want to cause his father, Richard, undue stress, he felt he must let him know the latest news. His dad remained company chairman, but although he was spending less and less time at work, he still made the big decisions.

'Dad. Have you got a minute?'

Richard looked up from his desk to see James standing in the doorway. As James walked to the chair across from his desk, Richard's silver hair caught a new sun beam shining slantwise through the office window. James was hit by a sudden thought, 'God! how old and weary dad's starting to look.' Richard's demeanour seemed to reflect the tired wood panelling and heavy oak furniture in his office.

'Of course, sit down. What's up?'

James remained standing gripping the rear of the seat in front of him. 'More bad news, I'm afraid. The Piraeus terminal has had to be shut down until we can certify the dock cranes again.'

'I don't understand. Has there been another accident?'

'Mateo just let me know that the central crane on the dry goods dock, loading crates of machine tools, let go and the whole lot fell into the hold of one of our ships. Four stevedores were hurt, three of them seriously. The cargo was completely wrecked.'

'Bloody hell! Are the men going to be okay?'

'I believe the injuries are quite serious. We'll know more

later,' James replied.

Richard sighed. 'Yet another accident. Was it the crane operator's fault?'

'No. It seems the hydraulics let go and the back-up safety mechanism did not engage. Our loss will be considerable; the customer has finished with us and revenue from the port will be lost until we can re-certify the equipment and open again.'

Richard shook his head. 'Christ! I can't believe it. God knows, we have invested heavily in increased maintenance and safety practices in the last two years to prevent these occurrences.'

'Dad, what do you think we should we do?'

Richard seemed a little surprised at the question. He looked at James directly for a few seconds and then seemed to make up his mind on what he was apparently thinking. 'You know James, I think we are at a crossroads in the company.'

'I don't understand. What do you mean?'

'Well, it's me that should now be asking you, what should we do now?' He paused. 'James, I've been spending less time here as you know. It's partly because I'm starting to slow down, and its partly doctors' orders; I'm supposed to avoid stress. In fact, I have an appointment first thing tomorrow morning at Queen Elizabeth Hospital with a cardiologist.'

James moved from the back of the chair and sat down slowly. 'Okay, dad. Has your condition started to worsen more than we know about?'

Richard shook his head. 'Not really. Here's the thing. I think it's your time now. Yes, accidents happen from time to time. It's the nature of our business, always has been. Of course, it's regrettable, especially where our employees lives' are concerned.'

'I don't believe we've ever had this number though in such

a short time. So far, only Yanbu has not experienced any accidents, at least not like this and not recently.'

'No, I don't think we've ever had a situation like this. When accidents happen, it's either mechanical failure or human error. You have to determine which it is and fix it.'

'Dad, I would like to get the board together as soon as possible. We need to collectively pool the facts that we know and try to make sense of these disasters. If we don't stop this now, we could start to get into financial difficulty.'

'Then do it, James. I won't be here in the morning, so take charge.'

'I'll try. Let me take some of the strain off you. We all love you, Dad. You better stay healthy!' James paused. 'But, what about Hal Spencer? Seems to me that he always wanted to take over from you?'

'Now that's where you're wrong. He would always support you. Hal's been a great CFO for this company for over twenty-five years now. He's a trusted family friend, as you know.'

'Okay. Good luck tomorrow. Call me afterwards.'

James left the office. Richard bent forward, putting his hand to his chest. His mouth opened and his eyes squeezed closed.

Chapter 3

Sultan Dastagir leaned over the stern of the 200,000-tonne dry cargo bulker, *Endeavour*. Owned by the multi-million-dollar international corporation Euro-Asian Freight Services and registered in Panama, the ship was loaded with a full cargo of rice and soya beans in each of its nine holds. With all the weight, it sat low in the dark-brown-coloured water. The smell of the Bombay port was always overpowering. The harbour water was a putrid mixture of rotten garbage, sewage and sea water. It was well known that while sanitation plants cleansed some of the city's sewage, millions of litres of waste-water sewage were still dumped, untreated, into the port and surrounding waterways.

Dastagir had been a deckhand for over twenty years – a career that had taken him to all four corners of the globe. He took a long look at the city of Bombay with all its hustle and bustle. Densely packed streets full of motorcycles, buses and cars belched out a never-ending thick brown haze of exhaust fumes. Dozens of gantry cranes used for loading and unloading the vessels in harbour protruded up into the evening sky. Dastagir was always sad to leave his home port. He had been back in port for less than a week and already he had been instructed to take on another trip. It was a race each time they reached port to see how quickly they could get back to sea. While the work was gruelling and took him away from his wife and five children, he managed to support his family – despite the low wages. While the ship's officers received bonuses, a lowly seaman like himself saw no additional money. In fact, over the years, he had seen his pay packets get smaller and smaller. A common occurrence in the somewhat loosely regulated industry of international cargo shipping. Once, when he questioned his pay, he was told by his boss to take it or leave it. Euro-Asian Freight Services employed cheap foreign labour and could have thousands of men waiting to take his place in a heartbeat.

Dastagir turned around to face the west. It was still warm, about twenty-five degrees Celsius. It felt good to watch the sunset even though it was only about six in the evening. The size of the sun always looked larger at this latitude. The clouds took on hues of gold and red. As the sun got closer to the horizon, it dropped down fast like a deflated ball. Soon after, he felt a chill run through him as he watched it finally disappear. Just at that moment, the deck bell rang snapping him back to the task at hand. He inserted the metal bar over the smaller lever on the winch and began to operate the rusted motor to bring up the now-slack and heavy rope that had tied the stern of the ship to its mooring for the last five days. The old electric motor creaked and groaned. How this company, Euro-Asian Freight Services, could allow this ship to continue running was beyond him. He was not an engineer, but even he could see that the decking and hatches were in need of severe reinforcement.

The constant salt-water corrosion and the battering of dock machinery that was used every time they loaded and unloaded bulk goods had completely worn out the vessel's equipment and structure. It was just a thread away from snapping.

Dastagir finished winching the heavy rope aboard, the motor sounding rougher than ever. He would not say anything about the ship's equipment, however, having recently been threatened by the first mate. All Dastagir had said was that he and his fellow sailors were concerned about their safety with the lack of maintenance and repairs of the ship. Just a week before, his mate had accidentally tripped over a loose deck hatch and fallen through into the hold below. Had there not been a full hold of well-packaged electrical equipment below, he would have died.

Dastagir continued to complete his deck duties. By now *Endeavour* was heading into deep water and the swell was beginning to build. She laboured on towards Rotterdam as the drift current pushed hard against the bow of the ship. With the north-east trade winds behind them and the prevailing currents, large amounts of spray were kicked up from the bow. The long, rolling movements of the ship tipping from side to side, the intermittent wall of sea-spray being thrown up and the constant drawl of the turbines were all familiar to him. This was his world, his home away from home. By now they were already several hours out of Bombay, heading south west across the Arabian sea towards Jeddah, the Red Sea port city in Saudi Arabia. The moon cast a dull light across the water and the stars shone brightly. Dastagir took a moment to look over the stern rail, thinking of his family. He missed them so much, but this was the only way they could survive. Hearing a sound behind him, he turned around to face a dark, burly silhouetted figure.

'Mr Nash. You startled me there for a minute!'

'Really, let's see what you make of this.'

Dastagir didn't have time to react; the almighty punch hit him square in the face. As he started to fall backwards, Nash grabbed him around his waist and flung him overboard. Still conscious but unable to comprehend what was happening, Dastagir flailed his arms madly but couldn't grip onto anything. His hands were full of fresh air as he fell into the dark, cold sea beyond the stern of the ship.

In the pale moonlight, Nash saw his head pop up through the foaming wash of the ship's propellers, his head getting smaller as the ship continued to sail eastwards. Nash gave a wry smile and held his right hand up to wave goodbye.

4

Chapter 4

James walked down the concrete steps to the office underground car park, on autopilot. He sank into the black leather driver's seat of his Range Rover and closed his eyes, feeling drained after scouring through the accident reports. His conclusion in each case was that the cause was mechanical rather than human error. But why now and why all within a short period of time? He didn't have any answers. Company losses would mount very quickly. It didn't help that the world economy was still sluggish after the recession in 1990. He knew that when companies went down, they went down quick. James was beginning to feel isolated at the helm of the company.

Driving out of Birmingham into the rolling Worcestershire countryside, the weather started to deteriorate. Low grey clouds scurried in from the west, bringing in driving rain. His left eyelid twitched, and his hands gripped the steering wheel. He pulled into the drive of his home at around 7.00pm, with the sound of gravel crunching under his tyres. As he activated the garage door fob, instead of driving straight into the converted stable block garage, he paused.

His wife Sarah had the lights on already in some of the rooms, but had not yet drawn the curtains. The Georgian house they had so painstakingly renovated by scrimping and saving looked warm, safe and inviting. That had been their choice. James, instead of wanting to be the rich, entitled boss's son, wanted to be treated like any other employee with the same level of salary and benefits. As he learned all aspects of the business, he felt especially good amongst the bluecollar workers. They were his friends and co-workers. He loved their collective humour and approach to life, often more than that of the managers.

Sarah had worked tirelessly as project manager of the renovation, having largely drawn the architectural plans up herself. She had also contributed a substantial portion of the manual labour. To lose this, their dream house that had taken three years to complete, would be heartbreaking.

His eyes moved to the family room window. The flickering light reflected on the ceiling and walls, suggesting that his three children were watching TV while Sarah prepared the dinner. *God, I love them.* James put the car away and trying to pull himself together, walked into the large kitchen-diner. He gave Sarah a gentle hug and a kiss on the nape of her neck as she stirred several saucepans simmering on the range stove. 'You know you are as gorgeous now as the day I met you all those years ago.'

She laughed. 'You can still say that to me after twelve years of marriage?' Her eyes were wide and sparkling as she turned to face him. Seeing his face, she stood back from him, tilting her head slightly to one side. 'You look upset. Something's wrong. What is it?'

James shook his head. 'I'll tell you later, after the kids have gone to bed. How was your day?'

'Oh, the usual. The kids were tired after school, the usual misbehaviour, but I finally settled them down to do their homework. They are all flat out in the family room watching cartoons.'

James put his head round the door, shouting, 'The monster is here!' in his best monster voice. All three children – Olivia aged four, Mia aged six and Mason aged eight – screamed and dived behind the sofa. 'I'm coming to get you! I'm hungry!' With that he crept up and put his head over the sofa and gave his best monster roar again. All three cowered and squealed, 'Please don't hurt us, Mr Monster.'

Then Mason shouted, 'Mr Monster, can you just eat the girls. They are so annoying!'

The girls squealed back. 'No, eat Mason. He's always teasing us!'

James grabbed them all, giving them big hugs and kisses and pretending to eat them.

'Dinner's ready!' shouted Sarah from the kitchen.

After dinner and when all three children had gone to bed, Sarah and James collapsed onto the sofa in the dimly lit lounge, both with a scotch in hand. The evening had gone unseasonably cold, so James lit a fire. As the logs crackled, flames flickered and radiated a warm orange glow from the inglenook fireplace all around the room, stretching up to the wood-beamed ceiling.

'Want to tell me what's bothering you, Jimbo? I know it's something serious.'

James sat silently for several moments, apparently deep in thought. Sarah looked at him lovingly, her deep-hazel eyes telling him that she wanted to help.

'I believe the company could be starting to get into serious trouble.'

Sarah's eyes widened, but she remained silent.

He paused, 'I can't quite put all the pieces together, but we have had more than the average number of accidents, all spread across our international terminals. Our accident-free days here in the UK are way down, yet overseas they are rising. It's not just the frequency of them either, it's the geographical spread and the seriousness of the accidents. All this after stepping up our training programmes recently. These things just don't add up.'

'Does your dad realise how serious things are?' she asked.

'Well, he knows about the accidents, but I haven't told him yet about the scale of the mounting financial consequences. I'm trying to shield him as much as possible until I fully grasp the situation that we find ourselves in. I saw him today and he looked tired and old. He's seeing a cardiologist tomorrow for a check-up. Even though he won't be there, I've called a board meeting for first thing in the morning to try to thrash out what's causing this sudden change of circumstances.'

'Let's hope your dad will be okay. At least he's seeing a specialist. I'll give your mom a call tomorrow. Hey, we'll get through this together!' Sarah stretched over and kissed James on the cheek.

'Thanks. It's always good to talk things through. Sometimes you see things more clearly than I do.' James took a sip of his scotch. 'I wonder how my ancestors would have reacted to what is happening now? One thing's for sure, each of them predicted how the shipping market would change and then carefully steered the company safely through those transformations. It's up to me to do the same, except right now I feel helpless. This is the first time in my life that I've come up against a situation as tough as this. I don't have a plan to move forward right now, let alone stop the business from failing.'

'Well, your lot sure were a tough breed, having descended from the Vikings. If ever there was a bunch of ruthless and brutal warriors, it was them. Remember you have their genes! Didn't your great-grandfather come all the way from his hometown on the east coast of Scotland to Birmingham to find work in the late 1700s?'

'Yes, he did. It must have been a huge step to venture so far away to an unknown world. Moving from being a blacksmith to starting a barge business exporting manufactured goods from Birmingham using the canal system. Later, my grand-father saw the decline coming in the barge business with the expansion of the railways. That's when the company became involved in ocean-going cargo ships.'

'It sounds like they took a few financial risks to do that,' Sarah said.

'That's certainly true. My father did it too when he bought into the four European harbour terminals that we now own. He's slowing down but doesn't want to fully retire. So it's up to me – and me alone – to find a way out of this mess. I just feel completely vulnerable right now.'

'You know the industry inside out; you'll soon find out the real causes of these accidents. When you have investigated more, I'm sure you will know what to do.' She threw both arms around his neck and kissed him hard. 'Come on, let's go to bed.'

They made love passionately with Sarah giving James all the

comfort her body and soul could give him.

While Sarah slept and the moon rose higher in the night sky, James tossed and turned in bed trying to disengage his overworked brain. He got up and walked down the hall to check on the children. Mason was sleeping soundly, his model spaceship on the bedside table. He had become obsessed with space after learning that the early mariners steered by the stars. Next, he checked the girls. Even though they each had their own rooms, they slept in the same room. They looked like little angels sleeping so peacefully. Olivia had kicked off all her covers, so James tucked her in again next to her little woolly lamb. Mia was cuddled up nicely with her teddy. James was struck anew with fear as to what might happen to them if the company went down.

He went downstairs to his study, in the dark. Outside, a ghostly kind of metallic-blue light drenched the garden from above. His mood darkened even further. *Why have these accidents suddenly started? I'm the one responsible for the workforce; they are my extended family. What about the employee that died? What about the injured? What if we go bust and all our employees are put out of work?*

James eventually went back to bed, but the dancing demons of the night continued to trouble him.

Chapter 5

As the first light of day started to creep over the house, James left home to drive to the office. The early morning mist wavered back and forth over the surrounding wheat fields and hedgerows. As he backed out of the garage, he turned the radio on, trying to clear his mind of all the still-unanswered questions swirling around. A CD by BB King was already loaded in the player. James loved his music, but somehow the 'The thrill is gone', with its heavy bass reverberating through the vehicle's speakers, didn't help him this morning. He turned it off.

At 8.00am, James stood inside the company boardroom pouring himself a mug of fresh coffee from the sideboard. He greeted the other directors as they entered and took up positions around the expansive maple wood table. Hanging on the wall behind him were paintings of the ancestors that had built and consolidated the business over the years since 1782. A world map dominated one wall, with another housing different clocks showing the different world time zones. The pastel-green wall colour and plush grey carpet seemed to induce a calm and sobering atmosphere.

James felt the mood of all the directors was subdued. *As it should be*, he thought. He quietly studied each of the six directors sitting around the table as they arranged their files and notes.

On the left sat Lynda Ferreira, Director of Human Resources. Lynda was in her forties and had earned her seat with international experience within the organisation. She had started at the Valencia shipyard in HR and quickly rose to prominence with excellent hiring, training and HR skills. Fluent in Portuguese, Spanish and English, she had met her husband, who headed up the Piraeus shipyard. They had moved to the head office in Birmingham, but frequently travelled to the company's international offices.

Next to Lynda sat Chad Greening, Director of Sales and Marketing. Chad had been with the company for over ten years and was well respected in the shipping industry. He had been in the logistics and distribution industry ever since leaving school. If there was one person who knew the industry inside out and all the competitors within it, it was Chad. He was single and a workaholic. He travelled frequently to meet with his customers and when prospecting for new ones, he rarely 'sold' but instead acted more as a consultant to the customer to advise them on their best distribution methods. If he didn't think a Macrae solution would add value and help the customer, he told them. That way he had built up tremendous credibility within the industry. He was perceived as being honest, transparent and loyal to both his customers and his own company.

At the other side of Chad sat Rob Bisset, Director of Operations. All the managers of the sub-divisions and associate companies reported to him; he was the 'go-to' guy. Rob had been with the company for twenty-plus years and had worked at every overseas branch. He was a practical, feet on the ground type of man, with a gift for languages. His father was French and an aircraft technician serving in the French Air Force and his mother was Italian. Consequently, Rob had moved around the world as he grew up in the different air bases in Africa, Middle East and Polynesia. Rob had moved around so much in his lifetime, he now appreciated the stability of his job and being able to settle in one place and bring his own family up in a stable home was important to him. It was something he had always wanted. Richard had the utmost faith and trust in him.

Opposite Rob Bisset sat Janet Rushton, Director of IT. Janet had been with the company for less than two years. She had been hired through an agency that specialised in IT recruitment after an exhaustive search to find the right candidate. The previous IT director had been let go, simply because he had failed to keep pace with the warp speed of IT development. The Macrae Shipping Company systems needed upgrading with better information systems and firewalls. Unlike the other directors, Janet had gone through a systematic background check. Hiring the wrong person for this position would be catastrophic; James had handled this hire himself. Janet Rushton had been the best candidate and, so far, everything was working out well.

Next to Janet sat Hal Spencer, the Chief Financial Officer. Hal was a grey-haired, somewhat overweight man in his late fifties. James had mixed feelings about him. Sometimes he would come across as patronising and yet at other times he couldn't be more helpful. James wasn't sure why these apparent mood swings happened. Was it perhaps that he was Richard's son;

the kid who didn't really have his heart in the business when he first started? Still, Richard had the utmost faith in Hal and so did the banks. The Macrae Shipping banking relationships were on a sound and stable footing. For now. James wondered how Hal would react to him as he took the lead from his father for the first time.

Martin Farley sat by Hal. Martin was Director of Legal Affairs. Like Hal, Martin had been with the company a long time and had been hired by Richard. In his late forties, happily married with a family, he was also a family friend. Over the years, as the corporate lawyer, he had steered the company well. He was well respected in the industry for understanding maritime law. When troubles erupted globally, such as in the Middle East, he had been able to navigate carefully, respecting international law with embargoes placed on countries such as Iraq, Iran, Syria and, later, North Korea. The United States and the European Union also kept him busy with constant updates on embargoes. Failure to fall in line with these international agreements, as Martin knew, could be catastrophic for the company.

James noticed some odd looks from some of the others when he sat at the head of the table, where his father normally sat. He took note that Hal Spencer then moved to the seat at the other end of the table, where he would normally sit when his father was present.

Hal looked straight at James. 'Morning, James. On your own today?'

James reminded himself of what his father had said yesterday: *It's your time now.* He took a deep breath, 'Good morning, everyone!' Making eye contact with each director, he continued, 'As you know, I've called this emergency board meeting to bring everyone up to date with the latest developments and come up with a complete plan of action on how to prevent further accidents and try to mitigate our losses. Richard will not be with us today. Firstly, we need to find the cause of these catastrophes. We have a lot of questions to ask ourselves. Were they caused by human error, mechanical failure or both? Are all the mechanical failures similar in nature? Was there a common denominator? Is there some sort of a pattern? Which of our personnel were on duty at the time of the accident? Were outside contractors on site? What was our security personnel doing at the time? And so on. Let's share our knowledge. We need to put a stop to this now.'

James paused to let his comments sink in. He then continued. 'Last night I dispatched Jason Ferreira to visit the Piraeus terminal to investigate the latest accident. Both Jason and I believe that none of these accidents or management failures should have happened, given the stringent health and safety measures that we instituted, company-wide, these past two years. All these accidents seem to be well distributed geographically. They stretch right across every one of our European foreign shipping terminals. Conversely, our UK-based operations have recorded 468 straight accident-free days. Yanbu has also been accident-free for the last 430 days.'

Hal Spencer interrupted. 'Well, that's just it, isn't it? It's no good saying they shouldn't have happened. They did happen. That's a fact! I've watched us pour money into the so-called "enhanced safety programme" and this is the result. Great investment, huh!'

James felt his neck grow hotter. 'Then how do you explain the improved safety record in the UK? It's the same programme worldwide. We've proved it works. I have the utmost faith in

Jason Ferreira. If anyone knows about improving safety, he does.'

Hal stiffened in his chair. 'So maybe it's a translation and interpretation thing. If you say the system works, then heads need to roll!' He turned his glare to Rob Bisset. 'You need to take charge, Rob, and sort your staff out. That's what you are paid for, isn't it?'

James interrupted: 'Hal! Please! We know you care about company finances, but in Operations we care about the three Cs. Complaint, in this case the accident, Cause and Correction. We are investigating the Cause right now. Until we know the answers to that, we cannot make corrections.'

Hal persisted. 'Listen, Master James, my dear boy. I'm old enough to tell you and you are young enough to listen! If your father was here, he would be firing people right now!' He pointed his finger directly at James. 'YOU have to make an example of these people to show you are strong and these oversights and accidents will not be tolerated!'

Shocked and belittled, James smashed the flat of his hand loudly on the boardroom table. 'YOU ARE NOT LISTENING TO ME! JUST STOP IT! We will not be firing anyone until we know the cause of these accidents. I've sweated, ached, laughed and cried with these people and I WILL NOT throw anyone under the bus until I know the truth. If you stepped outside your office more, you might even start to understand. Enough!'

Hal jerked his head back. His look of astonishment sent a powerful shockwave through the room.

James lowered his voice. 'Lynda, can you give us an update on Piraeus.'

Lynda blew out a long breath. 'OK, it's not good news this morning, I'm afraid.' She paused and swallowed hard. 'I'm sorry to say that one of the four cargo handlers injured in the Piraeus accident yesterday, died during the night. Jason is currently on his way to see the family of the deceased and visit the other three injured men in hospital. I can tell you that we are providing all necessary support, both financially and morally, to support the affected personnel and their families. We also have a grief counsellor on site this morning. Morale, right now, in all our overseas operations is at an all-time low. I'm sorry to say this, but everyone is asking the question, "do we even know what we are doing here?"'

Hal and James looked at each other with the gravest expressions on their faces.

Lynda continued, 'James, you asked the question about the timing of these accidents. In Genoa, we had the overhead crane accident and the forklift truck failure that left one employee dead and injured four others. These accidents happened just before we were due to meet with the local union to agree to a revised three-year employment agreement. The union immediately upped their demands for both the hourly rate and the number of sick days allowed per year. Then, in Istanbul, through a series of contract and clerical errors, we ended up losing a large amount of money just when we had gained a new customer. I know through talking with Chad that he had worked for three years trying to land this client and it would have made a huge contribution to the profitability of this company.'

James made a note on his iPad. 'Thank you, Lynda.'

'Chad. You are next. How do you see things through Sales and Marketing eyes?'

Chad sat upright in his chair. 'Firstly, I want to add my condolences to the families affected by all these accidents.' He then looked directly at Rob Bisset. 'If you ask me how I really feel about this, I'll tell you here and now. All these incidents seem very strange to me, especially since the company culture here is to place all employees' health and safety first. I simply don't understand it.'

'Chad, tell us what we need to know about what happened in Istanbul.'

'The draft contract and paperwork flow, with timelines, was approved and signed off by me. It was a new customer that, as you all now know, we have lost. I still have the original contract on my hard drive, yet the signed contract that came back from the customer was slightly different. The mistake passed through our vetting process and the result was a huge loss on the deal. Fact is, I'm still trying to figure out how it happened.'

James made another note. 'Hal, you need to do some forensic accounting to investigate what happened at local level as well. It's not just the financial loss, it's the loss of trust of our new customer in us. Our reputation has been severely damaged.'

Hal Spencer 'Yes, James, I will give it my utmost attention.'

'Rob, can you give us further details of all the accidents and failures.'

'As Director of Operations, no one is more concerned than I am over these sudden tragic circumstances. I deeply regret the loss of life and injuries. In conjunction with James and Lynda, we have extended all assistance that we can give to the affected families, including financial help. In addition, each of our general managers is investigating. I am not in a position to categorically give you the reasons for the failures at this time, but we're investigating with the utmost urgency. In each case, we are also working with the local police. I can assure everyone that once the hard facts have been collected, there will be a full report.'

Rob paused and looked at everyone in turn. 'One comment that sticks out with me was from Flavio Romano, our Genoa manager, when I spoke to him after the overhead crane and forklift failures. He told me that in both cases, not only had hydraulic hose connections failed, but their back-up safety mechanisms had also failed. We all know that should not happen. I'm having all the preventive maintenance reports reviewed in detail.'

James jumped in. 'Interesting. Mateo also told me that in Piraeus it was not just the hydraulics that failed, but also the back-up safety mechanism. I understand that the crane had only been checked and signed off two days before. I can tell you that I will be flying to Piraeus tonight to visit the injured employees. I will also see the family of the deceased. I will do the same at the other terminals, as well as digging deeper into the cause of these failures.'

James looked over at Janet. 'Janet. Where do we stand as far as IT is concerned?'

Janet looked down at her tablet and tabbed down the screen. She paused and then looked straight at James. 'As you know, when I started two years ago, we updated all of our hardware to include servers and laptops. We also completely stripped out the old software and introduced new systems with robust firewalls. So far, so good. However, we have seen increased attacks on our network firewalls from outside sources. These attacks appear to come from Russia, North Korea, China and the Unites States. Of course this doesn't necessarily mean the attacks originate from there, since any number of outside computers in any country could have been compromised. Our firewalls have not been penetrated as of yet.'

She continued. 'I would like to request more funding to hire an outside IT contractor to review our security and track down who is trying to compromise our systems. It would seem to me that if someone or some company is systematically trying to penetrate our firewall, then hacking into our systems would be an excellent weapon for them to hurt us with.'

James nodded. 'Okay, Janet, get me some quotes for doing this, but let's choose only UK companies that have a proven track record. It's too serious to mess about with unknown contractors who overpromise and underdeliver.'

Janet immediately replied. 'I'm on it.'

'OK, Hal, let's hear from you.'

Hal Spencer took a deep breath. 'Well, as you might imagine, we are under increasing financial pressure. The deaths and injuries to our employees have led to more insurance claims. These claims will be very damaging to our previous good record and I was told yesterday by our insurance agent that our premiums are likely to at least double, with immediate effect. Also, our deductible amounts will rise substantially. Our losses while the Valencia shipyard was closed amounted to a total of five and half million US dollars. If you couple that with the Istanbul contract debacle, that amount rises to twelve million and then add Genoa and Piraeus; we are likely looking at losses of around twenty to twenty-three million dollars. I need hardly add that our good name is being affected by all of this worldwide. This is a relatively small industry where everyone knows everyone else. Bottom line is, we are hurting and bleeding financially very heavily. I'm trying to keep a positive dialogue going with our banks, but they are going to get nervous.'

James closed his eyes and rubbed his forehead, looking down at the table. 'It doesn't help that we are investing in two new ultra large container vessels this year. Can we handle cash flow for the next quarter?' Silence prevailed with everyone looking down at the boardroom table. No one had realised that it was this bad.

Hal responded. 'We can just about manage the next quarter, however, after that, the company could be at risk if we do not secure additional funding.'

James's eyelid twitched again. 'My god, has it come to this already? Are you absolutely sure?'

'I'm sorry, James. It has. I repeat what I said earlier. Whoever is responsible for this needs to be rooted out and brought to justice. This is criminal negligence.'

James placed both hands on the table. 'Okay, Hal. Get hold of our bankers and let's set up meetings as soon as possible to arrange long-term financing until we can get ourself back on course again. Prepare a SWOT analysis for them. Strengths, weaknesses, opportunities and threats. We may as well give them the goods. God knows, we have worked with our banks long enough for them to know us. I've always found honesty to be our best policy. Also start to drag out our payables and let's cut spending right now.'

'I'll set it up as soon as possible, James.'

Next, James looked at Rob. 'Rob, let me see all preventive maintenance records and inspection reports for the equipment failures and stick close to your terminal managers and local police. Something is starting to smell here. Primary and secondary fail-safe systems don't just go at the same time. I'm starting to see a pattern here. You and I will meet the engine manufacturer this afternoon re the denied warranty claim and then I want you to man the helm while I'm away visiting the terminals. Take charge and don't rely on Richard. He is having a series of medical checks at the moment.

'Chad. Grab as much business as you can by cutting our freight rates, just for the time being. Any low-hanging fruit, grab it! Let's get together in my office after this meeting.'

'Lynda. You work on the morale of the company as much as you can and ensure the affected families have everything they need. While I'm away, keep me posted.

'Janet. You already know what to do.'

James looked down to his right. 'Sorry, Martin. I haven't forgotten about you. Can you add any knowledge to help us to understand how we have arrived in this position?'

Martin Farley looked around the table, seemingly to choose his words carefully. 'Firstly we need to consider that the company may be sued for criminal negligence. Nothing has been suggested at this stage from any quarter, but this could be a real possibility. For this reason, we must find the real cause of each accident. We're now a war cabinet; especially when we start to hear about possible similarities between these accidents. Secondly, I hadn't thought of it before, but there are rumours floating around the industry that two maritime shipping companies are being investigated for allegedly breaking international embargoes and shipping arms and, possibly, chemical weapons to Iraq under Saddam Hussein.

Martin paused, tilting his head to one side. 'On the face of it, it doesn't make sense to link this to our supposed situation, however there are two companies in our industry that have grown substantially in the last few years which does seem abnormal, given the world recession that we are just starting to emerge from. 'What if...' He let the question hang in the silent room. Gathering his thoughts further, 'What if either of these two companies wanted to expand further? Could they weaken us financially, then swoop in and take us over?' He tapped his fingers on the table, looking for a reaction.

James was the first to answer. 'You're serious, aren't you?'

'Yes, I am.'

6

Chapter 6

Under a darkening and foreboding sky, mid-afternoon over the South Atlantic Ocean, the atmospheric pressure was dropping rapidly. Waves had started to increase in height, fuelled by the building low-pressure system and consequent prevailing winds. With the gale force winds, envelopes of white sea-spray shot into the air like an impenetrable wall over the bow of *Endeavour*, the 200,000-tonne dry cargo bulker owned by Euro-Asian Freight Services. As visibility started to decrease even further, the piercing horizontal rain was adding to the deteriorating situation. The explosive cacophony of deafening sounds from the salt water and rain spray smashing into the bridge of the ship meant any communication by the officers inside had to be shouted at the top of their lungs.

Captain Thor Johansson stared through the bridge windows as best as he could. It became difficult to ascertain the difference between the division of the ink-black sea and the black sky in front of the violently pitching and rolling vessel. The windshield wipers swept backwards and forwards erratically, trying desperately to clear the huge volume of sea water blasting into them. His face was taut with concentration. He had been through many rough seas in his long career, but this time it was different. It wasn't the weather conditions that bothered him so much; it was the age and condition of his ship as she laboured north-east through the heavy seas.

He turned to his first officer. 'What does the latest weather fax tell us?'

'Sustained gale force winds, force ten.'

'Okay, re-check that we are all battened down, and the pumps are working properly.'

'Aye, aye, Captain.'

He then turned to his third officer. 'Keep a constant eye on the deck hatches. If we have one weak spot on this vessel, that's it.'

Johansson, a native of Gothenburg, Sweden, had been at sea all his life with Stena Line, one of the largest ferry operators in the world and headquartered in his hometown. Then, approaching the age of sixty, he was hit with the crushing news he had cancer. Remarkably, he came through it. Then his wife passed away from a brain aneurysm. Having lost the love of his life, he desperately needed a purpose to get out of bed each day and somehow carry on with his life. Winters were long and dark in Sweden and the older he got, the more he hated the cold. His two children were grown up and had their own families: his son now lived in England and his daughter in Germany. There was nothing to keep him in Gothenburg.

Trying to find another job as captain, or even first or second officer, proved difficult due to his age and health record. Then, one day, he was contacted by Euro-Asian Freight Services for an interview. He was offered the captaincy of a 200,000-

tonne dry bulker named *Endeavour*, though his pay was much lower than the industry average. He figured it reflected his age and health situation, but at least he would have a job and something to occupy his mind. He had heard the name Euro-Asian Freight Services before and it was well known that they operated an ageing fleet in order, as they believed, to keep costs down.

As the foredeck lurched steeply, he could begin to see the full height of the next wave towering before him. The waves now had overhanging crests with white foam streaming from their tops, driven by the gale force winds. His ship dove straight into the bottom of the deep trough. The hull shuddered from bow to stern as he tried to steer the hull directly into the wave. The diesel engines' vibrations through the steel hull changed all the time, as pressure on the screws varied with each climb and fall on the waves. *Endeavour* was three days out of Montevideo, Uruguay, with each of its nine cargo holds full to the limit with sulphate chemical wood pulp en route to Hamburg, Germany, to produce paper.

It had been several months since the tragic 'accident' of Sultan Dastagir. *Endeavour* and her crew had carried on as normal. It wasn't unusual to lose crew members at sea from time to time. No criminal charges had been laid by the authorities. It was simply classified as 'death by misadventure'. Case closed. His wife had been notified with commiserations and received a minimum of compensation and back pay from the company.

As Captain Johansson continued to strain his eyes to peer through the bridge windows, he continually focused on the direction of the ship to point directly into each of the next gigantic waves. His other officers were monitoring the deck hardware, compass and instruments. At approximately 5.20pm the third officer reported that the deck hatches on holds number two and four appeared to be moving slightly upwards as each wave swept over the decks. It was not long before the deck hatches started to part company with their locks. The ship had begun to take on water. They had to act fast; water and wood pulp was a lethal combination that would quickly clog up the filters and pumps. *Endeavour* was rapidly increasing in weight as the combination of cargo and water pushed the hull farther and farther down into the ferocious sea. Johansson did not hesitate.

'Issue a Mayday call immediately!' he shouted. 'Keep the engines and all the pumps at full rpm. All crew are to gather on the top deck and make immediate preparations to abandon ship!'

The Mayday distress call was picked up by another cargo ship, *El Cazador*, heading north out of Puerto Nuevo, Buenos Aires, carrying a full cargo of wheat. She received the position of *Endeavour* and managed to locate her on radar. At approximately 5.45pm, *El Cazador* was probably about one hour from rescue when *Endeavour* disappeared from radar. She was gone.

7

Chapter 7

'Hello, James. It's Mom. Listen, I'm still at the hospital. Dad's okay. He had an angiogram first thing this morning and they found a blocked artery to his heart. Luckily there has not been any lasting damage. Just letting you know that they are keeping him here and will perform what's called a balloon angioplasty to unblock the artery. He's going to need to rest for a while.'

'Oh, thank goodness he's there and in good hands. Give him my love and tell him not to worry. Everything is under control at work. Sarah said she would call you today.'

'She did already, James. She's going to do some shopping for us today and help out wherever she can.'

'Okay, that's good. I'll come and see you and Dad as soon as I can, but I have to visit the terminals and am going to leave after work today. Is there anything else you need?'

'No, we're good. Your dad is in safe hands. I'm so relieved they found out the cause of the chest pains before it was too late.'

'Yes, it took a while to find the problem but, thank god, they found it in time. Give Dad a big hug and a kiss from me. I'll come and see you when I'm back. Love you, Mom.'

James heard a tap on his office door.

'Come in.'

'James, I'm sorry about this morning,' said Chad. 'I work so hard trying to win customers and then keeping them happy. Seems I'm always battling Operations for one reason or another. Sometimes I don't think they have the same urgency as we do.'

'You know what, Chad, you don't have to apologise. Don't stop what you are doing. To be honest with you, I think we could improve our customer turnaround times. I need to find better ways to integrate our maritime deliveries with land transfers. I've got some ideas already, however our most pressing need right now is to stop these accidents and turn the company around. I really need your help.'

James left the office and ordered a roast beef sandwich and fresh orange juice from the nearby cafe on Berkley Street. He needed some fresh air, vitamin C and time to himself. He ate his lunch, quietly decompressing in a nearby park.

On his return, he ran into Rob in the corridor. 'Hey, James, I was just on my way to see you. The area manager, Kevin Renshaw, and his service manager and the warranty manager from the engine company will all be here later to review the denied warranty claim.'

'Good, bring them up to my office as soon as they arrive.'

James settled back in his office and studied the latest set of financial reports. Hal Spencer had been correct in his financial assessment, given during the board meeting. If things didn't change fast, the company would, indeed, be in severe financial straits.

Rob tapped on the door.

James looked up. 'Good afternoon, gentlemen, come in.'

The three engine manufacturer managers sat down around the small conference table in James's office. They all looked rather uneasy.

Kevin Renshaw clasped his hands together in front of himself. 'James, good afternoon.'

James smiled and joined them at the table with Rob. 'Hello, Kevin, it's some time since we last met. I hope you have brought us good news!'

Kevin looked down at the table and took a deep breath. 'I'm sorry to say that we don't. I know what you will say. I have discussed it with Rob. It was not the engine or turbines that caused the failure.'

'I don't understand, Kevin. The engine is in warranty. Period!'

'Yes, you are right. The engine is under warranty and within hours under normal operating conditions. However, the metal we found inside the engine does not match the titanium metal blades of the turbines or their aluminium housings. We found grey iron filings inside the turbines and the engine cylinders.' He let his comments hang in the air.

'So, what are you trying to tell me?'

'I'm saying that the ingress of this metal caused the failure and the only way this could have happened is that someone must have placed the metal flakes and swarf in the air intake system. Our warranty does not cover this. I'm sorry.'

'Are you saying the engine was sabotaged?'

'Yes I am. We further analysed the molecular structure of the foreign particles and there is no way that this is our responsibility.'

Picking the warranty report up, James shifted in his seat and then stood to his full height. 'So, this is a refusal to pay out anything at all?'

'I'm afraid so, Mr Macrae.'

Leaning forward over the table, James peered down at them. 'Very well. You can return the damaged engine to us and I will have an independent analysis done. We have always been a loyal customer to your company, in fact you are our sole engine supplier. How many millions of euros have we paid you over all these years?'

Renshaw shrank back from James. He felt his face redden. 'I know, I know, it's a considerable amount of money.'

James felt his anger started to rise 'You bet it's considerable! It's not just your new engines that power our fleet, it's all the service and parts we buy regularly every month to keep the fleet running!' He pointed his fore finger at each of the visitors in turn. 'You, you and you are going to go back to your office right now and tell your president to call me today and reverse this decision. If you don't, here's what's going to happen. We will change engine suppliers immediately on the ships that are currently being built and stop buying our service and parts from your company. Your competition has been trying hard to win our business for a long time. Do you understand?'

'Well yes, but how can the engine failure be our fault?'

'I heard what you said about sabotage, but just to come in here empty-handed without even an offer to help us out on this huge bill tells me just how much you value our business. Did any of you ever hear of the term "goodwill"?

There was no answer from the visitors.

'This meeting is over! Rob. See them off the premises now.' James pointed them to the door.

8

Chapter 8

'Edmond, can you come up to my office? I want to go over next year's budget with you before I leave for the Shanghai head office tomorrow night.'

'Will do, Hugh. Can you give me about fifteen minutes? I'm in the middle of some bank transfers right now.'

'Go ahead. I'll see you after that.'

Hugh Stanfield, owner and CEO of Euro-Asian Freight Services turned in his swivel chair and looked through the extensive floor-to-ceiling windows of his London office at One Canada Square. The skyscraper overlooked Canary Wharf on the northern side of the River Thames. His corner office was located on the forty-eighth floor, looking out over north London and east down on the docklands and the winding river Thames stretching out to the east.

It was a dull day with a low cloud ceiling as Stanfield looked down towards the Bethnal Green area, now renamed Tower Hamlets. He reflected on his poor childhood, growing up in the back streets of the poverty-stricken and overcrowded housing. With high unemployment amongst its largely unskilled workers, it was no wonder his life had involved crime from a very early age. Without that, he might still be there scrabbling every week to try to cover the rent. At the time, his father was an unemployed dock worker, and his mother was a seamstress in a textile factory in Spitalfields. There had been no real hope of improvement for himself or his two sisters and three brothers. He knew he would have to make his own way in the world. There wasn't much to steal from the other houses in the area, so, with his childhood friend, Jack Carter, they concentrated on stealing coats and other items of clothing from public buildings that could easily be sold to the traders in the East Street Market for cash. Mixing with other like-minded individuals, they also learned the skills of forgery and made money that way. Even now, he and Jack still had business on the side. Old habits of embezzlement and taking easy cash didn't die hard.

Stanfield remembered his first real job as a lowly clerk for Lloyds on an extremely poor wage. He still worked hard, learning every aspect of the business.

As he continued to stare through his office windows, he caught a reflection of himself looking impeccable in his tailored dark suit and tie. He was average-looking, but had developed a certain charm that he could use to inspire confidence with the people around him.

As Stanfield progressed within Lloyds, he took a promotion based in Shanghai. He was a quick learner of Mandarin and was soon fluent in the language. Once away from London, he had the opportunity to hone his skills of forgery, lies, and embezzlement. He managed to amass a small fortune and started his own shipping business, still working for Lloyds. One of the Lloyds associate businesses was a logistics and cargo brokerage company. Stanfield was able to steer cargo through this brokerage, to be transported on his own ships, instead of the company he worked for. It was easy for him to do this, and no one suspected anything.

One of his first vessel acquisitions was *Endeavour*, an ageing 200,000-ton dry cargo bulker. It had been built in the early 1970s during a boom in international trade and shipbuilding. This was the time when ship building costs and weight were minimised by using lighter high-tensile steel instead of the traditional mild steel. Corrosion and metal fatigue were prevalent, especially when exposed in rough seas. Stanfield had bought her when she was ten years old. She was already a tired hull and he knew it.

As he purchased more of these older ships, he arranged for falsified surveys, giving his ships safety certification when they would not pass a legitimate inspection. His overheads and running costs were low in the early days and if there should be a loss at sea, then the insurance would more than cover it with an inflated hull value that he had provided.

By the time he owned ten ships, he was – not surprisingly – finding it difficult to run his own business and work for Lloyds at the same time. While he had his own company management in place, he would now need to devote all his time to Euro-Asian Freight. He left Lloyds. Not a family man, his relationships with women were fleeting. Within his own business and his now extensive list of international contacts, he used his vessels to not only carry legitimate cargo, but also to smuggle guns and munitions, disguised as machine tools, to the hotspots of the world. The IRA proved very profitable in the early days, as was Iraq under Saddam Hussein. Times were changing, however, and by 1994 the IRA was embarking on the ceasefire process. Conversely, Iraq, after being forced to withdraw from Kuwait by the US-led military campaign, had started to build their arsenal of weapons up again. Stanfield saw opportunity.

From time to time he would receive threats from crew members that they would report him for safety violations. One crew member, a Sultan Dastagir, had been a real threat, claiming he would go to the authorities. Stanfield had had no other choice but to silence him for good. His henchman Dan Nash had seen to that. It wasn't long after that *Endeavour* sank altogether.

Stanfield turned his seat back to his desk, smiling to himself. Now in his late forties and still single, he was a self-made and respectable businessman with his own international shipping business. No one would ever suspect that he and his old friend Jack Carter also operated a very profitable arms smuggling business on the side.

'Okay, Hugh. I'm all yours.' Edmond Andreas, CFO of the company, entered his boss's office and took a seat in front of the desk.

Stanfield finished allocating a series of ticks, crosses and question marks on the budget estimates in front of him. He started tapping his pencil on the documents. Looking directly at his visitor, he said, 'Edmond, our last financial year was tough. I can't afford another one. The loss of our most lucrative contract, MidWest Cereal Suppliers, to the Macrae Shipping Company hurt us badly and will continue to influence our figures for the duration of the five-year contract awarded to them. To hear we lost the contract to a company charging higher freight rates is an insult to me personally. MidWest Cereals has been one of our mainstay customers for over ten years!'

'I know, Hugh. I share your concern, in fact I've never seen you so angry as when you returned from the meeting that day. The trouble is, Macrae's, by owning their own terminals, can offer quicker turnaround times than us and that's what MidWest Cereals focused on. If we had owned our own terminals, we could have done the same.'

'But that's just it, we didn't own our own terminals! It grieves me that that little shit James Macrae walks into his family's business and gets handed everything to him on a silver platter! Still, at least we've started to acquire terminals now; Zeebrugge, Belgium, being the first.'

Stanfield picked up the budget paperwork and slid it across the desk.

'Looking at your budget, I can't sign off on this for our new financial year. It's too conservative and your estimates of costs are inflated beyond belief. Don't take me for a fool just because I'm not here all the while. I have to split my time between here and Shanghai. I know what the real costs should be and this budget is padded to hell!'

'Hugh, I can assure you I would never take you for granted. You are a self-made, successful businessman, but you have to understand that costs are rising with inflation.'

Stanfield's eyes widened. 'Bullshit! The market is still slow, which means we can squeeze lower costs from our suppliers. Are you going to do that, or do you want me to do it for you?'

'Hugh. I can't pull a rabbit out of a hat!'

'Well then, you'd better go back and do the figures all over again! I will not accept these figures for next year's budget!' He eyeballed Andreas. With a clenched fist, he continued, 'What the hell have I worked all these years for? To make a profit of only a few million dollars on the total revenue that you are forecasting. With the amount of capital I have tied up, it's nothing short of lunacy!'

He leaned forward over the desk and continued to stare directly into Andreas's face. Through clenched teeth he hissed, 'Go back, cut costs and get me a minimum of twenty per cent return on capital employed. Do you get the message? You know exactly what to do and how to do it, right? God knows, I taught you!' He did not wait for a reply.

Andreas grabbed the papers and stormed out of the room, slamming the door behind him.

9

Chapter 9

Returning to his office after the outburst by Stanfield, Andreas felt bile rise in his throat. He threw up in the adjoining bathroom. In a cold sweat, he looked at the white face in the mirror. 'The bastard never knows when to stop. He's nothing but a ruthless, greedy motherfucker! No wonder everyone despises him!'

He tried to revisit the budget papers in his office, but instead swept them clean off his desk and across the room in a fit of rage. When was it going to stop? Couldn't Stanfield just accept that some years were not as good as others? Sometimes you just had to consolidate, take stock and regroup for another attack on the market as soon as it opened up again.

Andreas locked his office door and took the elevator down to Bank Street. He crossed the road and went into Grinders Cafe. He ordered a large black arabica coffee and sank back into an easy chair in a dimly lit, cosy nook at the rear of the cafe.

He had worked for Stanfield for twelve years at the London office and wondered why he was still there, although he already knew the answer. In that time, he had only visited

Shanghai twice. On his first visit to the office there, he had been surprised by the sheer physical size of the operation. The company was growing fast. He knew Stanfield could tap into funding relatively easily when most of his CFO peers outside the company would struggle to source additional funding in this difficult economic period. The old story of how banks would give you an umbrella on a sunny day and take it away on a rainy day was true to most of these CFOs, but Euro-Asian Freight Services did not seem to have that problem. This had made his job a lot easier and he was happy to be part of the success of the company.

He nursed his coffee and considered his options. Finally he got up and went to a pay phone at the rear of the cafe. He dialled the number from memory.

'Hi, old friend!' he murmured into the phone. 'I need you to meet me at our usual spot. Can you make it in half an hour?'

'Affirmative.' Click.

They met at a Mediterranean restaurant just off Trafalgar Way, behind Billingsgate Market. Large pictures of Italian landmarks decorated the walls, and all the tables were covered in red and white chequered tablecloths. With the subdued lighting, it was a good place for clandestine as well as romantic meetings. The restaurant was quiet at this time in the evening. Traders and back office staff were slowly making their way out of the city to their homes and it was still too early for the evening crowd.

The other man greeted Edmond. 'Hello, my friend, we haven't spoken for how long, twenty-four hours, is it?' He grinned smugly as though he knew what the outcome of this particular conversation would be. So, how can I help you this time, Mr Andreas?

'Ben, I'll get straight to the point. I'm under pressure to reduce costs in next year's budget. Inspections, repairs and maintenance appear to be the only areas that I can cut down on. I've trimmed everything else. Stanfield gave me a roasting this afternoon, which is why I called you. Can you delay the inspection on *Wayfarer*? She'll cost us a fortune to repair after what you told me last year. If we can just get a few more voyages out of her, I can delay the repairs until the following year. Then we can do minimum repairs, you give her a clean certificate and we can sell her off.' Edmond sat back with a smile on his face, believing he had found a huge chunk of money to save this year.

'God! I've taken some chances in the past with Euro-Asian on falsification of reports, but this one, well, I would have to think about it.'

'What do you mean, you'll think about it? You will do it,' Andreas retorted with an emphasis on the 'will'. Then he reflected further on what the inspector had said. 'Or are you just trying to tell me the price is going up? God knows, we've paid you enough in "commission", so don't get righteous with me!'

'Listen, Andreas, you seem to forget my position. There are only so many things I can do for you and keep us both under the radar. As chief inspector of the Blue Water Maritime Bureau, we are the biggest marine classification society in the world. "Managing" marine inspections can be done on a small scale, but delaying *Wayfarer* would be reckless. It could bring us both down. I can't afford to lose my credibility or position and you also have much to lose. Think about it.'

The inspector frowned and continued, 'What worries me more than anything else is the present state of *Wayfarer*. You know full well that we have pushed out vital structural repairs and maintenance far longer than any inspection company would have allowed...even the questionable ones. For a start, we only carried out temporary repairs to the hatches last year, with the proviso that they be replaced, together with the deck frames at the next service interval. What's more is the depth of the corrosion on the front bulkheads. I suspect that there could be a major weakness in the integrity of the main structure if this is not seen to this year. You know, as well as I do, that it is more expensive to repair later rather than sooner. I'm not joking and I'm not bullshitting you. This is not like before. We could massage the reports and cut costs, but they were within, what I call, reasonable limits of safety.'

'Listen, Mitchell!' Andreas hissed as his eyes contracted to cold, empty slits. 'I'm only going to say this once, so listen very carefully. You will do as you are told. Get me *Wayfarer* through this year!'

Mitchell sat up. Andreas was no longer the meek-looking, mild-mannered man that he had dealt with in the past. Suddenly he had shown a new, chilling side to himself. This guy wasn't the gullible, dry accountant he had taken him for. It was clear that when he was under pressure, he operated under a quite different set of rules. Maybe he was the CFO for a reason.

'Look, Edmond, I know what you are saying, but, believe me, when I say there are risks, they really are substantial risks. You remember when *Endeavour* was lost? Don't you think that I didn't ask myself what really happened? It was my inspection report giving her a clean bill of health before she sank! I can't help thinking that there was some kind of sudden, catastrophic structural failure. The ship went down too quickly. Normally you get a little time or warning due to the way holds are built with their own watertight compartments. Something big happened, as the crew only managed to get one Mayday call out and then she just disappeared. I'm worried the same thing could happen to *Wayfarer*. People's lives are at stake, for Christ sake! If that were the case, there would be a major inquiry and you and I could end up behind bars!'

'I don't ever want to hear you say that again. It's your guilty conscience that is playing you up. Let me make myself absolutely clear. You will pass *Wayfarer* with provisos or, at the most, very, very temporary repairs. We are talking just one more year of service and then she can be retired for a Saudi Prince to store his crude oil in until the price per barrel rises and he can sneak it out onto the world's market outside the OPEC quota. Otherwise, I will have to make a call to HMRC.'

'And just to add a small footnote to the conversation. I am an extremely good bookkeeper. I have come up from the bottom, you see. I know all the tricks about keeping correct records of operations, health, safety and finance. Should there be any recriminations on us from your side, we have our house in order. I also have insurance too, which I will not dwell upon, but let's just say that if anything were to happen to me...'

Benjamin Mitchell nodded acquiescently. What had started out to be a fairly safe exercise was now anything but. Something he had never considered would ever happen. He got up to leave.

Edmond went back to his office to re-do the budget.

10

Chapter 10

'I'm sorry, Mr Macrae, we are not in a position to pay out a huge warranty claim that is clearly unrelated to our product. We pride ourselves on our engine designs and performance and, in this case, I have to side with our technical staff.'

'As your major customer, I was asking for a goodwill contribution. Mr. Stevenson, as President of your company, you can make that decision if you value our business.'

'Mr Macrae, of course we value your business, but we can't just pay out money when clearly it wasn't our fault. Imagine if we did that with all our customers?'

James looked across the desk to Rob Bisset, who had heard the whole conversation on speakerphone. James silently drew his finger across his throat in a cutthroat action. Rob nodded in agreement.

'Thank you, Mr Stevenson. Good day.'

'Bloody hell! I thought they might make a contribution towards the claim. Christ! This is yet another drain on our capital that we can ill afford.'

'The clock is running against us alright, James.'

'With what we learned this morning, this now appears to be sabotage. Rob, find out more about the failed engine. I know the engine failed shortly after the ship left our Valencia terminal.' James thought for a second. 'Weren't you visiting the terminal when it happened? The chances are that the engine would have been sabotaged while the ship was docked, not when it was under power.'

'Yes, I was there,' said Rob, looking troubled.

'Well, did you notice anything unusual?'

'No, James, I didn't. In fact, it never crossed my mind. Like you, it was a surprise to hear what was in the warranty report, although the photos and metal analysis were conclusive.'

'Make sure all our security is Code Red on every vessel, terminal and office. We are clearly fighting a hidden enemy.'

'Yes, I'll get it done straight away.'

'Here's what else you need to do today. Change to the German engine supplier on the two new ships we are having built. They have been trying for years to win our business, even to the extent of promising us freight business to carry some of their raw and finished materials. Also, change the service and parts supplier on our existing engines immediately. See if you can get deferred payment terms as well. That should help us with our current cash position. It's clear that our past loyalty to Mr Stevenson and his company means nothing.'

'Consider it done, James.'

James Macrae left the office straight afterwards, going briefly back home to pack for his trip. Sarah hugged and greeted him. 'The kids will be sorry they missed you.'

'I know, but I don't have a choice. One of our employees

died last night after the accident and the others aren't in good shape either.'

'Oh my god, James. This is awful! I'm so sorry!' Sarah exclaimed, shaking her head. She stroked James on his left arm.

'I'm meeting Jason there to investigate why it happened. I will also visit the other terminals.' He moved forward and hugged her, kissing her on the forehead.

She stood back from James. 'Listen, I've got everything under control here. Don't worry about us. How did the meeting go?'

James pressed his lips together tightly. 'It's bad. We will be in financial trouble very soon and it's emerging that there are some troubling similarities between each accident as the back-up fail-safe systems all malfunctioned. I'm still trying to make sense on the timing of each accident as well. Just to add insult to injury, we had a major engine failure warranty claim refused. The engine had been sabotaged!'

'Sabotaged? Who would do that, James?'

'I honestly don't know. Martin Farley said that he heard that two shipping companies were being investigated for arms smuggling to Iraq. It seems strange as there are two other companies in our industry that have grown bigger and more profitable in recent years.

Sarah looked shocked, then looked up at the kitchen clock. 'Crikey, is that the time? I've got to dash and pick up the kids. Listen, I love you very much, so if I'm not back by the time you leave, stay safe and call me when you can.'

James smiled back. 'I love you too, my darling!' They hugged, kissed and parted. Inside he felt frightened and had done his best to hide it. He knew he was now venturing into uncharted territory.

11

Chapter 11

James parked his white Range Rover and went through Security at the private air terminal at Birmingham International Airport just before 6pm. He boarded the company Cessna Citation six-seater jet in the warm evening sun, greeting the company pilot, Leigh, and co-pilot, Craig, as he came aboard.

Leigh turned around in the cockpit. 'Hi, James, good to see you. We are good for our take-off slot. By the way, I heard your dad is in hospital. Is he okay?'

'Yes, he is. It was fortunate they got to him in time. He had a blocked artery.'

'Does this mean we will see more of you now?'

'Yes, I believe it does. We have a lot of work to do!'

'That's good. It's always a pleasure to see you and work with you. Keeping busy keeps us employed.' He put his one hand up to his headset. 'Got to go!'

James sat in one of the rear groups of four seats with tables in between them. He set a sketch pad on the table. As a visual learner, he could always think better with pictures and flow charts in front of him.

The flight to Athens took just over four hours and during that time James took the time to sketch out on a pad each of the events that had recently taken place. He made headings for each event. Location, date, time of day, description, type of failure, company deadlines at time of accident, motive? Next, he listed the two companies that had grown substantially during the latest recession. The last heading was 'odd events'.

James grabbed a chicken sandwich and drink from the galley at the front of the passenger compartment once he had completed his chart. He sat, ate and drank, trying to connect each event. A pattern was starting to emerge in front of him. Rather than jump to any solid conclusions at this stage, he picked up his copy of *Mercantile News*, that he had started to read yesterday morning when his world appeared to be on an even keel. He thumbed through the pages to where he had left off and saw a heading across the page that hit him straight in the face.

Euro-Asian Freight Services buys into Zeebrugge Harbour Terminal.
Euro-Asian Freight Services have announced the purchase of the Zeebrugge container terminal, Belgium's second largest port, effective this month. The terminal has been struggling for some years, outshone by the nearby ports of Rotterdam in the Netherlands and Antwerp in Belgium, Europe's two biggest ports. Hugh Stanfield, the CEO of the company said, 'The purchase of the Zeebrugge terminal is a major step forward for our company. Already a leader and major player in the global shipping industry, this is just the first of our acquisitions into establishing a global network of Euro-Asian Freight Services terminals with the latest

*handling equipment and facilities that will enable faster
turnaround times for our customers. We will be investing over
$700 million dollars on new equipment, new piers and a railroad
connection. In addition, we will be keeping the existing workforce
and are proud to have Zeebrugge in our expanding portfolio.*

James slid his pencil behind his ear. 'Holy shit! I didn't see that one coming. Where the hell did they get the money from to do that? The Zeebrugge terminal was down and out for the count.'

He looked down at his sketchpad again. Euro-Asian Freight Services was one of the companies that he and his staff had identified as growing abnormally fast in a slow market. The other company was Nielsen Shipping Lines. His eyes then scanned down to the last heading on his pad, 'Odd events'.

The Cessna Citation landed smoothly at Athens International private terminal, just after 10.00pm local time. James cleared Customs and Immigration quickly and picked up an Avis Alfa Romeo hire car. The air was still a sticky thirty degrees Celsius. His shirt stuck to his skin with the humidity and he could already taste the putrid smog. Cranking the AC as high as it could go, instead of driving due east through the congestion of Athens, he took Route 62 south west to the coast and then the 91 north east along the winding coast road to the shipyard.

Having grabbed the sandwich on the flight, he got straight to work at the yard, being met by Jason Ferreira, Macrae's Safety and Training Manager and Mateo Ariti, the General Manager of the Piraeus shipyard.

'Okay, what have we got so far, Mateo?' James asked.

'Well, Jason and I have carried out an extensive investigation and we can show you evidence of sabotage. The local police are involved, of course, as this is now a murder inquiry.'

The three of them jumped into a golf cart and drove from the port office through the main container handling port and onto an adjacent jetty, housing a number of jib cranes used to load smaller cargo vessels with dry non-containerised goods. Powerful lights illuminated the whole port with work continuing twenty-four hours per day, seven days per week. The area was full of Macrae ground crew, all wearing luminous-orange jackets and white hard hats. Each worker carried ID on the front and rear of their jackets. Security personnel were dressed in blue uniforms and circulated the port both on foot and in SUVs painted in luminous green.

The central crane stood with four outstretched legs with a square platform on top, eighty feet from the ground. From there, high above the platform, a large, slanted tower crane emerged like the neck and head of a giant dinosaur. At the back of the neck was a long hydraulic arm that enabled the neck to extend itself both forward and rearwards. The crane operator's all-round glass control tower sat above and protruded in front of the platform. This area of the dock was used to load and unload vessels with diverse types of dry goods. It also involved more human interaction using stevedores, unlike the highly mechanised and robotic container terminal on the adjoining dock.

They mounted the non-slip metal steps in single file to the platform housing the electric motors and hydraulics. Inside the brightly lit room they could see the machinery to raise and lower the crane jib and electric hoists to control the crane lifting cables. There was also a large turntable so the crane could rotate through 360 degrees. Jason had already carried out his investigation, having arrived two days earlier. He addressed the others directly and sternly.

'This was not an accident, it was sabotage. Here's why.' He pointed at the machinery with a powerful, narrow beam of light from a pencil flashlight. 'You see the black hydraulic hoses going to and from the hydraulic oil storage tank to the extension rams attached to the lifting and lowering arm of the jib. You can also see the stainless-steel connectors have been slacked off slightly to give the arm enough pressure to raise and lower itself and then, as the pressure builds in the hoses with the weight of the cargo, it lets go. Notice the oil stains around the joints and the floor. Every crane is fitted with a fail-safe device to prevent the hoist cables from letting go. We have taken the housing cover off the safety cogs that should have automatically prevented the cable from unreeling. Can you see where those stainless-steel countersunk screws have been unscrewed and the braking cogs have been slid away from the teeth of the cable drum?' Everyone nodded. Jason continued. 'Those cogs were slid along this key-holed spline shaft deliberately. We know because there was a weekly crane inspection only three days before the accident, or, in this case, sabotage.'

Mateo, the GM, confirmed that the police had reached the same conclusion.

James looked at Mateo and Jason and raised his eyebrows. 'I have some observations. Firstly, I take it you have checked with your security staff on the land side of the perimeter of the port prior to this event?'

Mateo replied. 'Yes, we have. Anyone who entered the port forty-eight hours before this had full authority for access. In addition, we have checked all closed-circuit tv recordings and there were no breaches of security. Facial recognition by our security staff confirms what we call a state of Green. Moreover, the police have interviewed our staff and reviewed the footage. They reached the same conclusion we did. I may add that the expertise of our security staff and our police force is of an exceedingly high standard. This port stands at the crossroads of Europe and the Middle East. Any likely international terrorist activities using the shipping industry to smuggle whatever, would pass through the Suez Canal to our south and eastward through the Med.'

James looked at the two others in turn, nodding his head slowly. 'My understanding would be that this sabotage was carried out by an experienced technician or engineer. This was precision, not the hand of an amateur.' Jason nodded in agreement and James continued. 'My next assumption would be that the culprit came from the sea or it was an inside job, since there was no apparent breach of security from the land side.'

Mateo jumped in. 'Each of our staff, both ground crew and security, go through stringent criminal and background checks. At this point we do not have any evidence that this was an inside job, but you never know. The police are interviewing and cross-checking everyone.'

James nodded. 'I'll have Lynda Ferreira carry out a personnel check.'

James continued, 'So, logically, that would lead us to the conclusion that the saboteur must have come in on a visiting cargo vessel, carried out the job and escaped when his ship left port. I wonder if this person is a regular crewman or perhaps a paid professional using the ship to enter and leave the port?'

No one made any comments and then James added, 'Of

course, it could also be a possibility that it was one of our own employees coming in on a ship, docking and leaving?'

Mateo replied. 'There were two Macrae ships loading at the dock at the time of the accident.' James added another note to himself to check if any of the same Macrae crewman were visiting the other Macrae ports at the time of the other sabotage incidents. Lynda would need to get back to him fast, in order to narrow down their search.

'Mateo, can you also give me a printout of the log for arrivals and departures two days before and after the accident of all visiting ships and their owners? Ships don't stay long in port, so we'll concentrate on these four days. Tomorrow morning I want to visit with the injured stevedores and also visit with the family of Hector, who died.'

James had a reservation organised by the Birmingham office at the Peiraius Port Rooms hotel. He went straight there for what was left of the night, as he was due to fly to Istanbul the next day at around noon. Back at the hotel, James stood in the rainfall shower for far too long, thinking. *If the saboteur came in from the sea it could possibly fit in with the theory that it was a competitor who was gunning for them.*

By 7.00am, James was up, dressed and driving back to the terminal. Even with only four hours' sleep, he felt rested. He drove in silence, his mind having rebooted itself after a period of rest. One sentence in the article he had read in *Mercantile News* about Euro-Asian Freight kept nagging at him:

Already a leader and major player in the global shipping industry, this is just the first of our acquisitions into establishing a global network of Euro-Asian Freight Services terminals with the latest handling equipment and facilities that will enable faster turnaround times for our customers.

He gripped the steering wheel as his mind sifted through the pieces of the jigsaw puzzle. He pulled up at a red traffic light on Antistaseos Avenue. Several pieces were dancing in his vision at the same time. First piece: two competitors growing abnormally fast. Second piece: Euro-Asian buying a European terminal and investing a whopping $700 million dollars into the operation. Third piece: Martin Farley had floated the idea that a competitor might want to weaken them and take them over. Fourth piece: sabotage from outside sources.

An airhorn blew behind him from a loaded Scania transport truck. The traffic lights had turned to green, and he had just sat there pondering his thoughts. 'Shit, I nearly had it!' He pushed the accelerator down and moved forward. There was still a missing jigsaw piece that he knew was there, but he had been jolted out of his trance too soon.

Mateo and Jason were already in Mateo's office, overlooking the terminal, when he got there.

Mateo greeted him. 'There's coffee and croissants there for you.'

'Great. Thanks!'

'James, following our conversation yesterday and the possibility of the attack coming from another vessel in dock, we may have found something on the CCTV footage. There was a ship here for two days before the accident, loading and unloading in the oil terminal.' He turned the computer monitor around to face James. 'If you look closely at the disembarking crew of the vessel *Aviemore*, most of the crew are Indian and Filipinos. You can see the captain and first officers, but there seems to be a Caucasian crewman who looks a little different. His bag looks smaller and the way he carries it suggests it could be heavy because he shifts his hold several times from hand to hand. With the angle of the camera, you can't really see his face, but his hair is dark and unruly. Not sure if it's the shadow, but, by the shape of his nose, it may have been broken at some stage. Not much to go on but, hey, we can't overlook anything.' Mateo paused the video and looked at Jason.

'Now, here's where it gets interesting,' Jason said. 'Look at the next video and see if you see anything familiar, James.'

Mateo pressed Play.

Jason continued. 'This comes later than the video you have just seen, but here you can see a man of about the crewman's size climb the steps to the tower crane. Only thing is, this person is wearing a Macrae hi-viz jacket and white hard hat, provided for our own dock staff. You can also see a bag, like the one that we showed you of the crewman from *Aviemore*. None of our own staff have reported their jackets, identities or hard hats missing and none of our staff say they climbed the tower at the recorded time.'

'Did you see anything familiar?'

'Spin the video back again and play it in slow-motion.' Mateo pressed Replay and the frames came up slower.

'There it is. Looks like the same guy!' exclaimed James.

'That's what we think too. We've looked at this a few times. We also think the bag is heavy as it would contain the tools necessary to sabotage the crane.'

James raised his eyebrows. The footage was certainly a start and might help them piece the jigsaw together. 'Can you get me the best still of this man?'

'Will do, James, although the image will be fairly grainy due to the low light conditions.' Next, he handed over a computer printout. 'Here's the list of ships and their owners you asked for.' There were a number of companies listed, but

James noticed that *Aviemore* was owned by Euro-Asian Freight Services. She had discharged a cargo of crude oil, had her tanks purged and then loaded a full cargo of refined petroleum. Refined petroleum was the main export of Greece. No ships from Nielsen Shipping had visited the terminal in that period.

Jason added, 'I also spoke with Lynda this morning and she confirmed that there were not any Macrae vessels in the ports when the accidents occurred. That seems to rule out that any sabotage was caused by our employees.'

James answered. 'Okay, let's check on *Aviemore* using marinetraffic.com.'

Mateo logged in. She's a super tanker of 500,000 deadweight tonnes heading north through the Med on the western side of Italy. She could be discharging her cargo in Genoa.'

'Okay, give me ten minutes, I need to call Genoa and then we can go and visit the injured stevedores.' Finishing his second cup of coffee, James called Flavio Romano, the Genoa Terminal general manager.

'Hey, Flavio, how are you?'

'Personally OK, but we are working flat-out to try to make up for the loss of revenue we incurred after the last accident. I've obviously stepped up security and we are still none the wiser as to who would have sabotaged our equipment. We don't think it was one of our own. When are you expecting to get here?'

'Right now, I'm in Piraeus and I'll head to Istanbul later today so I should be with you late tomorrow afternoon. Can you check your terminal reservations and see if a vessel by the name of *Aviemore*, one of Euro-Asian's fleet, is due there shortly?'

'Give me a minute.' James could hear Flavio tapping on his keyboard. 'Yes, she is due to dock in the next few hours and offload her cargo of petroleum.'

'Okay, Flavio. Can you keep a close eye on her crew? We are not really sure what we are looking for, but *Aviemore* was in port here in Piraeus at the time of the sabotage and we think it was a possibility that one of her crew could be responsible for it. We don't believe the threat came from the land side.'

'What am I looking for, James? Do you have a description of any kind?'

'Frankly, we don't, we are just following up hunches right now. It's all we can do for the moment. One thing is for sure; the sabotage was the work of an expert, a technician of some sort who knows his machinery.'

'Interesting,' Flavio replied. 'The same applies here; the accidents were carefully planned. Very precise, almost surgical, in their nature. We'll show you when you get here. Seems to me that the culprit or culprits would come from an engineering background, rather than just an ordinary deckhand. Okay, we'll keep an eye out. I'll also have the cameras focused on *Aviemore* while she unloads and her crew disembark.'

'Good, how is morale right now?'

'In the tank, I'm afraid. All the staff know what has been happening at the other terminals as well and they are scared. There's talk of a revolt by some of the stevedores with a work stoppage.'

James started to massage his aching neck. 'Bollocks! That's the last thing we need right now. Any more stoppages and we'll be crippled!'

12

Chapter 12

J ames put his hand to his chest as he felt his heart rate starting to accelerate. He tried to dismiss it as best he could. A work stoppage would only bring the demise of the company closer. Time was running out.

He climbed into the passenger seat of the Nissan Armada driven by Mateo. Jason was in the rear seat. 'Okay, Mateo, let's go and visit the injured crew, but first I want to visit Hector's wife.'

James knocked on the door of a fourth-floor apartment in the Neo Faliro district, not far from the port. A man, in his twenties, answered the door.

'Hello, my name is James Macrae of Macrae Shipping. I was hoping I could see Mrs Aetos?'

'I'm her son. Let me just see if she's up to it.'

James waited at the door.

'You can come in.'

James entered the apartment. There was an open-plan kitchen with an adjoining lounge. Mrs Aetos sat on a sofa facing the window. James walked around to face her. Her eyes were red as she clutched a damp handkerchief between her hands. He held out his hand.

'Mrs Aetos, I'm so sorry for your loss. Words can't express how I feel. I knew your husband personally. He was truly a friend and a good man.'

Mrs Aetos nodded. 'Thank you for your kind words and taking the time to visit with me and my son. Hector always spoke highly of you.

This is my son, Adonis.'

'Adonis, I am so sorry.'

Adonis nodded.

'I wanted to let you know that the company will look after you. We'll pick up all the expenses for the funeral arrangements and any other outstanding expenses. I will also ensure that we provide the best pension we can. Your husband was a hero.'

Adonis replied. 'Thank you, Mr Macrae, that is kind of you. How was my father a hero?'

'Have you not been told? It was your father that saved the lives of his co-workers. Apparently he heard the crane go and pushed others out of the way. They were all injured, but the push was just enough to save their lives.'

'We didn't know that,' said Mrs Aetos.

'I just learned what Hector did this morning. The company will be recognizing his bravery, and I believe the authorities will too.'

James shifted position on the sofa.

He paused and swallowed hard. 'I'm sorry to tell you both, this was not an accident.'

'I don't understand,' replied Mrs Aetos, quietly.

James tried to choose his words carefully. 'It's possible

75

the police will want to speak to you. You see, the crane was sabotaged, and Hector's death is now a murder inquiry. We don't know who's done this, but I can assure you that whoever it is will be hunted by the police as well as ourselves. We will never forget Hector. I'm so sorry.' James leaned over and hugged them both.

As he left, he gave his business card to Adonis. 'Adonis, my cell number is on the card. If you or your mother need anything, call me. I'm here for you.'

As James got back into the car with Mateo and Jason, no one spoke.

They pulled up in front of Tzaneio hospital and met Dario, Jonas and Spyro, the injured employees, in a ward on the third floor.

James was taken aback by their broken and battered appearances. The men's faces were black and blue, dried blood still congealed in their hair. Splints and bandages covered various limbs. Jonas was in a wheelchair, while Dario and Spyro sat in their beds, various limbs in plaster. He moved forward to each of them and touched them gently on the shoulder.

'God, I wish I could say it was good to see you. I'm so sorry for this and the loss of Hector.'

Jonas just sat in his wheelchair with his head leaning forward, looking at the worn lino floor.

Dario spoke. 'James, thank you for coming to see us. Mateo and Jason were here yesterday, and they are making sure we have everything we need. It's not just us either, they are looking after our families as well. We are all grateful to you.'

'Well, we are going to make sure you all get the best possible treatment; whatever it costs, I don't care. We will take care of you. Now, what's the status of everyone?'

Dario continued, 'Jonas has concussion and a couple of broken ribs. If he wasn't strapped up so tight, he might have tried to give you a hug.'

Jonas smiled.

James got up and put his hand gently on Jonas's shoulder.

Dario continued. 'As for Spyro, apart from a broken foot, leg and wrist, he's in great shape. He'll be back in the company soccer team in no time!'

Spyro smiled and did a thumbs-up with his good hand.

James smiled back. 'You know, Spyro, you pushed me to join the team when I worked here. Our games were some of the happiest times of my life, especially after each game!' They all laughed together.

Dario piped up, 'Yes and I remember when we all had to carry you back into the bus James after the one game when we won the cup. I've never seen anyone defy the laws of gravity yet! Not even you!' They all continued to laugh, Jonas trying his best not to.

'So how about you, Dario, how are you doing?'

'For me, you can see I've got a broken arm, but my right shoulder got smashed up pretty good. I believe it will be a long reconstruction, but, hopefully, I will get the full use of the arm back again. At least, that's what they tell me.'

'Well, we will do all we can to help. Now, you will no doubt get visits from the police as Hector's death is now a murder inquiry. The police agree with both Mateo and Jason that the equipment was deliberately sabotaged. I can assure you that whoever is responsible will be brought to justice.'

Back in the car, James commented, 'I don't know how you two feel, but it's like we are in a dark room fighting an opponent that we can't see, hear, smell or feel. I suppose we just have to keep punching in the dark until we hit something or someone.'

Jason answered. 'That's exactly how I feel too.'

'I was going to visit Genoa after Istanbul, but think I'll go directly there first. Jason, can you stay here with Mateo and oversee repairs to the crane. It seems the police have all the evidence they need, including photos, so let's get back to full operations as quick as we can.'

James contacted Leigh to file the flight plan for Genoa and let Flavio know that he would arrive later that evening. Just before he left the Piraeus yard in his rental car, Mateo caught up with him.

'James. Listen, I can see the stress you are going through right now. I consider us friends, not just co-workers. Everyone now knows about Richard's health problems and we all know everything has fallen on your shoulders, but you should know that everyone in this company is behind you. These attacks are against all of us. You are stronger than you think you are!'

13

Chapter 13

Dan Nash opened the steel, watertight hatch of *Aviemore* and stepped out onto the afterdeck. Lying on his back in the confined steering gear room, deep in the stern of the ship for the last three hours, he needed to fill his lungs with air other than stale diesel fumes. He had been overhauling the dual hydraulic steering pumps and actuators.

The thin cirrus shreds of cloud stretched high in the sky from the west like long spindly fingers, silhouetted against the deep-blue sky above. He revelled in the fresh sea air as a few seagulls trailed the stern, erratically darting and diving into the foaming wash of the ship.

He smiled to himself as he recalled his latest act of sabotage in Piraeus. Taking care of Dastagir and the sabotage of the deck hatches on *Endeavour* had netted him more funds in his offshore bank account than ever before. *Whisky and women, here I come.*

He lit up a Marlboro, enjoying the strong taste and ensuing nicotine hit. He remembered his first encounter with Stanfield when they met one drunken Friday night in a seedy Shanghai bar full of other sailors, hookers and desperadoes. The Lucky Star bar was located on the waterfront on Songpu Road, Wusong, close to the port. He had gotten into a fight with the Russians, but had seen them off. Sitting alone at the bar afterwards, he was drinking yet another beer when Stanfield approached him.

'You can handle yourself alright! I'm impressed. You fight like I've never seen before; mean *and* dirty.'

'Who the fuck are you?'

'Hugh Stanfield. How long are you in port for?'

'What's it to you?'

'Well, I might have a job for you.'

'I've already got a job. Don't need another.'

Nash turned and flicked the stub of his cigarette overboard. A seagull darted deftly after it. He stood in the lee of the bridge, shielded from the wind, and thought some more about his life. Originally from Kitimat, on the north coast of British Columbia, Canada, he was the son of a construction worker who had been employed to build the dam and surrounding facilities that would provide the necessary hydro-electric power for an aluminium smelter. His father was a tough nut and liked his drink. Growing up in a violent household where his father would return home from the bar pissed as a rat, beat his mother, his brothers and himself up, didn't give him much of a chance. He possessed the same violent genes his father had.

When he was old enough, he became an apprentice welder and hydraulics mechanic, working for Rio Tinto Alcan, the biggest employer in the town. Once qualified, he knew he had to get away from his family and Kitimat. His mother was already long gone, and he was now grown up and a lot stronger. The tipping point came one night when his father came home drunk as usual and started to push him around, demanding that dinner should have been ready.

'Where's my fucking dinner, you little bastard! And where's the rest of the little brats?'

Nash had stood tall and faced his father directly. 'Those little brats, as you call them, have all gone.'

'Gone where?'

'Somewhere else, that's where.'

'Don't fuck with me, boy! Where are the little bleeders and where is my fucking dinner?' His father pushed him hard across the kitchen table. He had flown backwards across it, knocking the surrounding chairs flying. That was it. No more. As his father came at him with his sleeves rolled up, he darted to the side and, as his father fell forward, he smashed him over the back of his head with the large teapot from the shelf.

'You fucking bastard!' his father had shouted, 'I'll kill you for this, you little cunt!'

He ducked the wild right cross punch coming for him and then counter-punched his father square on the nose, splitting it wide open. As his father went down, he kicked him in his ribs several times for good measure and one final hefty kick went to his crotch. He left him writhing in agony on the stone floor, covered in sweat and with blood trickling from his nose and head.

He left home. With Kitimat being an important port on the northwest shipping lanes connecting North America to the Pacific Rim, he had found a life at sea; welding and repairing hydraulic leaks on ships hatch covers, conveyor belts and other deck and engine room machinery.

He lit another cigarette and went back to remembering his first encounter with Stanfield in Shanghai. 'So, are you sober

81

enough to talk now, or do you want to meet me tomorrow?' Stanfield had asked.

Something about Stanfield intrigued him. He was drunk, but not so far gone to wonder why a smartly dressed man would visit a place like this and why would he talk in Mandarin to the local bar staff?

'Who are you?'

'Before I answer that, tell me about your skills. I sense that you are not an ordinary seaman,' Stanfield replied.

And so, he had told Stanfield about his skills and his background. From there, he had become an employee of Euro-Asian Freight, maintaining and servicing their tired but extensive fleet. As time went by, he carried out a number of questionable acts for Stanfield, gaining more trust from his employer each time. The financial rewards grew and for the first time in his life he had money in his pocket. Sultan Dastagir was the first man he had ever killed, and he found out that he didn't care about taking another man's life. Death meant nothing to him.

His cell phone vibrated in his pocket, jerking him from his memories. It was a burner phone Stanfield had given him.

'Dan, can you talk? Where are you?'

'Hi. I'm on *Aviemore* with a cargo of refined petroleum sailing west in the Med to Genoa. I'm doing routine maintenance on the steering gear.'

'Did everything go according to plan in Piraeus?' Stanfield enquired.

'Yes it did. That should help terrorise the bastards, right?'

'Good work.' He continued on, coolly, 'Here's what I want you to do next. When you get to Genoa, you need to turn around and jump ship onto our cargo vessel *Wenzhou*. She should be ready to sail from Genoa within a few hours after you arrive. She will have a full cargo of computerised machine tools ready to sail to Yanbu, Saudi Arabia. While the manifest states only machine tools, within the shipment are twenty crates of Beretta PM12's submachine guns and 9x19 mm cartridges. I want you to escort these crates from Yanbu across the border into Iraq through Medina, Hail, Sakaka and Arar. Transport is already laid on. Just make sure that Nabil receives them safely. You've met Nabil Quraishi before. Let him know that this will be the last shipment for a while. I'll arrange all necessary visas and paperwork for you to enter Saudi Arabia and Iraq. Come back with the trucks and then catch a flight from Jeddah to London as soon as you can. I'll let you know more details of what we'll be doing after that.'

Chapter 14

'Good morning, Mr Andreas!' The security reception desk officer looked surprised. 'You only left work at two this morning.'

'Yes, I know. Tell me about it!'

It was 6.00 a.m., the morning after his meeting with Ben Mitchell, chief inspector of Blue Water Maritime Bureau of Shipping. He had worked late into the night, not only to complete the revised budget, but also to complete his explanation on how the company could expand in a tightening economy. His boss was tough to work for, but they did have an understanding. Hugh Stanfield was ruthless, but Andreas was cunning and greedy.

The two men were alone in Stanfield's plush office with the door closed. The smell of coffee permeated the air.

'So, Edmond, show me your revised budget.' Stanfield asked as he stood up and adjusted the blinds on the eastern-facing windows looking down from the office tower onto Billingsgate market and the roof tops of east London. The river Thames reflected the bright sunlight back at him like a winding, glowing silkworm. He was calm this morning after sleeping well. Looking out through the window, he thought about the company that he had created. It was a powerhouse in the industry and would swallow anything within its way. His henchman, Dan Nash, had proven to be not only highly effective at his job of hydraulics engineer, but a dedicated and loyal enforcer. As a highly skilled operative, Nash was focused on infiltrating their adversary, Macrae Shipping Company, to bring them to their knees. Today he would start to tie together all the chaos he had carefully created to eventually takeover Macrae Shipping and its terminals that he so desperately needed.

He returned to his desk and picked up the budget file. After scrutinising the figures for some time in silence, he used his calculator and challenged Andreas on his estimates for expenses. This was the area he was most interested in. He knew the capabilities for next year's gross sales revenue. With his legitimate business, he had good contracts in place. The extra revenue he would make up with his illicit below-the-table business of arms dealings, an area that Andreas was not party to. Stanfield had been incredibly careful over the years at keeping his clandestine activities in different silos, or, as the IRA called them, 'cells'. It was a good model to follow, since no one person could see the full scope of the operations; only those that they directly interfaced with.

'How come you were able to reduce expenses so much between yesterday and today?' he asked, looking directly at Edmond.

Edmond sat straight up in his chair. He knew Stanfield would ask this question, so he had carefully prepared his answer. 'Firstly, I had a very conservative accrual for the insurance payout for the loss of our cargo ship *Endeavour*. To be honest with you, I was using this accrual as a financial cushion if we needed it next year if the world economy continues to worsen. As you know, we overvalued the value of the hull with Sterling-Judge Marine Insurance. Of course we had to pay higher premiums, but, knowing the eventual outcome of a total loss, it was worth it. So, we scored big on that one. In addition, the cargo was covered by a separate insurance company. The value of Bills of Lading I had over-inflated with bribes to the Uruguay supplier. Again, we made a substantial profit. All in all, the loss of *Endeavour* was a financial success! I just didn't think that the end would come as soon as it did.'

The two men smiled at each other, quite content with the financial outcome. Neither of them considered the thought that they had committed mass murder by sending the entire crew into the deep, murky depths of the South Atlantic Ocean. While Stanfield and Andreas both knew they had fudged the inspection and maintenance reports by bribing Ben Mitchell, Andreas was not aware of the role that Dan Nash had played in the sabotage of the deck hatches. Stanfield had always kept Dan Nash as his dirty tricks hatchet man very confidential.

'You make it sound easy, Edmond.'

Edmond perked up. Maybe for the first time in his life, he was becoming a 'someone'. He looked eagerly to his boss for praise. 'Well, I had to do some fucking fancy footwork with the Sterling-Judge insurance adjuster.' He continued, 'They have their own adjuster by the name of David Morris. Mr Morris proved to be exceedingly difficult in trying to undervalue the value of the hull. Seems he is an experienced claims assessor and carries out forensic audit inspections for the company. He spent some time going through all our service and maintenance records, and not just of *Endeavour*. Fortunately, we had our asses covered with the complete maintenance and inspection reports signed off by none other than Ben Mitchell. Also, with *Endeavour* at the bottom of the ocean, nobody will ever know the truth. To be honest, I'm not sure that we have heard the last of David Morris. He is a persistent son of a bitch. We will need to keep a close eye on him.

Stanfield made a note of the name David Morris on the pad in front of him.

'Good work! Do carry on with how these expenses have dramatically fallen since yesterday.' Stanfield wasn't letting Andreas off the hook easily.

'Well, secondly, I threatened Ben Mitchell last night to delay the major overhaul of *Wayfarer* until the next financial year. He will complete the paperwork for this year with some small repairs and sign off on them. This means we will avoid substantial overhaul and repair costs in a dry dock for the time being.'

'Can Mitchell be relied upon to keep this confidential or are we in danger of him blowing the whistle on us?' Stanfield queried.

'I have our bases covered; tax evasion. I didn't even have to bring up the sex stuff. Exposure would end his career, his marriage and lead to a lengthy stay at Her Majesty's Service. He will comply.'

'Will these figures hold water, Edmond? Can I rely on them?'

Andreas took a deep breath and replied forcibly, 'Yes you can.' He knew he had done his homework.

'Okay. I'm satisfied with the budget,' Stanfield continued. 'Now let's move on to the other task I set you. What is the latest intelligence you have picked up from your contact inside the Macrae Shipping Company?'

Andreas replied, 'Well I spoke with our contact early this morning. Apparently Richard Macrae is in hospital undergoing cardiac tests, so James Macrae has taken the reins.'

'Hmm. Now that's interesting!' Stanfield continued to tap his pencil on the pad in front of him.

'It seems there was an extraordinary board meeting yesterday. Bottom line is that they are suffering from several serious accidents that have affected their company very badly, with substantial financial losses. They only have liquidity for the next fiscal quarter. They believe that there are two possible companies trying to weaken them and take them over. We could be one of those companies since we have grown exponentially in the last few years.'

'Hmmm, even more interesting.' Stanfield sat forward and leaned further over the desk. 'Are you sure that your contact is on the level about their precarious financial situation?'

'Yes I am. Our contact has been honest about everything so far.'

'I'm impressed, Edmond. This is excellent news. Okay. Here's what I want you to do now. If Macrae can only cover the next quarter, they will need to source long-term finance with other banks and finance companies. Start to spread rumours that the Macraes are in financial trouble and that should create sufficient doubt amongst your banking fraternity. We just need to create enough doubt to stop them securing their future. In the meantime, prepare me a list and estimated valuation of all their assets. Use your contact as necessary, but be careful. Can you prepare this within a month? Make sure the report covers all their ports, equipment, offices, warehouses and exclude any goodwill. I'm leaving on the BA flight this afternoon, arriving in Shanghai tomorrow morning. I will be in the Shanghai office for two weeks. Get hold of me if you pick up any more information on Macrae Shipping.'

'Before you go, Hugh, what about the separate company we set up under Euro-Asian Freight to handle our new venture in Zeebrugge? As a separate cost and profit centre, we are going to need to source funding for all the upgrades we have promised. We will need the funding sooner rather than later.'

'I know, Edmond. I have the funding arranged already and will open it up to you once I'm back in Shanghai.'

'How do you do it, Hugh? I don't understand. How are we funding these? As CFO, I have to be concerned that we are not leveraging ourselves too thin.'

'That's noble of you, Edmond, but let me worry about that. After building this company from the ground up, I'm not about to throw it all away.'

Andreas stood up and shook his boss's hand. 'Okay. Have a safe trip.' Andreas left the office perplexed on how they could suddenly source over seven hundred million dollars just like that. Something funny was going on.

As Andreas left his office, Stanfield shouted to his secretary,

'Can you hold all my calls? I don't want to be disturbed for the next little while.' He closed his door and took a burner phone out of his briefcase.

'Hello, Jack. It's Hugh. Listen, are you free for lunch?' Stanfield could hear the clink of glasses and bottles in the background, so he knew Jack was in the pub they both owned.

'Can I call you back in a few?'

'Yes, do that.'

Stanfield and Jack had bought the pub between them over

twenty years ago with laundered money. The income had come from supposedly exporting TVs and computers. With Stanfield's growing knowledge of the shipping industry, they would load trucks up with merchandise, drive them to the docks at Dover, have their export papers stamped and then drive straight out of the docks again, back into England and claim back all the sales tax and VAT. The goods would then be sold inside the country at the higher price, tax included, without ever being exported. The pub had become their secret base and while Stanfield lived in Shanghai, Jack continued to run the pub and pursued on his crime path. Stanfield smiled to himself. 'What a fucking unit! Two childhood friends still involved in a life of crime, neither of them ever being charged with anything.'

His phone vibrated. 'Okay, Hugh, I can talk now.'

'Jack, I need you to do something for me, but I would rather discuss it in person. Are you free if I'm there around noon? It'll have to be quick as I have a flight from Heathrow later.'

'No worries, me old china. See you then.'

The midday lunchtime was busy with office workers out enjoying the warmth on their lunch breaks. Stanfield jumped out of the London black cab in front of the National Westminster Bank on Bishopsgate and strode back east towards Tower bridge, turning left onto Middlesex Street, a smaller side road. He walked through a maze of older buildings and offices and entered a narrow alleyway called Sandy's Row and then turned right into an even narrower worn-down cobblestone alleyway called Artillery Passage. It was no more than six feet wide. The old four-storey red and honey brick buildings on either side must have had some history to tell over the centuries. Older wooden shopfronts with small windows and doors lined each side of the alleyway and there, set amongst them, was the Bulldog and Beaver, known to locals as the Bulldog and Bollocks. The exterior of the brick and timber-framed pub was quaint and crooked. The door and window frames were painted black and small bull's-eye-paned glass windows were underlined with white window boxes full of overflowing red geraniums. The name of the pub was picked out in contrasting gold paint.

Stanfield stood back as far as he could to look at his property. He had not visited the pub for some time. Because of its inaccessibility, few tourists ever ventured down the real backstreets of the old city, but it was popular with the locals. Stanfield and Carter had bought the place for several good reasons. It was a legitimate business to launder money; people could come and go regularly without raising suspicion; and, lastly, there was access through a large set of wooden double doors for vehicles into a small warehouse at the rear of the pub. The road at the back of the pub was fairly narrow, but was accessible with a small truck. Vehicles could come and go unobserved.

As Stanfield entered the freehouse pub, he was met with a haze of smoke, loud chatter and laughing, mixed with the sound of clinking glassware. Jack was behind the bar with a white tea towel slung over his shoulder. Jack's face looked redder than ever. His skin was more pock-marked and his nose looked almost purple; too much exposure to smoke and alcohol. He pulled a pint of London Pride bitter and slid it across the oak bar to his partner.

'Thanks, Jack. The place looks great! How are you doing?'

'I'm well, Hugh. Business is good and we are always busy. What can I get you for lunch? We can go in the back while it's prepared.'

Stanfield ordered a ploughman's. They went through a door marked 'private' at the side of the bar through the kitchen and into a hallway leading to the warehouse. Jack unlocked a door to the side, and they entered a private office.

'Good to see you again, Hugh!' They hugged each other. 'So, what would you like me to do that needed a face-to-face meeting?'

'Jack, I need you to take someone for me and hold them for a while. I'm assuming you can safely hide them here in our basement.'

'Shouldn't be a problem. Since you were last here, I've fitted out one of the rooms as a living and bedroom. We could use that. It's secure and soundproof, being located so far underground. Let me show you.'

They went back out into the hallway again and then through another door that led down to the stone-walled cellar where the beer barrels were stored. A wooden ramp with iron side guards ran up at an angle from the floor to a set of trap doors mounted in the pavement above at the rear of the pub. This was where the barrels of beer were rolled down by the draymen from the delivery trucks outside in the street. The cold, damp cellar smelled of centuries of stale beer. Stored on wooden pallets on the floor were aluminium casks as well as the traditional oak wooden beer barrels. Some were already hooked up to the pumps above them in the bar. At the rear of the cellar, Jack opened an old cupboard. Inside the cupboard, he slid back a secret panel to expose a small room with a trap door in the floor. Opening the trap door, Jack flicked a switch illuminating a set of narrow stone steps leading down to another room below.

Hugh smiled to himself. 'You know, Jack, when we bought this place twenty years ago, no one knew this was here. It was quite a find. Here we were, buying a freehold pub in the old City of London, laundering money and we end up discovering a whole Roman spa and baths beneath the premises. It has been more use to us than had we informed the authorities that we had found it.'

They descended deep down, following the spiralling, worn stone steps into a large underground room with a classic stone vaulted ceiling. Built out of terracotta bricks, the baths opened out into a hall of huge proportions with vast colonnades and wide-spanning arches and domes. An intricate mosaic floor and marble-coloured walls adorned the entire structure.

Jack led Hugh to a small room at the side of the spa. The walls and ceiling were insulated and decorated. A couple of easy chairs and a bed filled the room. He had added a small bathroom to the side.

'What made you do this, Jack?'

'Actually, I thought I might have to lie low for a while and this was the best place I could think of to disappear. It turned out that the Old Bill nicked the wrong gang for the job, but framed them and so I didn't need to do a runner after all!'

'Bloody hell! Talk about your luck!' Stanfield looked around the room. 'This is perfect.'

'I thought you'd like it! Now, who is the victim?'

15

Chapter 15

As the Euro-Asian super tanker *Aviemore* slid quietly and slowly through the Multedo entrance into the port of Genoa oil terminal, Dan Nash stayed out of sight. He mentally prepared himself to take extra precautions after causing all manner of chaos at the Piraeus terminal and at the Genoa terminal on his previous visit. He didn't think anyone would have spotted him before, in his Macrae disguise, but he knew he still had to be careful. He checked his kit bag to ensure his Macrae hi-viz jacket and white hard hat were still there. He would lay low till the right opportunity arose to leave the ship.

The sun, now weakening in the afternoon sky, lit up the partially snow-capped mountains surrounding the port with long shafts of golden beams, shining slantwise through the broken clouds. The tall, historic lighthouse of Genoa stood tall at 380 plus feet above sea level and aided the pilots safely into dock.

On arrival, Macrae dock personnel boarded the ship and connections were made to the pumps to offload the full cargo of refined petroleum. Nash waited until they were finished and then simply blended in with the other Macrae personnel when they disembarked in the failing natural light. He tagged on at the end of the line. What Dan did not notice until he followed the last Macrae dockhand was that a white reflective stripe had been added crosswise to their jackets from the left shoulder to the right hip since the last time he was here. *Damn!* he thought to himself, but it was too late to turn around now.

Once on the dock, he moved swiftly to the shadow side of the adjacent warehouse. The high-pressure sodium lights were still warming up in the dusk, so had not yet reached their full luminosity. He checked for the position of any security cameras and did his best to find a blind spot. Next, he dumped the jacket and hard hat in a metal dumpster. From his bag, he took out a baseball cap and put on his Euro-Asian Freight Services coveralls and marched confidently across the dockyard towards the dry goods dock section of the terminal.

Just as he was crossing from the oil terminal to the dry goods dock, he had to present his identity and papers to Macrae security at a crossover post. Nash was a pro. 'Hi!' he said. 'Just going to embark on *Wenzhou*, routine maintenance.'

The guard carefully checked his Euro-Asian Freight Services credentials and passed Nash's passport to an assistant, who took a photocopy of it and kept hold of it for the time being.

'So why were you in the oil terminal when your vessel is in this section?' The guard asked.

Nash had to think quickly on his feet. He did not want to say he had arrived on *Aviemore*, which would link him to Piraeus. He was sure if he did, then he would be detained for further questioning. So far, he had gotten away with his sabotage, but the Macrae personnel were not stupid and would be on high alert by now. He was certain they would have worked out that the attacks were coming from the sea and not the land side. Indeed, they had already changed the uniforms of their personnel. He had brazenly got away with all manner of fights, robbery and sabotage in the past, but now it seemed there could be a possibility it could catch up with him. He remained cool.

Dan smiled confidently and said, 'Had to pick up some tools from another Euro-Asian Freight Services vessel in the port.' He still did not mention *Aviemore*, although it must have been obvious.

'Open your bag please. I need to inspect the contents.'

Nash immediately did as he was told and stood back. He knew he could not run. There was no way out of this, except to brave it out and play for time. At least he had ditched the Macrae luminous jacket and hard hat.

The security guard examined the contents of the bag and saw the pipe wrenches, hydraulic pressure gauges, couplings and seal kits in a separate section to his clothes.

The guard asked, 'So how does this job of yours work? Do you cross from one vessel to another as maintenance is required on the go?'

'Yep, that's pretty much it. Doesn't give me much shore time and my whole personal life is fucked up anyway. Might as well do this for a living. It pays better than a shore-based job.'

The guard was obviously satisfied and smiled back. 'You are so right. Anyone at sea in this industry can't possibly have a normal home life. On your way.' He handed him back his passport and papers.

'Thanks. Take care.'

Nash strolled towards *Wenzhou* without looking back and slowly mounted the gangway leading to the deck. He presented his papers to the security guard at the top.

'That's okay,' shouted the captain to the security guard as he recognized Nash. 'He can come aboard. He's one of ours.'

'Glad you could make it, Dan! We need you to take a look at the hydraulics on the deck cranes and hatch covers while we sail to Yanbu. The weather looks good so it should take us about five days.'

'Thanks, Captain. I should be able to service them and make any necessary repairs in that time.'

Nash left the deck area as quick as he could. He needed to be out of sight, at least until the ship sailed. It was possible that the Macrae security personnel would link him to *Aviemore* and Piraeus sooner rather than later. They knew where he was now and might come for him. He needed to treat every move from now on like he was a hunted fugitive. He threw his bag in his cabin below and strode purposely to the engine room, picking up a short lashing bar on the way. If needed, he could use it as a weapon. It was short enough to swing in a confined area. He made his way on the galvanised metal catwalk around the massive diesel engines to the ventilation shaft above the rudder trunk at the stern of the ship. He could hide there until the ship sailed. If they came looking for him, he could easily escape down the shaft to the rudder and leave the ship undetected. He crouched in the confined space, praying they would complete loading and depart as soon as possible. He started to bite his fingernails. It was just a matter of time before someone discovered there was an additional Macrae dockhand leaving *Aviemore*.

16

Chapter 16

J ames stared blankly out of the plane window. His whole mind felt numb and incapable of reason. He could not concentrate on anything and kept rubbing his stiff neck. Mateo had told him when he was leaving that he was 'stronger than he thought he was'. What the hell did he mean by that? He was simply devastated by his employees' suffering. Mateo was well into his fifties, was wise and didn't mince his words. If he said it, there must be some truth in it. The only thing that James could think of was an incident that had occurred when he was doing his apprenticeship in Piraeus. Tired of being bullied, he had lost his temper and badly beaten up one of the bullies. From then on, he was never bullied again for being the boss's son. Mateo had covered it up.

James thought more about the sabotage. *Why should I play by the rules? I'm going to go on the offensive and launch a counter-attack.* Being the good guy and waiting for the police might be too late to save the company. The fog started to clear in his head, but the pencil broke in half in his hand.

The Macrae private jet landed at Genoa Cristoforo Colombo

airport in the early evening, a few hours after *Aviemore* had docked. The flight from Athens had taken almost three hours. Flavio, having received notice of James's change of plans, sent a car to meet him at the airport. It was only five kilometres to the Macrae terminal.

James was met by Flavio, who took him straight to the main security office. Inside the lowly lit office sat security personnel, constantly reviewing the screens from the various cameras positioned at strategic points throughout the terminal. Radio contact was also maintained with each security checkpoint within the port.

Flavio stood in the centre of the office. 'Listen up, everyone. I want to introduce you to James Macrae, our president. You've already been briefed on what our focus should be and that is the vessel *Aviemore* and her crew. Let's have an update on our security situation.'

The security manager looked up from where he had been consulting with one of his staff.

'Hello, James. Right now we have a person of interest under surveillance from the vessel *Aviemore*. Following your instructions, Flavio, we focused on this vessel and crew. It seems that an extra Macrae dockhand left the ship after our own team had secured the outlet oil pipes to the cargo pumps. It wasn't apparent at the time, but when we counted the Macrae people boarding and then the number of Macrae members leaving the ship, there was one extra. This person also had on a Macrae security jacket and white hard hat. Due to the position of the sun, we only have a brief side image of this person.'

The security manager continued, 'Later, still within the "secure" area of the dock, we questioned a Euro-Asian Freight

Services crew member who was crossing from the oil terminal to the dry cargo terminal. It's possible that this person could be the extra person leaving *Aviemore*. We have a copy of his passport and Schengen visa, which gives him the right to enter Italy. So far, he has not gone through the official Port of Entry Checkpoint with EU Immigration, so technically he is still transit in the cargo terminal. What's more, he is a hydraulics technician, according to his papers and the tools in his bag. But he did not have any Macrae security clothing with him. Now he is on board the vessel *Wenzhou*. We have a full description of him coming up from the security checkpoint. He is a Canadian national, well-built, five-eleven with dark wavy hair and blue eyes and goes by the name of Daniel Nash. He moves about the Euro-Asian Freight Services fleet according to maintenance schedules and carries out any necessary repairs. According to the arrival manifest of *Aviemore*, Nash was on the vessel when it arrived from Piraeus. That would put him at the scene of the crime just committed there.'

The security manager then added, 'We have notified the Italian police and have requested immediate apprehension of the suspect. We are awaiting answers from the police as we speak. It is possible that, as he is now on *Wenzhou*, he could be armed and dangerous. We have also relayed this information to the Piraeus terminal to pass on to the Greek police.'

James signalled to Flavio into a quiet corner and asked, 'Can you get me on *Wenzhou* before she sails?'

Flavio checked a computer monitor and replied that she had berthed early, completed loading and had asked permission to exit the port already. Tugs and pilots were already escorting her out of the port. She appeared to be well on her way.

James issued immediate orders. 'Stop and delay her due to

technical difficulties!' His message was relayed to the pilots. The reply came back that the vacated berth was now being occupied by another incoming vessel and because *Wenzhou* was one of the larger cargo vessels with a deadweight of over 200,000 tonnes, they did not have the sea room in the shipping lanes to turn her around. Given the winds and tides, they would have to release her to avoid a major marine disaster.

James smashed his hand against the nearest wall. 'Get me *Wenzhou*'s manifest and find out where she is heading, or, if it's quicker, use the global sailing schedule app on our intranet. Also, get me on the line to the police handling this case!'

James put down the receiver. 'OK, bottom line is this. The suspect apparently does not have a criminal record, at least within the Interpol database. Interpol is cross-checking databases around the world but, in conjunction with the Greek police force, they do not have enough direct evidence to issue an international arrest warrant. He could be brought in for questioning, but any authorities anywhere at this stage would not be able to detain him for long.' He paused. 'Have this guy's description circulated amongst all Macrae facilities and let's try to hold him up wherever he pops up again while we secure actual hard evidence.'

Later, it came back that *Wenzhou* was heading to Yanbu, Saudi Arabia, carrying a full cargo of machine tools.

James huddled with Flavio back in his office. 'Seems to me we now have a main suspect, even though we can't get hold of the bastard right now. In any case, we still don't have any hard evidence but it sure stinks and makes it very probable that Euro-Asian Freight Services is the saboteur.'

'I agree, James.'

'Okay, let's get a conference call with...' He was going to

say Rob Bissett, his operations director, but stopped himself. Another piece of the jigsaw was circulating in his head. It was the piece that eluded him when he was in Piraeus, sitting at the red traffic light.

'Give me a minute, Flavio...'

As his mind focused, it became clearer. All the accidents, not just the odd one, had happened on or near dates that were important to his company. The accidents here in Genoa had happened just before the company was due to meet with the union to agree a new revised three-year employment agreement. It was clearly meant to affect negotiations and terms with the union. Then, in Istanbul, through a series of contract and clerical errors, the company ended up losing a large amount of money that also cost the company a lucrative contract that they had just picked up with a new customer.

He sighed and thought some more. In Valencia the municipal government health and safety board closed operations down after apparent violations of employee safety. It was a set up according to Jason Ferreira, the safety and training manager. That week cost the company millions in compensation and re-certification charges, again just before union negotiations. Furthermore, in Piraeus the accident happened just after they had gained a really important new customer.

James came back to the key question he had. How could a competitor like Euro-Asian freight know confidential internal milestones and deadlines? All this collective information would only be known to a few managers.

James got up from his chair and looked back at Flavio, who was now sorting out some papers on his desk. James decided he needed to trust someone. Flavio had worked closely with his father for over thirty years as well as himself, when he worked in Genoa for an extended period of time. Not only that, Flavio would not know all this crucial company information.

'Flavio, let me ask you a question. How could a competitor know when to sabotage us, given that every accident happened close to a company event or key date? You see, it's clear to me now that these events were calculated to coincide with dates that would inflict the most damage to us from a financial point of view.'

Flavio looked James straight in the eye. 'No competitor could possibly know all that information.'

'So, logically, what does that lead us to believe?'

'Only one answer to that. Not sure you want to hear it though?'

'Shoot, Flavio.'

'Someone from the head office in Birmingham must be giving the saboteurs inside information.'

'That's the conclusion I'm drawing as well.'

17

Chapter 17

J ames paced his sterile and neutral hotel room. With a double bed, small office desk and plain walls, it was one of those rooms where you could be anywhere in the world. His palms were sweating, and he was starting to tremble. 'Who the hell would leak confidential information to our competition and why would they do it?'

He wanted to call Sarah, except he was too angry to do it just at that moment. He went through the members of the board in his head.

'Our entire management team has been together for at least the last ten to twelve years. Chad joined us about ten or eleven years ago, but his salary is tied to profit; it wouldn't make sense for him to stab the company in the back. Janet only joined just over two years ago, but she came with impeccable qualifications. Not only that, she was also vetted by the executive recruitment company and her references were glowing.'

James took a scotch from the minibar fridge and drank a healthy slug.

'What about Martin Farley? He's been with us for over twenty years and as a corporate lawyer he's done a solid job. For him to do something like this would be contrary to his profession. The Law Society would terminate his licence immediately.'

Grabbing a handful of peanuts, he continued to pace the room.

'Lynda doesn't make sense either. These acts of sabotage actually damage her performance and create a problem for her husband, Jason. I think I can eliminate them as well.'

'Then there's Hal Spencer. Dad has relied on him for over twenty-five years and he's a family friend. He behaved like an asshole in the board meeting, but at least he was upfront and direct. He sure didn't mince his words. If it's him, wouldn't he keep a low profile?'

The scotch tasted harsh after the peanuts.

'What if Rob Bisset is the traitor leaking information to Euro-Asian Freight? Rob was visiting the Valencia terminal when the engine was possibly sabotaged at that time'

'Whoever it is has committed a whole series of grave crimes. Conspiracy to commit murder, attempted murder and corporate manslaughter. I'm going to get you, you treasonous bastard whoever you are!'

He took deep breaths and, feeling a little calmer, called Sarah. 'Hi, my love. How are you? I miss you!'

'Hi, James. I miss you too. I'm good, but how about you? I've been thinking about you ever since you left, wondering how you are getting on?'

'I'll tell you in a bit, but first things first. How are the kids?'

'They are all fine. Mia lost a tooth today so I guess the tooth fairy will come tonight. Olivia has been playing with a friend and so has Mason.'

'That's good! Did you speak with Mom today? I was wondering how Dad is?'

'Yes, I did. They are going to keep him in hospital for a little longer just to make sure he's fully recovered. He says he feels good though. What's happening at your end?'

'That's good news about Dad. At this end, I'm afraid it gets worse. It's now clear that every incident is sabotage and, likely, one of our competitors is behind it. What's more troubling is I believe that someone from head office is helping them.'

'What! Can't be. Who would do that to you and your dad?'

'Right now, Sarah, I'm thinking the main suspect could be Rob Bisset. There are too many coincidences happening all around him.'

'He just doesn't seem the type. I thought he was happy to settle down in one place. You are going to have to tread very carefully with this, James. I would keep it to yourself for the time being.'

'I'll have to do some digging, but you're right, Sarah, I'd better make sure before I pull the trigger.'

***

James lay on his bed planning his next move. Time to get down and dirty. Time was running out. He pulled up Google Maps on his laptop and honed in on Iraq and its surrounding neighbours. *So how would I smuggle illegal arms into Iraq?* He was trying to follow Martin Farley's reasoning from the board meeting that two shipping companies were being investigated for allegedly shipping illegal arms to Saddam Hussein. He knew Euro-Asian were growing exponentially in the economic downturn, but to purchase the Zeebrugge terminal in Belgium and then invest a further $700 million dollars was mind-blowing. Maybe they were financing their rapid expansion with the proceeds of illegal arms dealing?

He thought through all possible ways to do it.

Chances were that any arms shipments would be heavy and probably easily identifiable in small quantities if shipped by air. Too risky to ship by that method in his book. That would therefore mean shipping by sea, however that wouldn't work so well since Iraq's only access to the rest of the world by sea would be through Basra on the Persian Gulf. Doubtful anyone would try that since the Americans and their allies' navies are always on the lookout for illegal shipments to that part of the world via the Arabian Sea. Same story trying to reach Iraq through the eastern Med via Syria or Turkey, as Israel keeps that area well covered on their radar. He finally reached the conclusion that the best way to transport goods to Iraq would be via the ports of either Yanbu or Jeddah in Saudi Arabia. They could then be transported overland to the border with Iraq. With the huge import of heavy agricultural, petro-chemical refinery and desalination plant equipment, there is a very well-developed transport system in the Kingdom. Not only that, but the Bedouin also operate a huge number of older, locally built Mercedes transport trucks. Couple that with the trading heritage of the region for thousands of years, and there is a thriving trade between all Middle Eastern countries, including Israel, despite their varied religions. Trade is trade and money is money, I guess.

Maybe there was a link between Dan Nash and the Yanbu destination? James decided he would follow Dan Nash, now aboard *Wenzhou*, on his way to Yanbu. He was really the only lead they had. He estimated the voyage would take about five days, so he decided he had time to visit the Istanbul terminal and dig further into the debacle that had cost the company another shit load of money. He could then fly from Istanbul to Yanbu and visit with their Saudi partners, who owned the majority share of the terminal. It also meant he could be inside the terminal when the ship docked.

He rang Janet Rushton the following morning, prior to leaving his Genoa hotel. He decided he had to trust her. Her background checks before she was employed were impeccable.

'Hi, Janet. It's James, can you talk?'

'Hi, James. Yes, I can talk. I'm in my office with the door closed.'

'Janet, I need your help and I need you to keep this conversation confidential. It's clear our backs are against the wall. I know my father would never ask you to do this, but...'

He waited a few moments and continued, 'Do you know of anyone who is specialised enough to access each of the identified competitor company's IT systems?'

Janet's eyes widened. She sat contemplating what she had just heard. 'Wow! I never thought I would hear that within this company!'

'I know, I know,' James said, putting his hands up defensively, 'and I never thought I would ever request such a thing.' He paused and then continued, 'After realizing our whole company and livelihood is at stake, we are going to have to fight fire with fire. Whichever way we look at this, we are in a fight for our lives and it's clear there are no ethics or rules involved in this war. With the death of and injuries to our valued employees, I'm ready to do whatever it takes.'

'Since you put it like that, I see your point. Look, as you know, I moved my whole family from London to Birmingham for this job. It was no small undertaking, but I believe in you and I love your company. This must work for me, my husband and my family.' She paused, 'Maybe there is a way. I do have a contact that I trust who we can keep at arm's length from the company. He would know how to digitally hide himself if he was to attack their security systems and firewalls. What are we looking for?'

'That's the thing. I don't know. I guess, anything out of the ordinary or anything that mentions our company. Again, Martin Farley mentioned that two companies could be mixed up in breaking embargoes with Iraq, shipping either arms or chemical weapons. Maybe there's information along these lines?'

'OK, I get the picture. Let me see what I can do. Rest assured, this conversation never happened.'

'Wait, Janet. There's more. You have the ability to see all management's emails going through the firewall. I need you to give me access to see everyone's emails.'

There was a pause on the line, then a prolonged, 'Okaaay.'

'You have to trust me, Janet. We have to work fast, and we have to go on the offensive.'

'James, I trust you. I also trust your father. I'm with you both.'

'Thanks, Janet. You have no idea how much I appreciate this! Oh, before I forget, pick up some burner phones. We may need them.'

18

Chapter 18

The Macrae Cessna Citation banked slowly on its final approach to Ataturk Airport on the European side of Istanbul. James looked down at the array of minarets, spires and domes spread out beneath him. It was hard to believe the magnitude of the various cultures and architecture, all gathered in the one place, that straddled Europe and Asia and had evolved over many centuries.

The Macrae terminal manager, Jusuf Kahya, picked James up in his own Toyota 4Runner jeep. He was happy to see James. They had known each other for a long time. They drove to the Macrae Haydarpasa marine terminal on the Middle Eastern side of Istanbul. The terminal was strategically important, being positioned between the Black Sea and the Aegean Sea as the gateway to Europe and beyond.

Before they entered the terminal, James suggested they should go to lunch at the Restaurant Galatasaray and talk privately. They drove along the winding coast road, lined by cypress trees, to the restaurant and sat at a private table shaded by an umbrella on the edge of a white-washed stone patio overlooking the sea of Marmara. The light incoming sea breeze felt warm and comforting. James looked out at the rippling sea with the sunshine sparkling on its surface. Under normal circumstances he would have been happy just to close his eyes, drink the air and relax. Not so this time. They ordered a mezze of the delicious local specialities and helped themselves, chatting idly about their respective families and current affairs.

Over coffee, they got down to business.

'So, Jusuf, what's your take on what happened with the tampered contract that cost us our customer and millions of euros in losses?'

Jusuf looked James straight in the eyes and came forth, 'You are not going to like what I say, but I'm going to say it anyway.' Jusuf took in a deep breath and psyched himself up.

'I have not told this to anyone, not even Chad Greening. I have been waiting to tell you personally, James. The altered contract was not an oversight, nor was it any kind of accident, whatever we want to call it. It was a pure act of white collar sabotage. Our administration manager, Mirza Baig, claims the changes, whoever made them at our end, just slipped through the cracks. Firstly, although Mirza is a seasoned professional and has been with us for over ten years, he is a guy that just doesn't make mistakes. It's not like him. And, got to say, when I confronted him on it, he looked very uncomfortable. Another thing, when he knew you were coming in originally, yesterday, he did not turn up for work. Neither has he come in today.'

'Was he sick?'

'Not to my knowledge. This is a guy who takes health and fitness seriously. I do know that a serious relationship has just ended,' Jusuf replied.

'Does he live locally?'

'Yes, he has an apartment in the Maslak district on the European side of the city. He just moved there.' Jusuf continued. 'Here's the second part of what I think. The changes to the contract at this end were so subtle, it had to have been a calculated act from someone at head office in Birmingham. The contract promised the customer altered and unrealistic delivery and turnaround times with heavy penalty clauses that clearly favoured the customer.'

There was an uncomfortable silence from James.

Jusuf spoke first. 'There, I've said it aloud. Why do I think that? Well, the changes were so surgical in nature, they had to have been made by a highly experienced accountant. No one else would have had the intricate accounting knowledge to do this.'

Another silence followed. James sat back in his chair, put his hand on his head, closed his eyes and tilted his head backwards. He let out a loud, exasperated sigh. James knew that the original contract that Chad Greening had signed off on remained intact on the company's secure server. He believed Chad would not have done it, since it would have negatively affected his salary. This was a clue, that maybe Hal Spencer was involved, if Jusuf's assumption that an experienced accountant was true.

'Okay, Jusuf. I hear you. Listen, I want to go and make a surprise visit with Mirza Baig later this afternoon. I want to question him myself.'

Back at the terminal, James and Jusuf interviewed the other office staff and reviewed the tampered paperwork. Having got Mirza Baig's address, James then took a taxi via the E80 ring road and crossed the Bosphorus strait, separating the east and west side of Istanbul, via the suspension bridge to the European side of the city. The cab turned north and dropped him off shortly in the upmarket Maslak district. He looked up to see ten newly constructed apartment towers. From where he stood, they looked expensive, set inside an area of neatly laid out, well-manicured lawns, trees and outdoor swimming pools. James walked confidently along the footpaths joining the towers and found the one he wanted. The air smelled of freshly cut grass. He waited for someone to exit the front of the building and, just as they were coming out of the door, went in. As Baig had not turned up for work, he hoped he would be in his residence. Without announcing his arrival, he took the elevator to the twenty-first floor, found the apartment he wanted and knocked on the door.

'Who is it?' came a voice from the other side of the door.

'Property Management Company. We are checking all the apartments on this floor, following a report of leaking water from above. I just need to check your ceilings.'

The door opened and James barged in.

Mirza Baig stood back, eyes wide as he covered his open mouth with his hand. 'Errrr, Mr Macrae. I, I didn't expect to see you!'

'I bet you didn't! This shouldn't take long,' James said and walked confidently into the lounge. The floor-to-ceiling windows were covered by net curtains for privacy from the other surrounding towers.

'Now. Let's have a chat, Mirza. Sit down. You are going to answer four questions: One, why did you alter the Macrae contract? Two, why did you then claim you didn't catch the changes you had made? Three, who told you to do this? Four, who sent you the exact changes to make to the signed

113

contract?'

Baig's eyes bulged and his top lip started to quiver. He remained silent.

'Okay,' James said, quietly. 'We can do this another way. I'm tired of always being the nice guy and when my company, with all my employees' livelihoods, is at stake, I'm running out of patience. Do you understand?'

Mirza stuttered, 'But, b-but I didn't do anything.'

'I don't believe you, Baig!' James shouted. 'You're a professional, you don't make mistakes like this! Telling everyone that this slipped through the cracks is a lie and you know it!'

'Mr Macrae, y-you have to believe me! That's what happened!'

James stood up and grabbed Baig's shirt collar with both of his hands. He yanked him forcefully up towards him. His face reddened and he spat his words out inches from Baig's face. 'Let me be kind and start you off with a little bit of help. We know you have just moved into this very expensive apartment block in a swanky part of town. Places like this don't come cheap, so let's also ask where you got the money?'

Baig hung his head,but said nothing.

'Okay, have it your way!' James rammed Baig's head hard back against the wall and punched him hard in the stomach. Baig's head fell forward and James pulled him close to him again. He shouted, 'I can't hear you!'

Still nothing so James kneed him in the groin and punched him hard in the stomach again as Baig leaned towards him. With his height and build, he knew he was hurting Baig but didn't want to leave any marks. Baig bent over, crippled, grabbing his stomach and groin, and fell to the floor.

James lifted his right leg up and started a kicking motion towards Baig's ribs, 'Do you want some more?'

'No! Please! No more! I'll tell you!'

'Okay, so let's start at the beginning, shall we?' James pressed Record on his phone.

'I'm so sorry, Mr Macrae, honestly!' said Baig, whimpering. 'I couldn't help it! I fell in love with a Chinese girl I met in a downtown nightclub. We were hugely in love and planned to live together. I'd never felt that way before. After a while, she introduced me to her brother. He became a friend and promised me 50,000 Euros if I would make some small changes to one of our contracts. I was blindly in love, and saw it as an easy way for a down-payment on this new apartment. My girlfriend and I were so excited about our future together.'

Baig was quiet for several moments, still sobbing and shaking. James spoke softly to him. 'Mirza, who told you what to insert into the contract?'

'The changes came via an anonymous email to my own personal email address, and a few key words were inserted into the Macrae contract. To be honest, with my past record with the company, I believed I would be able to bluff my way through and then just claim it was an honest mistake not to pick out the changes. I didn't realize at the time, that such small changes could affect the bottom line of Macrae's as much as it did. I was paid the money direct into my bank account and purchased the apartment.'

He was quiet again, but James did not want to interrupt him. Baig cleared his throat and started to talk again, 'I moved in with my girlfriend, but once the contract had been doctored and signed off, she disappeared. I have not seen or heard of her or her brother since. I've been such a fool, but I was so in love. Then, when I heard that you were coming to investigate, I became scared. What seemed like a worthwhile risk at the time is now the end of me. I'm so sorry and ashamed.'

James listened to his story and then called Jusuf. 'Jusuf, can you call your contact in the police force. Baig has a confession to make.'

After Baig's arrest, James and Jusuf returned to the terminal and sat in Jusuf's office overlooking the docks. One by one the powerful lights came on all around the docks. Overhead lights shone down from the huge tower gantries and cranes onto the cargo ships below. The terminal was a living being twenty-four hours a day.

James looked through the floor-to-ceiling windows. 'I'll go and talk to the men at shift change and let them know what's happening. We need to reassure them that we are working towards a solution and we have their backs.'

Jusuf tapped his fingers on his desk. 'So, what do you think now, James, given what we now know from Mirza Baig?'

James exhaled, hard. 'Well, there are two things bothering me. Why would this Chinese girl and her supposed brother be involved in the contract fraud and, secondly, Flavio has the same belief you do that someone in the Birmingham office is involved. We now know every single accident, call them what you will, was an act of sabotage. The question is who is the traitor in head office?'

***

James stayed in Istanbul overnight. He rose early in the morning and accessed the Internet. Janet had sent him access to each of his director's company emails. He concentrated on Rob Bisset first, but every communication that Rob made was professional and entirely within the company's interests. Indeed, it was clear that every move or directive he was giving was to get the company back on track as quickly as possible. Next he studied Hal Spencer's correspondence, but could not see anything untoward there either. He even checked their 'junk' email but could find no evidence of company treason.

James called Janet Rushton next. They used their burner phones.

'Hi, Janet, can you talk?'

'Hi, James, yes I can. My door is closed. I do have some news, although it is somewhat inconclusive. My contact is a night owl and worked through the night. He was able to breach the firewall at Nielsen Shipping completely undetected. He spent most of last night poking around and could not find anything suspicious. He was able to view their latest business plan and there was no mention of Macrae Shipping. All their expansion and acquisitions have focused on the smaller, niche shipping companies. All funds for each of these transactions were all completely above board as he could link them through all their bank transfers. He went through their general ledger and latest balance sheet, including their last audit report. They appear to be clean.'

'Good work, Janet! Anything on Euro-Asian Freight?'

'Not really, yet. Their firewall is proving more challenging with lots of trip wires. My contact says, for a company like this, it seems very sophisticated. He even made the comment that it was getting close to some international secret service levels. Strange. He will keep trying.'

'Okay thanks, Janet. I really appreciate what you are doing. Let me know if you need anything further. Give me a shout when you have any more info.'

James called Sarah. 'Hi, my love, how are you today?'

'Good thanks, Jimbo. You'll be happy to know everything is under control at this end. I do have some good news. The part-time work I've been doing for my old company seems to be paying off. They've asked me to do some more research on Canterbury Cathedral and work with their stone masons. It's good because I can do the work at home, while the children are at school. So, how are you getting on?'

'That's great news. Congratulations! As to here, the situation is still unclear. We have one man under arrest in Istanbul for fraud, but this incident doesn't shed any light on the other accidents. I'm going to fly to Yanbu next to try to pick a thread of a lead we have on a possible suspect. In any case, I can check up on our partners.'

'Where are the police in all this? Can't they handle it?'

'Well, that's just it. Each police force investigating each of these accidents is working separately. Since we don't have a firm suspect at this time, they can't issue an international arrest warrant. Whoever our enemy is, is very clever. With time running out for the company, I need to follow this up myself. It's the only choice I've got. I'm even more frustrated because I know we have a traitor in the head office. I'm convinced it's either Rob or Hal but I have no concrete proof. Rob's spending money like water.'

'How do you know that?'

'Well, Chad mentioned that he is now moving into a much bigger house in an exclusive area and apparently sending his three children to a private school.

'So, why don't you just come straight out with it and ask Rob where he got the money from?'

'I've thought of that. No doubt he would have a ready-made answer and I don't want to alert him that I'm scrutinising his private life. I need to catch whoever is doing this in the act.'

'Ummm. You know sometimes I see Rob's wife at yoga class. She isn't always there but when I next see her, maybe I can find something out.'

'Okay, it's worth a try. By the way, I haven't called Dad yet. If I do, he will only ask me about the company, and I want to keep him as free from worry as much as I can.'

'I think you're right. Got to go. Take care, my love. I love you!'

'I love you too.'

Chapter 19

David Morris, the Sterling-Judge loss adjuster, had just sat down for his Sunday breakfast of bacon and eggs, toast and coffee. The sun was already warm and shining through the open kitchen window. *I have precisely nothing on today.* As a single guy in his mid-thirties, he could do whatever he wanted. *Maybe a ride later.*

He was just about to eat his first bite of breakfast when he heard the report come over the airwaves from the BBC.

'A report is just coming in from Muscat, Oman. A tanker carrying millions of gallons of oil has exploded and caught fire in the Arabian Sea, leaving four sailors dead and eighteen missing. The blast occurred as the Panamanian-flagged *Solstice* sailed about 250 miles east of the Omani island of Masirah, bound from Oman to South Korea, according to the Lloyd's of London shipping intelligence unit. The company owners, Euro-Asian Freight Services said that *Solstice* was carrying a crew of six officers and twenty-nine sailors.'

David dropped his fork onto his plate. 'My god, they've done it again! It's another vessel insured with us.' As a professional insurance adjuster, he did not believe a word of any of the ship survey reports that slippery fucker, Edmond Andreas had given him before, concerning their ship *Endeavour*. Neither did he believe that *Aviemore* had passed its latest safety certification. He knew that the insurance claims by them were criminal, but he couldn't prove it. All the evidence was at the bottom of the sea. He could go after Ben Mitchell, the Blue Water Maritime Bureau chief inspector, but the guy had such an awesome reputation in the industry, that nobody would believe him. Maybe, just maybe, if *Solstice* hasn't sunk, he could get a true report for himself on the state of the hull. He wondered if it was possible for the wrecked hull to be towed back to Muscat?

David finished his breakfast and, half an hour later, as he was cleaning up, the BBC news announced that fifteen survivors had been picked up from *Solstice* by a Kuwaiti livestock ship after the super tanker was found burning. The *Solstice* was still afloat and clean-up crews were on their way to prevent a huge oil spill.

Hugh Stanfield had also heard the same report on the BBC world service. *Damn, that was not supposed to happen!* he thought. *That's one ship we would never have sabotaged. She was just too big a vessel and the risk of oil spillage of that magnitude would be unthinkable.* This time it must truly have been an accident. Dan Nash had never even stepped on *Solstice.* At least they did not have to cover anything up on this loss.

David Morris arrived at his Bristol office for work at 7.00 a.m. Monday. He was anxious to get on the newswire to learn all he could about the *Solstice* accident. He discovered that the ship's cargo was still intact and that the ship was now about eighty miles off the United Arab Emirates port of Fujairah, being towed by a Dutch salvage ship. He also saw another report from United Agencies that the fire had broken out in the engine room and quickly spread to the crew's quarters above it. The fire had spread so quickly that smoke had entered the HVAC system and twenty Filipino crewmen had died, being unable to escape. On passenger ships the fire detection system would have stopped the HVAC fans, however this was not a legal requirement for non-passenger ships.

David did not know what to make of this. Was this another Euro-Asian Freight Services fraud? After all, the hull was well over fifteen years old. Whatever it was, he decided he would lean heavily on both the company and Mr Edmond Andreas. He was tired of being taken for a fool. The cargo of oil would probably be pumped off onto another vessel and the chances were that the ship would be sold for scrap. He decided he would inspect the vessel personally to investigate the source of the fire as soon as possible. He got clearance from his boss to fly to the Emirates and carry out a full inspection of the vessel. The risk of loss was too great for the insurance company to ignore.

***

Nash continued to crouch in the confined space of the ventilation shaft at the stern of the ship. He was stiff, but his hearing was on high alert. So far, he had not heard any voices or shouts. All appeared to be quiet. Eventually, after a nerve-wracking amount of time, *Wenzhou* prepared to leave dock. Once the turbines were working at full speed driving the ship further away from Genoa, he began to relax. They would cruise at approximately twenty-two knots. He had had a close escape. It would take approximately five days to sail to Yanbu.

Once far away from the Italian coast, Nash took out another cell phone and contacted his boss. Via satellite, Stanfield took the scrambled call immediately. 'Everything alright, Dan?' he asked.

'Just about. I was able to barely escape. Listen, they have my identity, as I was challenged transferring from the Genoa oil terminal to the dry cargo terminal. I can't take any more chances now. Can you arrange for another set of identity papers, as we discussed prior to this operation?'

'Already done. You will have to enter Saudi Arabia using your current ID and papers though. This will not be a problem, however, as the arrival of you and the shipment has been arranged to coincide with a shift of immigration and customs officials that have received regular compensation from us. Nabil Quraishi has a package for you containing your new identity and Schengen visa, together with a Glock pistol.'

As they exited the Suez Canal in the half light of the dawn, the huge orange ball of the sun was rising fast on their port side. The Red Sea revealed itself and widened southwards in front of them like a giant open and gaping jaw. The rolling waves increased slightly in height and the gap between their peaks widened. White caps were beginning to form on their crests. On the eastern side of the ship the land was flat and undulating with the light-brown barren desert of Saudi Arabia. The land became shrouded with particles of abrasive sand from the east, further cutting down the visibility. Nash could taste the tiny sand particles as he inhaled the breeze coming from the land across the gently rolling dark blue sea, despite its name being red.

On the approach to the port of Yanbu, there were several cargo ships sitting at anchor, either waiting to load or unload.

Instead of joining the queue, *Wenzhou* sailed straight into port. Clearly there had to be some 'backsheesh' involved. Knowing Stanfield, Nash knew this would be the case. 'Efficient business', he called it.

Nash's entry visa was already waiting for him and had clearly been arranged some time ago by Euro-Asian Freight Services management.

As the full cargo of machine tools were off-loaded, they were taken from dockside into a large, bonded warehouse. Dan accompanied the cargo, along with the first officer of *Wenzhou*, with multiple copies of the bills of lading and certificates of origin, all with the necessary stamps and certifications. The Saudi customs personnel took their time to review all the documentation. There were several questions for the first officer, however all went smoothly.

Later, a show was made of opening certain crates of the cargo. All contents were checked against the bills of lading.

'Okay, Dan,' said the first officer. 'Transport has been arranged by our own company broker to ship the cargo to the end customers. You see those crates there with the designation AZ 36789 stencilled on the side; those are your responsibility. You will be contacted shortly. Nash waited by the cargo and very soon he was told that two transport trucks had been admitted to the port to pick up the cargo and himself. Within minutes the two dull-grey painted Mercedes L1924 trucks appeared with short bonnets propped open by Pepsi cans and bungee cords. The cargo bodies consisted of typical high-sided wooden stake bodies used by the Bedouin to carry general cargo. Nabil Quraishi jumped down from the driver's side of the cab of the lead truck and shook Nash's hand firmly. Smiling, with a full black beard and shining brown eyes, he was dressed in a white thawb and wore the traditional red and white cotton ghutrah and agal on his head.

In perfect English, he said, 'Hi, Dan, it's been a while. Good to see you. *Ahlaan, welcome.*'

'You too, Nabil. How are you and how is your family'? After several minutes of the traditional Arab greetings, all the crates were loaded onto the two trucks. By early afternoon, they left the shipping terminal by the main gate, cleared the final security check and headed south on Medina Road. There were many low-rise industrial buildings and after approximately a mile, they were joined by similar trucks both in front and behind them.

'What's going on, Nabil?' Dan asked.

'Just a regular precaution. These are trucks owned by all my extended family. We are not just taking this arms shipment, but many other items such as tyres and spare parts that are difficult to source in Iraq. It's very lucrative for us, however we still need to be careful. We switch the order of the trucks from time to time, just to confuse anyone who happens to be scrutinising our activities. Not only that, but we are also all heavily armed. With a heavy US presence in the Kingdom after Operation Desert Storm to drive Iraq out of Kuwait, you never know who is watching us, either on the ground or by satellite. You will see that our route varies often through open desert at night. It has been the way of our people for centuries.'

As they reached the outskirts of the city, there were acres and acres of prepared new black top roads, complete with street lighting, all waiting for the future development of housing and industrial estates. With billions of dollars in oil revenue, Saudi Arabia was investing in its future infrastructure.

Nabil added, 'The Saudi authorities have built us Bedouin all kinds of free housing that we could move into right now if we wanted to, however, we are not dwellers who stay in houses and settle in one place. The desert and stars are the home of our ancestors and will remain so.'

The convoy of trucks pressed on and turned left, heading north-east away from Yanbu and the coast towards the holy city of Medina. The terrain was still fairly flat with sand and broken brown rock for as far as the eye could see. There were few palm trees and extraordinarily little vegetation. Just a scorched dry landscape that suffered every day under the blazing hot sun. The cab was filled with a stifling heat and smell of diesel fumes. Coupled with the humidity, it felt extremely uncomfortable for Nash. For Nabil, this was normal.

After a few miles they passed a rough section of scattered run-down breeze block buildings with tin rooves that were obviously roadside car and truck repair workshops. Tyres, exhausts, oil, air and fuel filters, spring shops and oil change shacks were everywhere. The black oil-stained roadside was littered with battered pick-up trucks and old cargo trucks in many states of repair. Grimy mechanics circled around their customers' vehicles. One vehicle was having some heavy arc welding repairs to the chassis carried out right on the road. Hot molten metal showered the street with flying incandescent sparks. Dan Nash looked down from his truck cab and felt like it was a film set for a wartime movie. Then he spotted a brand-new parked Toyota quad cab pick-up, with four Chinese men standing close to it, looking at the convoy of trucks. It seemed odd to him, although Nabil said there were thousands of immigrant workers in the country working either in the oil fields, agricultural development or the expanding network of desalination plants providing more and more fresh potable water to both the population and the arable land. Dan did not think any more about it.

Unknown to anyone, there was also a set of eyes looking very carefully at both the convoy and the Chinese group. He stood at the upper end of the street behind a mobile gantry with a suspended block and tackle, holding up a dirty Mercedes twelve-litre diesel engine. Dressed in a grimy t-shirt, shorts and a baseball cap, James was looking specifically for Dan Nash as part of the convoy. His t-shirt stuck to his body in the high humidity.

James had flown into Yanbu two days before *Wenzhou* docked. He had met with his Saudi partners. It was a relief to see that operations had been running smoothly with no accidents or abnormalities. Profit from the terminal was healthy as trade through the port was busy. With Saudi having the lowest cost per barrel of crude in the world, money was plentiful for both exports and imports. It was good for Macrae's and good for their Saudi partners.

James had watched the ship dock and unload. He watched from a distance, looking for a crewman that resembled the grainy photograph he had in his hand. Eventually he saw a man that had a similar profile to that he had seen on the videos in Piraeus and Genoa. He also had a similar nose shape to the photo. It did look like it had been broken a few times. The man was also the same one that had crossed from the oil to the cargo terminal in Genoa. James had the copy of the passport that security had copied at the security point there. Nash also carried a bag similar to the one before. *That has to be Nash. There's no one else like him. I wonder if he will get stopped by Customs and Immigration before he leaves the dock?* He had watched Nash enter the bonded warehouse and then get picked up by the two Mercedes trucks. While the crates were being loaded onto the trucks, James left the warehouse area and waited patiently outside the Yanbu dock yard in one of his company pick-up trucks. Eventually he saw Nash in the lead truck, sitting in the passenger seat.

He overtook the convoy on a smooth four-lane highway before the road became two lane and the road became constricted with the 'shade-tree' workshops encroaching from both sides of the road. Traffic both ways was crawling along at this point. This would allow James to carefully inspect each vehicle passing through. While he waited from far away, he was looking for anything unusual. He spotted the white Toyota quad cab pick-up and four Chinese men pointing back down the road from which he had just come. The men did not approach any of the vendors and why would a new pick-up stop here? Surely it would be taken into a high street dealer for service, not such a place as this. James, however, did not look out of place. In fact, he blended in perfectly as he was driving a well-used Toyota pick-up.

James continued to watch the convoy of trucks weave their way slowly through the run-down automotive and truck repair district. A few children kicked about a roughly rounded shape of a ball made of old rags and held together with grey duct tape. He briefly marvelled at their skill. And then there Nash was, sitting in the passenger seat of the Mercedes truck. The driver was an Arab. Standing by the open driver's window of his own pick-up, James grabbed his camera with the telephoto lens and, using the motor drive, shot off several photos of Nash, the truck, the driver and registration plate. He also noticed the Chinese group of four men pointing at the truck. *Hmmmm, interesting*, he thought. He shot some photos of this group as well as their pick-up.

Somehow, James needed to get a close look at the contents of the truck. If Euro-Asian Freight was smuggling arms to Iraq, this might be evidence to prove they were involved. He also needed to get Nash on his own and bring him to justice. *One step at a time*, he thought. After waiting for the convoy of trucks to pass, he held back to see if the Chinese group would follow them. Not knowing why, they did. Sure that no one else was following, he tagged behind them and stayed far enough back to be unobtrusive. The road took them eastwards toward the holy city of Medina, but, just before the city, it branched two ways. The one way directly into the city was strictly for Muslims and the other way was for non-Muslims to bypass the city. The convoy took the direct Muslim route. The Chinese group and James took the city bypass route. Figuring the convoy would continue to head north-east to the city of Hail, en route to Iraq, James pressed on. He overtook the Chinese pick-up when it stopped by the side of the road at the junction of the bypass, where it reconnected to the direct city route. They had stopped and parked in the shade behind a group of palm trees. Two of the men were urinating. Without looking at them, James drove on towards Hail.

Before too long, the road started to rise upward, the sur-rounding sun-cracked and bleached rocks getting larger and larger with drifting sand between them. On rounding more of an incline and sharp bend, he was suddenly facing a range of rocky mountains approximately 1500 metres high. The steep escarpment ran all the way southwards to the east of Jeddah and then further south to the town of Abha and the empty quarter right on the southern border of the Kingdom. The narrow two-lane road ahead wound its way with tight hairpin bends upwards to the top of the escarpment. The road became steeper and more dangerous, with no natural or fabricated safety barriers to prevent vehicles going over the side. Every driver would know that with just one wheel out of place, you would be over the precipitous edge and plummet straight to the valley bottom hundreds of feet below. Death would be the only outcome.

The terrain started to become greener, with more vegetation. At the same time the air became cooler and less humid. Troops of monkeys perched high above them on the cliff face peered down at the traffic below. James could easily see the wreckage of old cars, trucks and buses that had gone over the side and strewn the jagged rocks way below them. The pace of traffic became slower on the narrow road, simply because there was nowhere to overtake. You could only go as fast as the slowest truck. Trucks, using only low-range gears, plodded their way slowly upwards, belching out clouds of black exhaust fumes. About two-thirds of the way up there was a large pull-off area for vehicles to rest and cool down.

James pulled over and parked his pick-up as far forward in the area as he could. Using his telephoto lens, he looked back down the road and waited for the convoy of trucks with Nash aboard. After half an hour he spotted them as they wound their way upwards, slowly towards him. On reaching the rest stop they pulled in, but they could not all park together. There were too many other vehicles already parked and scattered about in various locations waiting for their engines to cool down. James thought, *No wonder they all had open hoods with Pepsi cans holding them open. They would need to direct every square inch of air to both the radiator and the engine block.*

James held back and then walked towards the truck with

Nash in it. He had a tyre lever in his hand. All the Arab drivers of the convoy were chatting animatedly in Arabic. Nash was out of the cab, stretching his legs and taking a long drink of water from a plastic bottle. Avoiding eye contact, James walked to the back of Nash's truck, out of sight of everyone. He peered through the slats of the stake body at the wooden cases stowed inside the body. Quickly he inserted the bar through the gaps of the stake body and started to prise open one of the cases. There was a loud creaking sound as the nails were lifted out of the sides of the crate. Suddenly, there was a loud crack as one of the top pieces of wood broke in two. He froze and then quickly stepped away from the truck, leaving the tyre bar jutting slightly out from the stake body. He waited close by, but out of sight; heart pumping faster and faster. He knew he was completely on his own and outnumbered.

Chapter 20

Nash came from the other side of the truck to find out the cause of the sound. He waited, listened and looked around. Not seeing anyone near the truck, he went out front again. He did not notice the lever that had been left there.

James stealthily returned and exerted more pressure on the bar. This time, with the nails already loosened, they came out soundlessly as he lifted the crate top just enough to see inside. James could already smell gun oil and lifted the greaseproof paper aside. There, right in front of him, sat an arsenal of submachine guns. They were stamped with Beretta PM12 on the stock. Bingo! Quick as a flash he took photos of the guns with his phone. He also took some photos of the side of the truck with its distinctive painted decorative and unique colours. Finally, he got another shot of the number plate. Walking back to his truck with the tyre lever, he waited to see what would happen next. This would not be a good place for him to confront Nash. One, Nash was with too many men in his group and, secondly, he could not escape fast enough on this road either upwards or downwards. The traffic was just too slow. No other choice but to follow the convoy and wait for another opportunity.

After another hour, the convoy started moving again, having given their engines ample time to cool down. As they passed him by, James had his back to the convoy, pretending to look into the valley below. No one took any notice of him. Just as he was returning to his truck, he saw the white Toyota with the Chinese occupants take off some distance behind the convoy. Were they following the arms or were they following Nash? It was a question he could not answer. He started his truck and left about five minutes after the white Toyota. There were several vehicles between him, the Toyota truck with the Chinese men and the Nash convoy of trucks.

Later that afternoon, the road had levelled out on the plateau as they headed further north-east, towards the city of Hail. James did not see the white Toyota of the Chinese. Before long, the convoy halted again at the side of the road, together with several other cars, pick-ups and trucks. All occupants had left their vehicles and, taking their own prayer mats with them, faced southwards towards the holy city of Mecca. James held back and exited his vehicle. He could hear the words 'Allahu Akbar', meaning 'God is great' being spoken loudly. Nash was standing on his own away from the men. All the men praying had their backs to him and were kneeling down with their heads to the ground.

Now was his chance to grab Nash and escape. He believed that with the element of surprise he could get a hard, fast blow to Nash's head with the heavy iron bar and gain the upper hand. He jumped back into his own pick-up, started the engine and grabbed the tyre lever off the passenger seat. He revved the engine and started to pull forward onto the road towards Nash, but, before he could get to him, a white Toyota pick-up passed him at speed, and quickly pulled up next to Nash. Nash was startled as all four doors opened from the truck and the four Chinese men accosted him. James thought he saw a syringe being quickly stabbed into Nash's right leg. Nash collapsed and, within seconds, he had been piled into the pick-up and was gone.

Holy fuck! Now I know it was Nash they wanted, not the arms. This is just not making any sense. He decided he didn't have any other choice but to follow the white pick-up truck. He followed them safely at a distance into Hail. Before long they pulled over to fill up with petrol. The light was starting to fade. He needed some way to be able to identify the vehicle at night. Being a white quad cab helped, but the tail and brake lights looked the same as any other truck. Luckily, this one had a 'Back Rack' fitted to it, the 'Back Rack' sign being luminous on the top rear cross bar. *Alleluia!* He could hang back without having to tail them too closely. Having filled up his own truck with portable fuel cans at the previous rest stop, his tank was still nearly full, so he pretended to fill up with petrol on an adjacent fuel island. Nash still appeared to be slumped over in the rear seat between two of the occupants.

It was now dark, and the Chinese pick-up edged its way back onto the road. James followed at a safe distance. The one obstacle now that could hinder his pursuit was that he had noticed that the Toyota had diplomatic registration plates. *Damn*, he thought, *if we get stuck in a roadblock, which was customary in the Kingdom, the Toyota will be able to sail straight through, while I'll have to wait to be checked.*

James strained his eyes in the darkness as he followed

the white Toyota pick-up in front of him. Before long he realised that they were heading south-east on Route 65 to Burahdah and possibly Riyadh beyond that. He knew if they went to Riyadh, the capital, that it was about a five-hour drive. Maybe one more fuel stop, maybe not. This meant that the Chinese were heading away from the smuggled arms convoy, which was clearly on its way to Iraq. As he looked ahead of him, with the driver's window down, he heard the sound of several helicopters approaching the area overhead. When they had gone, he saw a convoy of Saudi and American armoured personnel carriers travelling towards him. They were in a hurry. Still the Toyota headed south-east. Occasionally he would drop even further behind them when the traffic was sparse. The evening air was now cool, with the temperature dropping quickly once the sun had set. To the left and right of the road, plantations of date palms came into view, picked out by the headlights of the passing cars and trucks. The air became filled with the sweet aroma of the dates.

As they reached the outskirts of Buraydah, there was a police checkpoint. *Damn. I knew this would happen!* James said to himself. He slowed down and was about six vehicles behind the Toyota. As expected, the Toyota quickly cleared the roadblock. James waited patiently in line and, when the time came, presented his passport, Iqama and company papers. All were in order, so he set off in hot pursuit of his prey. Taking a chance, he followed the road towards Riyadh but there was no sight of the vehicle. He drove faster and faster, swerving occasionally around stray goats in the middle of the road. 'Doesn't make any sense to stay in Buraydah. It has to be Riyadh as the pick-up has diplomatic plates and the Chinese would have their embassy there in the capital.' Over an hour had passed and he still had not spotted them. He was beginning to think that Dan Nash had escaped again. Once in Genoa and once here. He slammed his fist on the dashboard. 'Fuck! Give me a break, for God's sake!'

He pressed on and then, as if his prayer had been answered, he saw that the Toyota had stopped and the men were relieving themselves at the side of the road. Nash was among them, his head and shoulders slumped forward. James noticed that two of the Chinese men had guns pointed at him, which they tried to quickly conceal. *Too risky to take the group on right now*, James thought, so he continued past them. Just outside the town of Al Majma'ah, James ducked into a gas station and filled up quickly. As he did so, the Toyota sped by. James followed again at a safe distance. On reaching Riyadh, he had expected the vehicle to drive to the embassy section of the city, but instead they headed for King Khalid International Airport. Rather than go to the main passenger terminal, they drove to the private air terminal situated between the main passenger terminal and the Saudi Airline Cargo terminal to the north. Unable to enter through Security, James parked his vehicle close by and peered through the chain-link fence. Driving straight on to the tarmac, three of the Chinese men and Dan Nash exited the Toyota pick-up and climbed up a portable stairway into a white private Dassault Falcon 20 jet. There were no markings on the plane except the regulatory commercial registration numbers. James took note of them. Within minutes the Falcon had taxied away onto the runway and taken off, leaving a trail of dust and exhaust fumes behind it. It was just after midnight local time.

James released the grip of his fingers from chain-link fenc-ing and lowered his hands gently to his sides. He was dumbfounded. The only lead he had was gone. 'What the hell am I going to do now?'

21

Chapter 21

Davis Morris, the Sterling-Judge Insurance Company insurance adjuster, was sitting in his Bristol Head Office on the east side of the River Severn. He broke off what he was doing to look through his office window, considering his next sentence. He looked up towards the Clifton Suspension Bridge. Nearly 150 years old, it was an engineering feat for its day; slung over the River Avon in a steep gorge over one hundred metres below. He looked at the wrought-iron structure and the semi-circle of chains suspended from the red sandstone towers supporting the road across. 'It's a good job Ben Moore isn't the inspector for that! If he was, it wouldn't be here anymore.'

He was typing up his inspection report of *Solstice*, complete with photographs, after travelling to the United Arab Emirates. He had been able to contact the Dutch salvage company and was able to board *Solstice* and carry out his inspection of the stricken ship. What he found wasn't what he had expected. The fire was clearly an accident and had spread quickly to the crew's quarters above. He did not believe it was arson. What he did find, however, might help him nail Euro-Asian Freight Services and, maybe, Ben Mitchell the chief inspector of Blue Water Maritime Bureau classification company. David knew that for an annual inspection of a 300,000-tonne crude carrier for corrosion, an inspector would have to climb more than 10,500 metres. To examine all the welding, he'd have to walk or crawl 1200 kilometres. Even using electronic testing, it would take 70,000 man-hours to survey the exterior plate and main welding. So David, as an experienced surveyor and claims assessor, concentrated on the notorious fatigue 'hot spots'. It took him a full day, but he had found substantial corrosion on parts of her infrastructure that had been crudely patched. The patching was clearly an attempt to hide the rust rather than rectify the weakness and strengthen the forward bulkhead. He took photos and measured the depths of the corrosion. Clearly, the integrity of the structure was already compromised. It would only be a matter of short time, or an earlier storm, before this vessel sunk out of reach as well. He attached copies of the inspection that Ben Mitchell had signed off on, only two months before. Ben Mitchell had passed *Solstice* as being completely seaworthy. He claimed her structure was sound.

Before submitting his report to his boss, David Morris sat back in his office chair and meditated. On behalf of his company, he could certainly wriggle out of paying for the loss of *Solstice*, based on his report by utilising the standard insurance contract exclusions clauses. But that wasn't enough. He was sick of the unscrupulous behaviour within the shipping industry that was costing the lives of hundreds of nameless sailors and the mounting losses to the insurance companies. It was a cancer within the industry. He finally decided that he would submit his recommendations that his company should turn down the insurance claim when it was eventually filed. The claim would finally end up on his desk for the loss of *Solstice.* He also decided he would carry out another inspection of the vessel, *Wayfarer.* He had only received the signed off inspection report from Euro-Asian Freight Services one month before. Ben Mitchell had been the signatory. If he could get aboard when she was next in port, he would check her out himself. This would be the only way he could stop Euro-Asian Freight and maybe help the industry to clean up its own bad behaviour.

David knew it was only himself that could bring Euro-Asian Freight Services to justice. The United Nations had a body called The International Maritime Organization (IMO) to which all shipping nations belonged, but it did not possess any enforceable rules to regulate the industry. So he had to press on with his own quest. He picked up the phone and phoned Edmond Andreas at his London office.

'Mr Andreas. I see you've done it again!'

'What do you mean? We've done it again. I don't like your tone, Mr Morris.'

'You know. You've totalled another ship again.'

'If you mean *Solstice,* that was a tragic accident. We are gathering all the facts before we submit our insurance claim to you.'

David decided to see if he could hit a nerve. 'I suppose this ship was another one previously inspected by Mr Ben Mitchell?'

There was a marked silence at the other end of the phone and then Andreas said, forcefully, 'What's that supposed to mean?'

'Come on. You know.'

'No. I don't know.'

'Yes, I thought that was what you were going to say. Well, I look forward to receiving your claim. Good day, Mr Andreas.'

Edmond Andreas replaced the receiver and gently tapped his head with his fist. He sat quietly at his desk to consider his next move. After a while he picked up his phone again and called Hugh Stanfield at the Shanghai office. He left a voice message:

'Hugh, we have a problem.'

***

David Morris was finishing typing up his report when his phone rang. It was his boss Peter Owens. 'Hi, David, I need to see you in my office.'

'Sit down, David. Listen, I've just received a complaint from one of our clients about you.'

'Oh, that's not unusual, given the nature of the job I have.'

'No, it certainly is not, however this one is different. Normally I get customers call me disputing your insurance valuation assessments. Indeed, calls come to me daily with disputes for payouts, not just for you, but all our adjusters. It's standard for the industry, as you know. Everyone thinks their property is always above average and worth more than anybody else's. My job is to back you up and ensure the valuations are fair and in line with standard industry practices.'

'So what's different about this complaint?' David asked.

Peter looked at David directly. 'David, you have been with us for over ten years and you are an experienced claims assessor. You are one of the best forensic audit inspectors I have ever met. That's without question. What's different about his complaint

141

is the nature of it and who it is coming from.'

'How so?' asked David, looking perplexed.

'Well, you are being accused of persistent harassment, to the point of being insulting and libellous. The company wants you taken off their account with immediate effect. What's more, the complaint is coming from the Chief Financial Officer of Euro-Asian Freight Services. He says he has been dealing with you personally. What I don't understand is this, why would the CFO be dealing with you direct? Normally we deal with the directors of marine operations who understand the mechanical nature of their equipment. What do you think, David?'

'Yes, we normally deal with the directors of Ops, but, for some reason, I am always being directed back to an Edmond Andreas, the CFO. Yes, we did have quite an exchange of views, but I assure you it was him that tried to intimidate me, saying I was a useless assessor and that I didn't understand the marine insurance industry. Funnily enough, I was just typing up my report and I have been detailing every step that I took with Euro-Asian over these past few months. The particular assessment I assume he refers to is the *Endeavour*. Two aspects stood out to me. One was their valuation of the hull and mine. Yes, we certainly had differences of opinion on that one, but we eventually agreed a figure between their valuation and mine. The second point that struck was the service and maintenance records of their fleet.'

'I don't understand?' Peter replied.

'Well to me their records look too perfect. Sounds crazy, I know, but, based on my experience, their fleet has less maintenance carried out and less repairs than any other fleet I've ever been involved with. Per nautical mile, they spend less money on their fleet than anybody else.'

'Umm. I saw they just had that explosion on one of their vessels in Oman. What did you find when you visited the salvage?' Peter asked.

'That's part of my report too. *Solstice* follows the same pattern as the rest of their fleet. She passed her annual inspection only two months ago, yet there were clear weaknesses in her structure. Attempts had been made to make it appear as though repairs had been carried out, except they were all cosmetic.'

'Are you saying you have caught Euro-Asian Freight Services in a fraud?'

'Yes, I am. But before we go off shooting live ammunition, I need some more evidence to make the charges stick. Here's my problem. Firstly, I don't believe the loss of their ship *Endeavour* was an accident. She supposedly had substantial repairs carried out before she was lost in the South Atlantic. I can't prove anything as she's at the bottom of the ocean. Yes, there was a bad storm but there were other ships in the region that got through it. Captain Johansson was only able to get one May Day off and, within minutes, she had disappeared from the radar. To me, that points to a major structural fault.'

'Go on, David.'

'Secondly, there is the evidence I've just described on *Solstice*. I've completed my full engineering report and am just waiting for Edmond Andreas to put the claim in. He says he's working on it.'

'I don't get why you are holding back, David. That's not like you.'

'Here's the thing. Every inspection that is carried out for Euro-Asian Freight Services is done by Ben Mitchell of Blue

Water Maritime Bureau. Not only are they an accredited marine classification company, but Ben Mitchell is highly respected in the industry as a whole. If I didn't know better, I would think he's taking back-handers.'

'Holy shit, David! I see your point. What do you want to do?'

'I want to inspect *Wayfarer,* their 300,000-tonne carrier. She was signed off by Ben Mitchell only a month ago. If I'm right, I'm going to find major structural faults in her construction that have been miraculously signed off on. I would have done it sooner, but she's not due to dock for another week. She will be in Immingham, Grimsby. Once I have that proof, I can go after both Euro-Asian Freight Services and Ben Mitchell.'

'That makes sense. I'm going to leave you on their account, in spite of what Andreas wants. I want you to know I've got your back.'

David had already gotten up to leave when Peter stopped him. 'Listen, David, be careful. I don't like the sound of this.'

22

Chapter 22

Having lost his only solid lead, James got back into his pick-up and rested his head on the head restraint. He sat in the dark for a few moments before he started the engine. Maybe the pursuit of Nash wasn't a total failure after all? All the circumstantial evidence pointed towards Euro-Asian Freight and he now had proof of their arms smuggling. He had the photos. Why not contact the British Embassy in Riyadh, present them with what he knew, and maybe they could shut down Euro-Asian's operations before his own company went under? He called the embassy straight away and spoke with the night manager.

James located the Riyadh Oberoi Hotel near the airport and took a room. He needed a shower, dinner and a good sleep to prepare himself for the next day. He awoke early. His body clock was still on European time, but he was well rested. He had made an appointment to meet the British Ambassador at 10.00 a.m. His phone rang.

'Hello, James, it's Janet. How are you getting on?'

'Hi, Janet, I'm good, thank you. What's happening at your

end?'

'My computer contact has been back in touch with me. That second company we last talked of still has not yielded any further information. My contact believes that their firewall is protected by Chinese government software. It has all the signs of that.'

'Oh? That sounds very unusual.'

'Yes, I agree. It does sound strange. I was thinking though, because the company's head office is in Shanghai, maybe there's a link there?'

'Umm, I guess that could be a possibility.' He was silent for a few moments. 'Okay, Janet, thanks for the update. Keep me posted. Cheers.'

'Will do. Stay safe James!'

Next, James called his mother. 'Hi, Mom. How are you?'

'Hi, James. Good to hear your voice. Good news! I picked up your dad from the hospital today. He seems much better. In fact, Stan is here with his wife. They came over in the lunch hour to see how we both are. The Spencers really are such good friends. They brought flowers and even a dinner so I wouldn't have to prepare anything later.'

'That's excellent, Mom. Take care. Can you put them both on?'

Hal came on the phone first. 'Hi, James, good to hear from you. Are you still in Saudi?'

'Yes I am. Just finishing up some business so I should be back sometime tomorrow. Thanks for looking in on Dad and Mom. I know they really appreciate your friendship.'

'James, while you are on, I've made appointments with our two banks for us to go and see them. When you are back in the office, I can walk you through the report I have prepared for them.'

'That's great, Hal. Thank you. I appreciate it.'

'Hi, Dad! Good to hear you are out and feeling better! Sounds like everything worked out well.'

'Hi, Son. Yes, all went well. They kept me in for a little longer than we expected, but all is back to normal now. How are you and how is work?'

'Oh, I'm good. I'm in Saudi right now and had a good meeting with our Yanbu partners.'

'How about the other business?'

'Don't worry, Dad, I've got everything under control. Every-one is working flat out to step up business, so we'll be fine.'

'That's good. Love you, James.'

'I love you too, Dad.'

James then called Sarah. 'Hi, my love. How are you?'

'Who is this stranger on the phone or is this my long-lost husband!' she said with a chuckle in her voice. 'It's good to hear from you. I miss you. I'm good; working on the Canterbury project.'

'That's good. I miss you too. How are the kids?'

'They are well. They got spoilt rotten by your mom last night when she babysat. Typical! I wonder if we will do the same when we have grandchildren?'

'Probably. Did you run into Rob's wife at yoga last night?'

'Actually, I did. I don't think you have to worry about Rob selling you out. Her father passed away some time ago, and it seems they were able to finally sell his London house and wrap up the estate. She told me they are investing heavily in their children's education.'

'Phew, that's a relief. Could it be Hal I wonder? But I just spoke to him before I called you and he and his wife are being so sweet to Mum and Dad. So that doesn't add up either. Anyway, I should be home sometime late tomorrow. I love you, Mrs Sarah Macrae!'

'I love you too, Mr James Macrae.'

James entered the grounds of the British embassy in the Al Safarat district of Riyadh. He passed through a heavily reinforced steel security gate into a courtyard surrounded by palm trees, neatly trimmed hedges and bougainvillea, overflowing with bright-red flowers. The hot dry air was filled with the fragrance of honeysuckle. He was escorted to the fourth floor to meet with the British Ambassador, Peter Renfrew-Stevens. He was a veteran in the British Foreign Service and had been posted overseas for most of his diplomatic life. In his early sixties, with greying hair and a quiet, confident manner, he greeted James warmly. It was also clear that all the office furniture had followed him around the world. There were carvings and framed photographs from many places, including the Far East.

'I hope you don't mind, Mr Macrae, but I've asked Brian Morgan, our trade attaché to join us this morning.'

'No not at all,' replied James, knowing full well that Brian Morgan was probably nothing of the kind. As with all foreign embassies, there were several spies in every country masquerading as attachés.

Brian Morgan entered the office shortly afterwards. *Typical rosy-faced, jolly chap*, thought James. He would be the sort of middle-aged, posh public school guy that would mingle well with any type of company and be just another 'good ole, congenial Englishman'. 'G & Ts, jolly good show, ole boy' and all that crap.

Sitting around a conference table with coffees, James said that he should first introduce himself.

'No need, James. We already know all about you and your family shipping business. You are a credit to British industry.'

'Thank you, Ambassador. To be honest with you, I'm not sure where to start? I find myself and my company in a very difficult position.'

Over the next hour and a half, James explained in detail his visits to Piraeus, Genoa, Istanbul and Yanbu, detailing the sabotage and the suspicion of the Euro-Asian Freight Services employee Dan Nash. During the conversation, Brian Morgan's whole demeanour changed as he took over the meeting. He was no longer the typical rah-rah English stereotype. He recorded the conversation and wrote notes from time to time.

'What makes you think Euro-Asian Freight are arms smugglers? That's quite an accusation to make, Mr Macrae,' said Morgan bluntly.

'Well, you see, Mr Morgan, we live in an industry with only a small number of major players. We keep an eye on each other all the time. The grapevine is a small one. Firstly, we heard that two shipping companies were possibly being investigated for breaking arms embargoes to Iraq. Secondly, we focused on the two competitors that have grown substantially, especially at a time of worldwide economic slowdown. Euro-Asian's expansion is impressive, to say the least. My reasoning is based on other factors too. They lost a major contract to us because they could not guarantee fast turnaround times to the customer. We could do that because we own five marine terminals. Then they bought out Zeebrugge, investing millions of euros in a down-and-out terminal. It's apparent to me that they would like to replicate our business model so they can offer customers the same advantages. For a company to expand in this way, it would need a tremendous amount of cash. You know as well as I do that the banks have been gun shy to lend vast quantities of money in a down market. Coupled to that, our suspicion of Dan Nash leads me to believe they are trying desperately to weaken us financially so they can take us over. As a private company my father has always repelled any takeover bids. Euro-Asian would know this.'

'Umm.' Brian Morgan looked at the ambassador. They sat in silence for a while. James could see they were both fully engrossed and were now digesting and carefully filtering the information.

'James,' said Morgan. It was now first names rather than 'Mr Macrae'. 'Do you have any conclusive proof of what you have alleged?'

James wondered if he could trust Morgan, and decided he needed to if he wanted their help.

'Actually, I do.'

Both the ambassador and Morgan sat forward in their chairs. 'Can you share it with us?' asked the ambassador. James produced the photographs he had taken with his digital camera and phone. He had transferred them to a PC memory card.

The ambassador ran the card through a virus check first and then put them up on his large-screen monitor. As they painstakingly went through each of them, James explained the circumstances. Morgan continued to take notes and record the conversation. They both tried to stay impassive, but it was clear to James that they were surprised by what they had seen. Another attaché was brought in who took away the memory card to make hard copy photographs.

Finally the ambassador spoke, rubbing his chin at the same

time. 'Without question, this is a complicated set of events. Events that, on the face of it, don't necessarily connect, like arms smuggling and the sabotage of Macrae's property.'

'You are right, Ambassador. They don't readily connect, but, if you look at it this way, they do. As I mentioned, Euro-Asian Freight Services has grown substantially within the last few years, way above the industrial average. They could only have done it with huge injections of cash from outside the normal channels. I might as well tell you that our company has been severely weakened financially and we're an easy target for a takeover. The bottom line is this. I need your help to stop Euro-Asian now before they come for us. You have the proof. Why can't you freeze their assets and arrest their owner Hugh Stanfield?'

'Okay,' Brian Morgan said, 'I'm going to contact MI6 immediately and pass on all this evidence and information. They will be in touch with you in due course.'

'As for me,' said the ambassador, 'I will contact the prime minister and foreign secretary and brief them accordingly. I will also inform both the Saudi and American authorities of the group of Bedouin that are transporting the illegal arms through the Kingdom.'

James got up to leave.

'One more thing before I go. Why would Chinese nationals running on diplomatic plates take off with Dan Nash? Here is the registration number of the plane that left last night from Riyadh.'

The ambassador and Morgan looked blank.

23

Chapter 23

David Morris returned from Immingham as fast as he could. He wanted an urgent meeting with his boss, Peter Owens.

'So, David, you managed to complete your insurance assessment of *Wayfarer* while she was docked at Immingham.'

'Yes, Peter, I did. Take a look at my preliminary report. I will need a few days however, to complete the composite report on all the Euro-Asian vessels. I still have to consolidate the metallurgy reports, add my survey results and photographic evidence.'

'Okay, David.' Peter Owens sat behind his desk and quietly studied every detail of the report and photographs. Finally he sat back and said, 'we have enough evidence here to suspend all our insurance coverage with Euro-Asian with immediate effect. We also have enough evidence to go after Ben Mitchell, who reported only one month ago that *Wayfarer* was completely seaworthy. He then read aloud one passage written by David:

'This twenty-six-year-old vessel has substantial corrosion

that has wasted away most of her metalwork. It looks like a lace curtain. Several holes have been plugged with cotton waste instead of being patched with steel. The manhole covers were patched with plastic, which doesn't prevent leaking. It is the worst case I've seen in my career to date.'

There was silence.

'It's damning, isn't it?' Peter said and, without waiting for a reply, he continued, 'These actions are entirely criminal. We will not be under any liability to pay out for any insurable losses that Euro-Asian Freight Services might claim in the meantime.'

Peter then pulled out David's previous report on the stricken vessel *Solstice*, in the Middle East. He checked the original engineering reports and photographs that David had made. He also checked the previous survey of the vessel that Ben Mitchell of Blue Water Maritime Bureau had signed off on only two months before. Descriptions and photos of the same bulkheads did not match at all from the two reports. It was as though Ben Mitchell had inspected a completely different vessel than the one David had inspected.

Next, Peter and David went over a composite report of repair and maintenance costs on similar spec'd vessels of comparative years. Euro-Asian's costs per vessel were way below the industry average. Peter stated that they could be especially useful to have as testimony in a court of law and might lead to some interesting revelations under cross-examination of an impartial qualified subject matter expert.

Following this, they discussed the loss of *Endeavour*. Everything they discussed, however, was based on supposition, since all the real evidence lay at the bottom of the South Atlantic. Ben Mitchell's inspection reports would never be able to be verified. Peter thought some more about this for a few minutes.

'You know, David, we may be able to shed some light on this after all. We received a letter from a Mr Sultan Dastagir some months ago. He was a deckhand on the vessel at the time. I have a copy of the letter here. What's interesting is that he states that *Endeavour* was in a very unfit, unseaworthy condition. He notes that the hatch covers and their locking mechanisms on several of the nine cargo holds were severely corroded. We tried to contact Mr Dastagir after receiving this letter, however, it appears that he was lost overboard from the very same ship somewhere in the Indian Ocean shortly after he wrote the letter.

'Hmmm,' David murmured. 'I wonder if that was truly an accident or maybe murder? Let's get hold of the crew list.'

Peter made notes as they went along, then said, 'Good. Let's see what you can turn up and finish the final report as soon as you can. We will then present all the evidence to the police. Euro-Asian Freight needs to be shut down.'

**

James returned to England from Saudi Arabia as soon as he could. It was early evening with clear skies when the company jet landed softly on the tarmac at Birmingham International Airport. The air was warm. James hopped into his Range Rover and decided he would go into the office on his way home. It was still light when he reached the underground car park at the Gas Street office.

He was surprised to see how many people were still working. As he passed Janet's office, she jumped up from her seat.

'James, it's so good to see you. Welcome back.'

'Thanks, Janet. Any further news from your friend?'

'No, unfortunately not. He's hit a roadblock. Seems like Euro-Asian Freight Services servers hide behind heavily en-crypted Chinese Government firewalls. We don't understand it.'

James raised his eyebrows. 'I don't understand it either. Euro-Asian is a private company started by a Londoner by the name of Hugh Stanfield with offices in Shanghai and London. I can't imagine him tied up with anyone except himself. He's ruthless, yes, and selfish too. He certainly is not the sharing type.' James thought some more. 'Tell your friend to back off now and consider the job complete. He did well and at least it eliminated one of our suspects. Take whatever we owe him through the petty cash account, and I will sign off for it personally.'

Walking through the accounting section to get to his office, James passed Laura. Laura oversaw Accounts Payable and Accounts Receivable. 'You're here late, Laura. What's up?' Laura looked up at James and said quietly, 'James, can I see you in your office?' Once in the office, Laura remained standing. 'James, I'm still here because something's not right.'

'How do you mean?'

'Well, everyone knows in Accounting that we are heading for a cash crunch. It's easy to spot with the software systems we have. So why aren't we dragging our payables out to say sixty or ninety days and turning the screws up on our accounts receivable? I've asked Mr Spencer why, and he has told me that all payables should be paid within thirty days and not to chase our receivables and upset our customers. I've been doing this job for a long time now and when I chase receivables, it is not done in a threatening way. On the contrary, our customers know me well and we get along well. So, I'm trying to do what I think should be done without alerting Mr Spencer. I love this company, James, and I want to help.'

'I see, Laura. OK. Let's keep this to ourselves for the moment. You continue to do what you are doing. I agree it makes sense. If Mr Spencer queries anything right now, just tell him that I told you to do this. OK?'

'Yes, thank you, James. I knew I could speak to you.'

'Laura, is there anything else that might seem odd or out of place right now?'

Laura hesitated. 'Not sure if this is relevant, but Mr Spencer frequently leaves his office to make phone calls on his cell in the car park. He never used to do that.'

'Keep an eye on things for me. Thanks. I have absolute confidence in you. Thank you again for giving me a heads-up.'

Next, James ran into Martin Farley, Director of Legal Affairs.

'Hey, Martin, how are you? Don't want to go home either, eh?'

'I wish, but I'm still wrestling with the legalities of the customer contract that was screwed up in Istanbul. I've been talking directly to the customer's lawyer, trying to come to some sort of an agreement on financial obligations. It's early days yet, but if I can pull this off, it may save us a few million dollars. Don't get your hopes up, though. Hal Spencer thinks I'm wasting my time, but you know me, I never give in!'

'Let's keep our fingers crossed. Do you have any further information on the rumour about the shipping companies' smuggling arms?'

'Not really, but everyone can't believe Nielsen Shipping would be so stupid. They are an extremely ethical company and have been highly regarded for years. Can't say the same about Euro-Asian Freight. But bottom line, no further news.'

James sat in his office for a while, checking the emails of both Rob Bissett and Hal Spencer. It was clear Rob Bissett was working flat out to bring in more revenue. He had gone with Chad on a visit to a potential customer and, by offering extremely competitive freight rates, they had secured some new business. While it wouldn't help the cash flow in the next sixty to ninety days, it would strengthen the company after this. Moreover, he had contacted the German engine manufacturer and changed the engine supplier to Macrae's as soon as he could. He had even secured their freight business to bring in their raw materials and carry their finished engines to some of their world markets. These were not the actions of an internal saboteur. Then there was the explanation of his change in financial status with the inheritance from his father-in-law.

James got up from his desk and walked around his office. His eyes squinted and his lips tightened. The changes Mirza Baig made in the Istanbul contract had been provided by a skilled financial expert and now Laura's information that she had just given him was pointing him towards believing that Hal Spencer might really be the person leaking information to the competitor.

He picked up his phone and called a private detective agency.

24

Chapter 24

The next morning, James leaned over his desk and picked up his phone. 'Hal, let's get together in my office and go over the figures that we want to present to our bankers tomorrow.'

'Okay, James, give me ten minutes and I'll be there.'

Hal Spencer put the finishing touches to his SWOT analysis and his presentation folder that they would use for the meetings with each of the Macrae bankers. They had one meeting scheduled to begin at 10.00 a.m. and a later meeting scheduled for 2.00 p.m.

James spent some time studying the latest quarter's figures and then the projected cash flow for the next quarter. He pushed his chair back from his desk, took his reading glasses off and got up. 'Christ, Hal, this looks bad but when it's in black and white in front of you, it's a shocker! Show me the printout of our payables and receivables, together with the ageing report.'

Hal produced the computer print-out. James put his reading glasses back on and reviewed them. 'Nothing looks out of the ordinary except this one entry. How come we owe so much money to a competitor? I know we help each other out from time to time, but this is a whopping sum!'

'James. These are the true figures. Yes, you asked me to give an honest set of accounts and I've done that. Both banks know our carrying capacity, average expenses and average revenue per month and if we showed any major variances with those, they would delve in deep. They also know our cash position and how much room we have left on our credit lines.'

'Yes, you are right of course, Hal. Honesty and integrity are what we've worked so hard to earn over the years, but what about this payable of 5.5 million US dollars to Euro-Asian Freight?'

Hal smoothly added, 'Regarding the payable to Euro-Asian, we had no choice but use them when the Valencia terminal was shut down by the Spanish authorities for health and safety reasons. They were used to keep our two biggest customers' supply chains running. Had we not used them, we would have lost millions more if those supply chains had been broken and our customers had sued us. Euro-Asian Freight Services was the only carrier that had the spare capacity to help us out at that time.'

'I knew we were doing that, of course, but I had no idea that we owed them that much. Have you got any suggestions before we meet the bankers?'

'Honestly, no, I don't. We must just put a brave face on and show them the analysis of our strengths, weaknesses, opportunities and threats. I believe the SWOT analysis is very realistic and can help our case.'

The following day, James and Hal sat down at the main

159

boardroom table of the National Industrial Bank. They were surrounded by a total of eight bank officials, including the new account manager that had been assigned to Macrae's. It was a bleak meeting. James tried hard to lighten the tone of the meeting, talking about their history and profitable past relationship. Somehow, this time, it didn't work and when James suggested they go to lunch afterwards, which they normally did, he got a frosty reply.

The bank chairman replied, 'I'm sorry, James. Frankly, it's not appropriate at this time. You may as well know now that the bank cannot increase your line of credit and neither can we extend the credit period. Bottom line, we just don't think you can turn the company around. We were prepared to listen to you today, but there is nothing here that changes our position.'

James looked grave and responded slowly, 'Sounds like you had made up your minds before we got here?' James got up to go, then sat down again. He was going to ask the question that he had waited for Hal Spencer to ask, but he never had. 'You know,' he said with his hand on his forehead, rather like Peter Falk did regularly in the hit TV crime series, *Columbo*. 'There's just one thing bothering me. I don't understand why you are cutting us off when you know full well that the value of our fixed assets is way above our liabilities. There's something that's not adding up here. Would you agree?' He let the statement hang in mid-air.

The chairman looked a little uncomfortable, adjusted his shirt collar and said, 'Your current liabilities far outweigh your current assets. You will have no liquidity left after the next quarter.'

James got up finally and said, 'That's a cop-out and you know it! There is nothing to stop you taking a position on our fixed assets.'

'I wouldn't say that, but you must admit that you are perilously near the edge and if we extended the line to you, our shareholders would be squealing from here to the London Stock Exchange and back. Also, it doesn't look good when you show that you owe one of your main competitors 5.5 million US dollars. I'm sorry, Mr Macrae, but our decision is final. We wish you good luck.'

A series of cold, limp handshakes followed with a lot of hollow and meaningless words.

James and Hal found themselves back in the street in a state of shock. James was particularly choked. It was the first time in his life that he had ever been in this difficult position.

'You go to lunch, Hal, I'm going back to the office. I can't eat anything right now. I'll see you at MidCom just before two.'

Hal Spencer watched James shuffle off; he looked like a broken man.

The second meeting started off well at the MidCom Commercial Bank. James and the now chairman of the bank, Henry Harrison, had known each other for a long time; since he was a good friend of his father, Richard. As Macrae's business had grown, so had Henry's rise within the bank. Richard and Henry had a lot of respect for each other. There was an array of bank managers in the meeting, together with the account manager for Macrae's. He had been on the account longer than any other previous manager and it was fair to say he knew the shipping industry and the Macrae company extremely well. The accounts were presented and discussed at length, as was the SWOT analysis.

As the meeting was ending, Henry summed up. 'James and Hal, you have given us a lot to think about here today. We will not be making any quick decisions, although we realise that you need an answer soon. We respect that, and, furthermore, we promise that we will not keep you waiting long. We owe it to you to give due consideration to your position that is both fair to you and fair to the bank.'

James thanked him and, as they were leaving, Henry said to James quietly, 'let you and I have a private word in my office.'

Hal went off on his own and James and Henry sat in Henry's office, overlooking Victoria Square. They were alone.

Henry looked at James directly. It was clear that he was in the process of trying to choose his words carefully. James sat in silence, waiting.

'James, we've gone through a lot together with yourself and your father over the years and I feel compelled to tell you some things that may distress you.'

James blinked hard, raised his eyebrows and sat up further in his chair. He still didn't say anything.

'You need to know, my friend, that there are some vicious rumours floating around the industry about Macrae's. Some of those rumours could be very damaging and could colour people's thinking about doing business with you – and I'm not just talking about the banks. Quite frankly, the mood of this bank was to call in your line of credit before this meeting, but I persuaded the group to hold off until you had a fair chance to present your case. I meant what I said: that we would give your presentation fair consideration.'

'Tell me about these rumours, Henry.'

'Listen, our account manager assigned to your account is picking up information from all over the industry that you are in real trouble financially. There are stories of misman-agement, inefficiency, and an accident record that is beyond belief. For instance, we've heard about the different accidents at your terminals and a major contractual screw-up in Istanbul. I'll be honest with you. Today you showed a fifteen per cent reduction in your running costs per nautical mile. On the face of it, that is commendable. But, and it is a big but, at the same time you have had these accidents with your cargo-handling equipment that has cost lives. There's talk of you cutting corners everywhere!'

'Henry, that's just not true! Can't you see that?'

'James, I said earlier that you might get distressed. Do you know what they call you in the industry?'

'No, I don't.' said James quizzically.

'They call you Master Scissors because you are always cutting corners.' Henry was not laughing when he said this. 'I'm not joking, James. Do you now begin to see how these rumours are going to affect you?'

'Yes, I do. Lynda Ferreira has also warned us that many of our employees are questioning what we are doing. Yes, there are consequences. I can see that.'

'Henry, here's the true picture. It's the complete opposite of what you have heard on the grapevine. As president, I have invested heavily in increasing our maintenance and safety procedures over the last two years. It was my suggestion to take Jason Ferreira out of Operations and put him in charge of safety and training. Frankly, I think it was a good decision. Yes, it's cost us more money to do that, but it's a worthy investment. Our preventive maintenance procedures are the best in the business.'

'James, it doesn't add up. Here's why. If you've got proper safety and training procedures in place, how come you have had all these accidents?'

'Henry, we are convinced that we have been sabotaged.'

'Sabotaged! By whom?'

'We don't know at this stage. We are working with multiple police forces and government agencies. I'm deadly serious when I tell you this. Take our previous accident-free days in the UK; our safety record is hugely improved since these new policies and procedures were introduced. I alone have made these decisions although Richard gave me full backing. We believe someone is after our European terminals to take them over.'

James continued. 'Here's another example. Instead of cutting costs, we actually increased them when it came to investing in IT. I was the one who fired our previous IT manager and hired a top-drawer manager from the industry. We then spent more money on servers, security, software and training than we have ever done. We have certainly not cut corners! I know I'm going on a bit here, Henry, but it hurts to hear what you have said. God, you know me well enough. Our family culture has always put safety and ethics high on the list. Happy employees and customers always mean more productivity. Cutting corners only leads to ruin. You see that, don't you?'

'James, I'm sorry to tell you these things, but you needed to hear what the industry is saying about you. Yes, I believe you have done all these things and I must tell you that I admire you tremendously. You are the future and, furthermore, I trust you. Look, what you have got to do is this. Find out who it is that is sabotaging you and get me the police reports that confirm this. Also, find out where the source of these rumours is coming from and, in the meantime, I'll try to keep our bank from foreclosing on you. Remember this though, James, I can't make the decision to keep you afloat alone, it will be a group decision.'

25

Chapter 25

Ugh Stanfield stepped out of the Shanghai restaurant into a humid, sticky afternoon. The air was heavy, hazy and laced with dense exhaust fumes mixed in with the smell of the port. The Din Tai Fung restaurant was one of his favourites, situated on Nanjing West Road in Pudong; close to his office. He looked around as he came out into the bright light of day, burping in appreciation of the excellent pork with truffle dumplings he had eaten. As it was only a short distance back to his office, he decided to walk. He would wash, dry himself off and change into a fresh shirt back there.

Back at his office desk, his direct phone line rang. He immediately picked up. 'Hugh Stanfield. Good day.'

A firm voice on the other end commanded, 'Stanfield. This is General Jiang's secretary. You are to report to the Chinese Communist Party Headquarters for a meeting with the general tomorrow morning at 8.30 a.m., here at his office in the Zhongnanhai compound in Beijing. Is that understood?'

'Yes, it is. I will be there.'

There was a click on the other end and that was it. Conversation over! The tone of the request was not friendly. On the contrary, the government representative who called him was hostile and left Stanfield in no doubt that this was not a request. It was a blatant summons.

He sat at his desk, somewhat taken aback, and contemplated what had happened several years before and how he had arrived at this point. He remembered he had been working on several new contracts for potential customers that he hoped to acquire. His office door was closed, and he had told his personal secretary he did not want to be disturbed. He had heard shouting outside his office door; his secretary was trying to stop whoever it was from entering. The next thing he knew was that three Chinese officials dressed in army uniforms burst through the door, unannounced. The leader was dressed in a smart olive-green uniform of jacket and pants, complete with flat cap circled with a red band, gold braid and a gold insignia. His jacket had shoulder boards with three embroidered gold stars and a wreath. The other two were in smart uniforms, but clearly of a lesser rank. One of them closed the door behind him.

Stanfield stood up. His lips tightened into a thin line. 'Who the hell are you?' Stanfield had demanded. 'This is a private office!'

The senior official shouted. 'Sit down and shut up, Mr Stanfield!' His eyes were cold, and he was sneering with the one side of his mouth.

'I will not shut up! Get out, get out now. Mingmei, call the police!'

The official lowered his voice. 'We are the police. Now sit down and listen.' The two soldiers moved around behind his desk, while the senior official sat down.

'How dare you gatecrash my office! What do you want?'

'Quieten down, Mr Stanfield. Please. Just listen to what I have to say.'

'Alright, you have my attention.' He had sat down.

'My name is General Jiang. I am here on the personal directive of our chairman, Chairman Deng Xiaoping. Your company is being taken over by the state.'

'What! This is outrageous! What the fuck do you take me for? I've spent years building up this business. I've bust my balls to do it. Do you think I'm just going to roll over and play dead?'

'Mr Stanfield. We are perfectly well aware of the effort you have put in to build this successful shipping business. That's why we are here. Let me put our proposal another way. You will be taking on a partner. It's just that we will be the bigger partner.'

'A partnership? I don't get it.'

'This is what the new arrangement will look like. The Chinese government will own the majority share of your business. You will remain as president, owning the minority share. We will be an invisible partner. To the outside world, Euro-Asian Freight Services will still be wholly owned by you. Optically, nothing will change. You will answer directly to me.'

'Sounds like Deng Xiaoping has made his mind up. What if I refuse?'

'Simply put, if you don't comply you will be ruined, imprisoned and re-educated.'

'Ummm. Will I receive financial compensation for your share of the business?'

'Mr Stanfield. We are not monsters. You will be compensated

fairly. Before too long you will come to appreciate that we have common goals. You will still be a rich man.'

And so the 'partnership' had begun. He had had no choice but to accept. He was instructed to continue to run the company with the same name, however he received substantial injections of capital from the Chinese government and set up a chain of shell companies underneath Euro-Asian Freight Services. They were to achieve the expansionist objectives of both his new secret partners and himself. He had accepted the inevitable and now saw it as an opportunity to further feed his greed. At this point, the Chinese were unaware of his illegal arms deals.

To Hugh, China was an enigma. He could never decide if China was a truly communist or capitalist society. One thing was clear, however. He had a mandate to aggressively expand the company worldwide. The Chinese planned to dominate the world economically, not just with manufactured goods, but to control all the transportation lanes and global communications. While Hugh continued to work as the front man, the Chinese quietly monitored his activities in the background. To the outside world and the rest of the international shipping industry, nothing had changed. Euro-Asian Freight Services was still an independent private company owned and operated by Hugh Stanfield.

In the years that followed, some of their smaller competitors were swallowed up easily, however others proved more of a challenge.

Stanfield snapped himself back into the present. He was still shocked by the phone call demanding his presence at such short notice in Beijing. Nothing like this had ever happened before. He tried to think positively about what he could present in the meeting. His sabotage and intimidation plan to bring Macrae Shipping to their knees was going well. He would show his partners just how to achieve their economic and geopolitical objectives. Yes, Macrae Shipping had refused to sell in the past, but now his tactics would leave them no choice but to submit to their demands once Euro-Asian Freight Services revealed their offer to bail them out. Not only that, his last secret shipment of arms to Iraq had been particularly lucrative and had netted him a substantial portion of cash.

He immediately left for the airport to fly the two and half hours to the capital city. He would grab a hotel room at the Mandarin Oriental, a short distance from the government building. On the flight, he made short notes in bullet point format to summarise his progress to his partners. He could also show them the revised business plan for the next financial year that he had gone through with Edmond Andreas before he left the London office. All in all, he felt particularly good about the future.

***

Back at the Chinese Secretary's Office that same afternoon, the Chairman and President of China, Deng Xiaoping, stormed into the central government meeting room completely unannounced. His face was purple with rage and he spat his words out, spraying the room in an explosion of venom and spit.

'You damn fools! You fucking, fucking morons! What on earth do you think you are playing at? This Macrae venture was nearly brought off the rails because of your inability to control Stanfield and his henchman Nash!'

The three top Chinese generals sitting around the meeting

table were immediately taken aback. They had expected Deng's secretary to chair the meeting on the next steps for Euro-Asian Freight Services, not Deng himself. Their utter shock was reflected in their blank, astonished faces. They were frozen for words. Finally General Jiang stammered, 'I, I d-don't understand. You wanted us to bring the Macrae Company to its knees, so we could further your expansion plans in Europe.' Those last words hung in the air only momentarily before they were blasted down by a further barrage of acrid expletives.

'Yes, but you fucking stupid idiots did not listen properly, did you?' Deng Xiaoping remained on his feet, circling the boardroom table like a tiger waiting for the kill. He stared each general down, one by one. His eyes, filled with fury, pierced them to the backs of their skulls. 'Your directive was to be invisible below the radar within Euro-Asian Freight Services and take all necessary steps to weaken Macrae by purely commercial means. Yes! Purely commercial means! My new Long-Term China Economic Plan for China is to dominate the world, which we can only accomplish if we are seen to be supportive friends with all other countries. The longer those countries see us as close friends, the easier it will be to take them over! Instead, you have murdered innocent people and then, to top that off, allowed Stanfield to smuggle arms to the IRA and Iraq. Just think for once, you stupid bastards!' He paused and pointed his finger forcibly at all of them, one by one, stabbing the air in a constant motion. 'What will happen if the outside world gets to know that the Chinese Government is knowingly killing innocent people and smuggling arms to take over all the strategic ports in Europe? Our mission was to do this purely through subversive competition and economics.

Now we could have every international door slammed in our faces. They will see us coming from miles away!'

The second general finally opened his mouth. 'The deaths of the Macrae employees were very unfortunate. We just wanted to suspend their business to create financial hardship so they would have no alternative but to sell out to us. As to the arms smuggling, I'm sorry but we don't know anything about that.'

'Look at me! All three of you! Look at me!' he shouted. 'It was your job to know. It was your job to control Stanfield! You want to know about the smuggling? Well, I will tell you. While you were sitting comfortably on your fat arses, your man was smuggling a shipment of illegal arms through Saudi Arabia into Iraq. My own agents knew, why didn't you? Here's what happened: I dispatched our agents to take out Nash, so Euro-Asian Freight Services could not be connected to the illegal shipment. Next, I, yes, I, fed incorrect information on the geographical location of the arms to both the Americans and Saudis to divert them away from finding the arms. We allowed the shipment to go through to prevent our involvement being observed by outsiders. Luckily, the whole dam mess was taken care of!' Deng paused as if to consider his next words. 'You have failed me, you have failed China, you have brought shame on yourselves.'

Silence remained in the still air of the boardroom. Finally Deng said quietly, 'You have been replaced. The secret police outside this room will now take you to Qincheng Prison. You have been stripped of your positions. You have lost all your family privileges and you will spend the rest of your miserable lives incarcerated! Such is the price of your failure.'

Chapter 26

James returned home after the meetings with the banks. Sarah was sitting at the kitchen table with the children. They were all doing a jigsaw puzzle together. James gave them all kisses on their heads as they pored over the puzzle and went straight to the lounge and poured himself a scotch. Sarah came in a few minutes later.

'What's wrong, James?'

James didn't reply straight away. He took a sip of scotch and rested his head on the back of the sofa.

'Sorry to be so distant but I didn't have a good day. Things are starting to pile up on me. I had disastrous meetings with our banks today. Neither are jumping to help us, so I haven't yet secured any long-term financing. Our lead that I followed from Italy to Saudi has completely disappeared. Our debts are piling up. It just goes on.'

'I'm so sorry, James. What can I do?'

'I'm not sure anyone can do anything more than we have done. None of the police forces have come up with anything either except to confirm all these accidents were deliberate acts of sabotage.'

Sarah put a reassuring hand on his shoulder. 'Do you have anything further yet on who has been leaking confidential information to the saboteurs?'

'That's another thing getting me down right now. I'm pretty sure it's not Rob Bissett, but Hal, I'm not so sure. I've had a private investigator on him. All he's found so far is that he has offshore accounts, but he can't access them. He's also observed him buying prepaid cards and disposable cell phones. Trouble is, while it's suspicious it doesn't prove anything.'

'Sounds funny to me,' said Sarah. 'Although it's hard to believe it would be him. God knows, he's been a true family friend!'

'I know he has. It doesn't make sense.'

Just as Mason walked in the room, James sighed. 'I think I'm going out of my mind right now. I've never felt so depressed.' Mason left the room and went to his bedroom.

'Oh, James!' Sarah stroked his head, still resting on the back of the sofa.

'I've got a meeting with MI6 in London tomorrow afternoon. This is the result of my meeting in Riyadh with the British Ambassador. I'm not optimistic. Most government employees are all talk and no action. I'll stay in London tomorrow night and be back the following morning.'

Mason walked back into the room and handed his dad a framed picture of a poem. 'Dad, maybe this will help? It's the poem you both gave to me on my last birthday. You said it would help me in life.'

James picked up the picture. It was Rudyard Kipling's poem 'If'.

If you can keep your head when all about you

Are losing theirs and blaming it on you,
If you can trust yourself when all men doubt you,
But make allowance for their doubting too;
If you can meet with Triumph and Disaster
And treat those two impostors just the same;
If you can bear to hear the truth you've spoken
Twisted by knaves to make a trap for fools,
Or watch the things you gave your life to, broken,
And stoop and build 'em up with worn-out tools:
Yours is the Earth and everything that's in it,
And – which is more – you'll be a Man, my son!

James read it aloud as a tear rolled down his cheek.

27

Chapter 27

The InterCity Express from Birmingham slid into London's Waterloo and pulled up slowly against the buffers at the end of the platform. As James walked on the concourse under the massive roof structure of steel and glass, the huge, circular four-faced clock with its Roman numerals gave the time of 1:10 p.m.

A chauffeur, holding his name up on a plaque, greeted him at the exit turnstiles. James was taken by the government car through rain-soaked streets to MI6 HQ at Century House, the twenty-two-storey MI6 office block on Westminster Bridge Road in Lambeth. The car turned down into the secure underground car park.

James was taken through Security and then up to the conference room on the twenty-second floor. The walls surrounding the room appeared to be very thick, deadening the sound.

'Good afternoon, James. My name is Jack Fox, MI6 director. On my right is Alan Fortesque-Edwards, Under-Secretary to the Foreign Secretary, and this is Jeremy Hirons, one of our senior MI6 operatives. Now, I already know that you have signed off on the Official Secrets Act before this meeting and I can't over-emphasise the importance of this gathering both from a personal safety point of view, your company existence and national security. We did receive a full report from your meeting in Riyadh with the British ambassador, but perhaps you could give us a summary of the situation as you see it.'

'Thank you, Mr Fox. Gentlemen, I find myself and my company to be in terrible danger. Murder, sabotage, fraud and intimidation are only a few of the words to describe the monstrous situation we find ourselves in. We are haemorrhaging badly, and my company is on its last legs.

There was no visible reaction from the others.

James then relayed all the information he had gathered on his visits to the various Macrae terminals. He referred them to the local police at each port and reported on his chase of the prime suspect through Saudi Arabia and how Nash had been abducted by Chinese nationals using a pick-up truck with diplomatic plates. He also detailed evidence he had gathered from Mirza Baig in Istanbul and the involvement of Chinese individuals.

James continued. 'One final point. My colleagues and I believe that Euro-Asian Freight are behind this sabotage. We say this for three reasons. One, it was an employee of Euro-Asian Freight that caused the sabotage by the name of Dan Nash. Two, I provided you with photographic evidence of their arms smuggling activities. Three, their company has grown exponentially, way above any legal means, in a challenging world economy. Bottom line, we believe they want to weaken us to the point where we have no choice but to sell out to them. I may as well add that our banks are very likely to call in our credit lines very soon. In fact, our one bank has already turned their backs on us. With little liquidity left, we will be bankrupt next month.'

Jeremy Hirons took notes all the time James spoke.

Jack Fox remained impassive. 'Thank you, James. We clearly understand the gravity of the situation. I can tell you that the Toyota pick-up that was used to abduct Nash was an officially listed vehicle of the Chinese Embassy in Riyadh. The registration number of the Falcon 20 jet that you supplied us with, taking off from the private terminal, is also a Chinese government-registered aircraft.'

James spread his hands out either side of him. 'So, what does all of this mean to you?'

'Let me share with you what we know, James. China is a paradox. The country is not a communist state. Far from it, but neither are they a democracy. The Communist Party has instilled the message in their population for years that 'they will liberate the world'. In our language 'liberate' means 'takeover'! Now, under the leadership of Deng Xiaoping, they are becoming ruthless capitalists. The Chinese Communist Party runs everything: the people, the economy and foreign policy. Instead of dominating the world by using military tactics, they want to expand economically. They watched the previous failures of expansion in recent years of the Japanese, Germans and the Russians, trying to use military force. So the question we have is this. What if they could revive the Silk Road for geopolitical purposes?'

James stroked his chin. He remained silent.

Alan Fortesque-Edwards continued where Jack Fox had left off. 'Our intelligence from several other foreign countries points to the Chinese escalating and extending their economic and military tentacles worldwide. We know that they have secretly approached Pakistan, Iran, India and Turkey to finance the construction of a high-speed rail link that will interconnect each country with one another and help springboard Chinese influence across Asia and into Europe. The rail link would give them a direct route to Istanbul, the gateway to Europe. Deng Xiaoping is on a mission and his rhetoric towards the west, to use diplomatic language, is 'cordial and warm'. It is completely the opposite message of his predecessor, Chairman Mao. We believe that China will want to be seen as a friendly economic benefactor to these countries. It seems they will use gifts and cheap loans to help these countries develop their own infrastructure, however it will also provide a Chinese pipeline to the rest of the world that could be used for both economic and, maybe, military purposes at some future date. We also believe that they will leverage these transit countries so high that if the country cannot pay back a loan, they will accept payment by ownership of such locations of economic and military importance such as port facilities.'

Jack Fox stood up from the table and walked towards a map of Europe on the wall. He used a red laser pointer. One by one, he pointed at Istanbul and the other Macrae terminals. He turned to face James directly. 'Right now, you are in their way. You say you have refused to sell your business several times. What if the Chinese know that and need to weaken you sufficiently that you have no choice but to sell? If the Chinese had bases in Piraeus, Genoa, Istanbul and Valencia, not only do they have a strong foothold in Europe, but they would command the Mediterranean, have influence over the EU, have a pipeline from the Middle East and sway over North Africa as well. Economically they could control transport rates to further their interests in becoming the next superpower.

Far better for them to make you submit this way than to wage a military war and take possession that way. Not only that, but your bases could easily be used for Chinese military or naval purposes at some later date. The methods they use we refer to as *hybrid warfare*.'

James tapped his fingers on the table. 'I know the Silk Road existed at the time of the Roman Empire until round about the eighteenth century. I also know that, recently, the Chinese have talked of perhaps extending rail links to Central Asia, Middle East and Europe, but I believed they were just rumours. For them to do that, they would need to persuade an awful lot of foreign governments to cooperate with them. No way any one of them would allow that unless the Chinese bankrolled it. If we look at the current world players with America as the present-day superpower, Russia is struggling to hold their union together, China would seem to be the next in line. From what you say, it is a likely scenario for them to take us over.'

James got up from the table and walked to the map. He tapped his fingers on each of his locations. 'I have a question.'

'Shoot,' said Jack Fox.

'Where does Euro-Asian Freight Services fit in? I can't get my head around that.'

Alan Fortesque-Edwards nodded towards Jack Fox.

Fox responded. 'Our Hong Kong intelligence unit believes that Euro-Asian Freight was taken over by the Chinese government some years ago. With the company being based in Shanghai, it was easy for them to do so. They control the owner Hugh Stanfield. He would have had no choice in the matter. Any actions he takes would be a directive from the Chinese government and they can hide behind him acting as an independent private company. To the outside world, including you James, nothing has changed.'

James opened his mouth and moved his head to one side. He started to say, 'Stanfield built a good shipping business from the ground up. He is self-made. I can't imagine him wanting to share his business with anybody else...' And then he remembered Janet Rushton had told him that it appeared that Euro-Asian servers were protected by heavily encrypted Chinese government firewalls!

James sank back into his chair and decided not to say anything else. He did not say they had tried to illegally hack into their systems. Running his left hand through his hair, he quietly said, 'Oh god! It's all starting to make sense to me now.'

Jack Fox continued. 'We also believe that certain elements within Euro-Asian Freight Services are operating without the Chinese ownership's knowledge. Seems the arms smuggling is a private operation of its owner, Hugh Stanfield, who used Nash to help convey the arms into Iraq. If knowledge of the Chinese being involved in illegal arms operations, that were in contravention of US and European embargoes, became public knowledge, then it would set their "friendly expansion" back by decades. It would also explain why Nash was abducted by the Chinese using guns and drugs to do it. Based on your evidence, we have put out an arrest warrant for Nash. Unfortunately we, as one nation, based on this evidence, cannot shut down Euro-Asian Freight Services on our own. We will need to consult with our partners in Europe and the US. We are doing so as we speak.'

James sat up. 'Mr Fox, this is all very well but unless our company receives help now, not only are we going to go bankrupt, you will lose our ports to the Chinese. We don't have the resources to fight Euro-Asian Freight Services when they come to take us over. Our cash flow is in dire straits and, believe it or not, Euro-Asian Freight Services is one of our creditors from something business-related that they helped us out with some months ago. Never did we believe, at that stage, that we were being set up.'

'Mr Macrae, we hear you loud and clear!' Alan Fortesque-Edwards jumped in. 'On behalf of the Foreign Secretary, the British government does have the ability to protect you. Our lease agreement with China for Hong Kong will end in 1997. There are terms within that lease that we can use to hold up the handover of Hong Kong back to the Chinese. We know they are anxious to get their hands back on the territory as soon as they can. Again, it's all part of their new Silk Road policy.'

'So, are you saying that we are completely safe?' James asked.

'I'm saying we can prevent the Chinese from taking you over for the next few years,' Fortesque-Edwards replied.

'Sorry, sir, but that doesn't answer my question.' James replied. 'We need a huge cash injection right now. Politics aside, we will be taken over just purely under market conditions. Can you help us now from a monetary point of view or, at least, with a British government guarantee that we could show our bankers?'

Alan Fortesque-Edwards repositioned himself in his chair. 'We could, but, given our slow bureaucracy, I doubt that we could do it in time.'

'Can you at least try, Mr Fortesque-Edwards?' asked James.

'Yes. We realize this situation is critical. I must brief both the foreign secretary and prime minister after this meeting. We will get back to you as soon as we can.'

'Thank you.'

Jeremy Hirons looked up from his notes. 'James, is there anything else that you think could be important?'

James placed his hands on the table. 'I believe there is. It's clear to us that Euro-Asian have access to confidential information from within our company. The acts of sabotage all happened around critically important dates. Moreover, the tampered contract in Istanbul was skilfully manipulated by a finance professional. I've had my main suspect under surveillance by a private detective. He has gone as far as he can and discovered that he has several offshore bank accounts. Of course, my detective cannot access them.'

'Can you give us your detective's details please? We can get the necessary warrants issued to investigate further. We'll get on it straight away.'

'Help me, please!' James exclaimed.

Jack Fox responded. 'We will. Remember, we work twenty-four hours a day, seven days a week.'

28

Chapter 28

Hugh Stanfield left the Mandarin Oriental hotel before
8.00 a.m. for his meeting with General Jiang. It
was a bright, clear and crisp morning with only a
light breeze. He walked west along the busy West Chang'an
Avenue, past the vast slabbed area of Tiananmen Square
where a few tourists were absorbed in taking photographs.
He then turned right onto Fuyou Street and entered the
Zhongnanhai West Building Compound. The offices were of
a much plainer construction compared to some of the more
ornate neighbouring buildings in the sprawling compound.
Many of the support staff for the government were housed
here. He cleared Security and was ushered into a bleak,
windowless meeting room on the third floor. He was alone.
After waiting several minutes, two men entered the room. One
was in a general's military uniform. He had three embroidered
gold stars on his shoulder boards, the same as General Jiang
had had. The other person was wearing a smart business suit
and tie.

'Stanfield!' There was no greeting and no 'Mr'. 'I am General

Shen and from now on you report to me and only me. This gentleman is Mr Meng. Mr Meng is the private secretary of our Chairman, Deng Xiaoping. General Jiang and your previous partners and handlers have all been replaced. That's all you need to know.'

Stanfield's mouth hung open. He was completely taken aback. Shen looked dangerous, as though he was highly trained, and battle-scarred. He was clean-shaven with a receding hairline and his skin was pock-marked. His eyes were cold, empty and distant.

'I don't understand,' Stanfield stammered, 'My partners and I had been working closely together since the beginning of our relationship and had a good understanding. I ran the business and they made requests for me to carry out certain instructions.'

'So you think you have done a good job?' the general asked

'Yes I do,' Stanfield replied firmly and started to regain his composure. 'I have made notes and can give you a full report, not only on the financial performance of Euro-Asian Freight Services, but also our progress in weakening Macrae Shipping. We will be able to take them over very soon. That is what I was asked to do and that is what I have done.' He sat back, folded his arms and nodded to himself.

The general pulled up the chair, leaned forward and looked directly at Stanfield. His piercing and vacant eyes locked directly into Stanfield's gaze. The private secretary took a seat on the right of the general.

'But that is not all you have done, is it?' the general asked.

'I'm sorry, but I don't know what you mean,' replied Stanfield.

'Yes you do. You know very well what I mean. You were

asked to weaken Macrae Shipping using all normal commercial and competitive means available. We even told you to lose money on deals where you competed directly with Macrae if it would take business away from them. Instead, you resorted to violence, murder and intimidation. These are not normal commercial and competitive ways of doing business, are they? Do you concur?'

Stanfield went cold. He shivered and swallowed hard. His throat became dry. 'I thought that was what you wanted.'

'You did, did you? You, Stanfield, went well beyond your instructions. Never were you asked to commit murder.' The general remained stone-faced.

'That was an accident.'

The general slammed his large fist onto the table. A loud bang ricocheted around the empty room. 'Enough of this bullshit! And was illegal arms smuggling an accident as well?'

'I've never been involved in arms smuggling. Yes, I've been ruthless in business but never resorted to anything like that. Never!'

Shen's voice started to rise. 'So now you are a liar. A bare-faced liar! Do you think we Chinese are stupid? Do you think we are a Third World country still, full of simple peasants waving red books in the air?'

'No, certainly not!' Stanfield retorted, his face reddening.

'Then why do you lie to me?'

'I'm not lying.'

The general got up from his chair and leaned over the table within inches of Stanfield's face. 'Yes you are and here is the proof.' On that he turned around, marched to the door and returned with two other army officers. Between the two men stood Dan Nash.

Chapter 29

James was pissed off with all the bullshit that he had been given by Alan Fortesque-Edwards in their meeting at MI6. As far as he was concerned, Margaret Thatcher's observation on politicians was one hundred per cent correct in that 'politicians and diapers had one thing in common. They should both be changed regularly and for the same reason.'

The meeting had not gone well. All it did was confirm his suspicions of Chinese involvement and any help either MI6 or the British Government could give them, in spite of their good intentions, would be too late to save the destruction of Macrae Shipping and, worst of all, the people who he really cared about.

James stayed with Jack Fox and Jeremy Hirons at MI6 headquarters after Alan Fortesque-Edwards had left the meeting.

All he could think about was the saying, 'It's always darkest before dawn.' He tapped a pencil on the blank writing pad beside him. He looked at the MI6 director. An idea was beginning to form in his mind. 'Jack, I guess I can call you that, right?'

'Yes, James, you can.'

James held his forefinger up. 'I have an idea. Euro-Asian Freight has an office in London, I believe at Canary Wharf, right?'

'Yes, they do.'

'That means, therefore, they have to submit annual tax returns and yearly audits, if requested, from the HMRC.'

'That would be correct,' replied Jack.

'Can we get hold of all of their tax returns for, say, the last two years?'

'I think I know where you are going with this one. Let me make a call and I'll get Jeremy to pick them up. If I am correct, they would have the files at the tax office at Lower Thames Street, Billingsgate.'

While they waited for the files to arrive, Jack went back up to his office and James remained on his own in the conference room and started to sketch out a plan of action. Yes, it was good MI6 could help in certain areas, but he knew he had to force things to happen faster.

Within a noticeably short time, Jeremy Hirons returned with the information that James had requested. Such was the pull of the MI6 director. It was impressive.

James and Jeremy spread the contents over the large desk. All the tax returns had been signed off and approved by HMRC. All the Euro-Asian entries were signed off by the CFO, Edmond Andreas. James became frustrated; there was nothing in the documents that could help him as far as he could see. He scratched his head. Fuck! There must be something! A small clue that maybe could open a door, nail Euro-Asian Freight, so he could at least get a warrant, injunction or restraining order, or whatever you wanted to call it, to close them down, even if it was only temporary. Jack Fox put his head around the door. 'Anything?'

Jeremy piped up. 'Not yet, Jack, but we're not giving up. Somehow we have to stop these bastards before they destroy Macrae's and we lose the ports to the Chinese.' Jeremy sifted through some more papers, 'Hang on, I may have found something.'

Jack, James and Jeremy were looking at a file entitled 'Company Expenses'. There were numerous receipts and invoices within the file. Some airline ticket stubs were included that were listed to Hugh Stanfield. On several of them the British Airways flight left from London Heathrow via Zurich to Shanghai. The file also contained some airport limousine receipts. On one of the Zurich receipts was an address on the Bahnhofstrasse in the old city.

'Here's what I think,' said Jack. 'Stanfield has maybe got some sort of a base in Zurich. He could also have a numbered Swiss bank account or multiple accounts. Pound to pinch of shit, he is financing his illegal arms smuggling deals through Zurich. Swiss banks are notorious for their secrecy. They love their money! Half the Nazis in the second World War kept their illicit funds there. Stanfield has probably managed to keep out of sight from foreign governments by using this method. Jeremy, can you work this angle and follow up the lead. Good work!'

'Jack, before you go, you mentioned earlier that you have issued instructions through every UK police force and Interpol to have Dan Nash arrested?' James asked.

'Yes, I have. I might as well tell you though that I doubt Nash can use his own identity anymore. He knows you identified him in Genoa, and I would bet that he already has a new passport and papers. Obviously this is going to make it much harder to spot him. Something that you don't know, however, is some new secret technology that we are testing along with MI5. Due to our experience with the IRA troubles, these villains pop up here and there and then just disappear again. They are masters at disguising themselves. So, we are pilot testing a new software program that is coupled to a set of security cameras. It relies on facial recognition. It intricately measures the dimensions of the face through such points as ear to ear, eye to eye, nose etc. In theory we can then identify a person even if they are travelling on false papers. Right now, the test program is being piloted at Heathrow, Gatwick and Belfast airports, as well as the port passenger terminal at Holyhead. It's going to be difficult to spot these villains in real time, but at least we will know if they are in or out of the country and we can then match the face to a new identity.'

'That is excellent news!' James exclaimed.

'One last thing,' Jack said. 'I will set up a work-in-progress room so we can collate all of the information that we have so far and pinpoint all the information, facts and evidence that we still need to bring this case to a satisfactory conclusion.' Jack then left the meeting room.

'Thanks, Jeremy,' James said. 'Good thing you spotted the expense file. Listen, you were in the meeting today and heard that there is no quick solution for helping Macrae's fight off a takeover. I have to say that the under-secretary to the foreign secretary, what was his name, Alan Fortesque-Edwards? Well, he did some pretty fancy tap dancing. He knows the British Government wants to collaborate with China from a trade point of view, but they also need to be aware that they are competing with them too. That's an exceptionally fine line to follow.'

'Yes. It was pretty disappointing,' Jeremy replied. 'I understand your frustration. Listen, you've got me to help. Let's see if we can bring down Euro-Asian Freight Services between us sooner rather than later. At least you and I don't have to follow protocols, red tape and all that government bullshit. We can do whatever we need to. In fact, I think that's why Jack picked me to help you. He knows I don't always play by the rules, but he could never admit that. I think you've got more friends in high places than you realize.'

They combed through more of the tax files. Jeremy came upon an invoice from 'The Bulldog and Beaver' made out to Euro-Asian Freight. It was for supply of food and beverages for a Christmas party that had taken place at their Canary Wharf offices. 'That seems strange.'

'Why would it be strange?' asked James.

'Well, I can tell you that there are some very unsavoury characters involved with that place, although I don't think they've ever been found guilty of anything. I would have thought a company like Euro-Asian Freight would buy from a much more reputable establishment than the low-lives there.'

***

Sarah opened her eyes. It was dark, what time was it? She thought she had heard a noise but couldn't be sure. Was it one of the children? She lay there, half-awake, and listened. It was no good now, she'd have to get up and check on them. She'd lie there fretting otherwise. She swung her legs out of bed and pulled on her silk kimono, then pushed her feet into her fluffy slippers and plodded over to the half-open bedroom door. She screamed.

Chapter 30

J ack Carter kept the Ford Transit van deliberately under 70mph on his way back to London via the M40. The journey would take less than three hours so he could be back at the pub by 5.00 a.m. All was quiet in the back of the van. He smiled to himself. He didn't know why his partner, Hugh Stanfield, had wanted this woman kidnapped, but she was one hell of a looker. Tempting, very tempting.

After receiving the house address from Stanfield, Carter had driven up from London the previous morning. He had been told that the woman would be alone with her three children. He had parked his van off the road some distance away from the house and casually walked by to check everything out. He wore a tweed jacket, flat cap and carried a wooden hiking stick. To the casual observer, he looked like a local out for a walk. He saw the gravel drive so decided he would park on the grass verge of the road when he returned later, rather than make a sound driving over the gravel. The house was situated on its own, surrounded by wheat fields. No nosy neighbours to worry about. Next he checked out the position of the alarm system and motion detector lights. He was able to access the garden shed unseen from the house and found a ladder in there. Good. It meant he didn't have to use his own extension ladder from the van.

He returned to the house at midnight, parking his van quietly on the verge. He left it unlocked and, taking his bag of housebreaking tools, went to the shed, staying away from the security lights. He used the ladder to climb up to the alarm box and quietly took off the cover. Next, he sprayed foam into the alarm to prevent it from going off. He moved stealthily around to the window he had spotted earlier on the blind side of the motion detector lights. Using his diamond cutter and suction pad he removed a circle of glass big enough to put his gloved hand through and release the catch. All was quiet in the house. No dogs. Bringing his bag inside with him, he entered the room and crept quietly around the ground floor. Next, he slowly made his way up the stairs, using his hand on the stair rail to try to take as much weight off his feet as he could. Creaking floorboards and stairs were always a hazard. A low night light shone within one of the bedrooms. He peeped inside and saw two girls sleeping soundly in their twin beds, all tucked in with their cuddly toys. He checked the bedroom opposite and saw a small boy sleeping with a toy rocket resting on his bedcover. Slowly he closed both bedroom doors. Along the landing, past the family bathroom, was another slightly open door. As he made his way towards it, a floorboard creaked. Quickly he stood to the side of the bedroom door with his back against the wall. He took out a bottle from his pocket containing Desflurane, a rapid onset anaesthetic and poured some of the contents into a face mask. Within a few minutes he heard someone come from the other side of the door. The woman had screamed when she saw him but was silenced quickly as the anaesthetic took hold of her. She went limp as he let her down gently to the floor, trying not to make a sound.

He waited momentarily. The children had not woken up. He carried her downstairs, collected his belongings, grabbed her coat and outdoor shoes from the coat rack and carried her out to the van. He placed her in the rear compartment, threw her coat and shoes in and locked the doors. He placed his housebreaking kit in a separate compartment and left as quickly as he could before anyone discovered she was gone.

Jack was pleased. The abduction had gone smoothly. He had stopped only once to give her some more anaesthetic when she started moaning. Once back in the pub, he could give her another whiff and keep her in the cellar, locked up until Stanfield called him. It would be a good day's pay! All he had to do after that was dump the stolen van.

***

Mary, James's mother, answered her home phone the following morning.

'Nana, Mommy isn't here.'

31

Chapter 31

Stanfield was shocked. The last person he expected to see in the Beijing government offices was Dan Nash. Nash should have been on his way from Jeddah to London by now.

General Shen put his face inches in front of Stanfield's face. 'Do you still want to tell me you are not lying?'

Stanfield's colour drained from his face. Damn it, he was caught, and Shen knew it.

Meng, Deng Xiaoping's male secretary, spoke next. 'I will make it easy for you, Stanfield. Our chairman is incredibly angry with you. You are now perilously close to joining your three previous handlers in Qincheng Jail. Let me put it another way, one more mistake and you are finished. We don't care where you are in the world. We will come and get you. I can't imagine what will happen to you if we put you in the same cell as the other three demoted generals. A slow death would probably seem likely. The same goes for Mr Nash here.'

General Shen issued orders for Nash to sit down next to Stanfield. The two other army officers remained in the room.

His tone lowered, he said, 'Now, Mr Nash, do you want to tell Mr Stanfield everything you told us when you received our special water treatment?'

Dan Nash wriggled uncomfortably in his chair. 'I'm sorry, Mr Stanfield,' he stammered. 'I had to tell them everything.'

Stanfield remained frozen. Finally he summoned up the courage to speak back to the general. 'What would you like me to do now?' It was all he could think of to say.

General Shen sat down next to Meng. 'Right, now we've got that out of the way we will proceed with the original master plan. This time you will play by our rules and not yours. Understood?'

'Yes, sir. Understood,' Stanfield said weakly.

'And, Mr Nash. Do you understand?'

'Yes I do, sir.'

'Right. As far as we know, no one else knows you have been smuggling arms. That means that this illegal act will not reflect badly on Euro-Asian Freight Services as a company. You are the front man of the company to the outside world. You must be seen to behave with the utmost honesty and ethics. That goes for you too, Nash. There are to be no more acts of sabotage or arms smuggling. Do you both understand?'

Stanfield and Nash replied that they did.

'Now let's examine every loose end that needs to be tidied up. Tell me every little detail where you could be identified and associated with these acts of sabotage and murder.'

Stanfield reflected quietly to himself. Since the Chinese takeover, he had been stupid to think that he could just carry on as before being the sole owner of the company and doing whatever he wanted without due consideration for his silent partners. The Chinese takeover of his company had paid him well; unfortunately he was a prisoner of his own greed and malice. He now knew that he had to play by their rules. He could still have a good life, but only if he obeyed the Chinese one hundred per cent and no less. He had pacified himself.

Stanfield gathered himself together. 'Firstly, Dan Nash was identified in Genoa by Macrae Shipping. He must be their prime suspect. I have no doubt his description and details are all over Interpol by now. I already had sent a new identity for him. European passport, Schengen papers, life story and background. Dan, you should have picked them up in Yanbu, right?'

'Yes. I have them,' Nash replied.

Shen responded. 'Yes, we have inspected them already. The forgery is very well done and will pass any checks anywhere. We will also want to know where you got them. Right, that takes care of that angle, although you will need to alter your unruly hairstyle, Nash. I'm also glad that Nash is no longer identified in these papers as a Euro-Asian Freight Services employee. That was essential. Now, what other details need to be taken care of?'

Stanfield spent a few moments thinking. 'We have another problem. For our company to grow so quickly, we have committed insurance fraud. Our insurance company has a claims inspector and auditor that knows it and is trying to obtain actual proof. His name is David Morris and he is based at his company's head office in Bristol, England. My CFO, Edmond Andreas, called me a few days ago to say that he believes that Morris will try to inspect one of our ships that suffered an explosion in the Persian Gulf. He also thinks there's a good chance he will inspect another vessel by the name of *Aviemore*. She recently passed an annual inspection, but we bribed the inspector to pass the vessel, even though we all knew it would fail. His name is Ben Mitchell of Blue Water Maritime Bureau. I was dispatching Dan to London from Saudi Arabia to arrange fatal accidents for both men.'

'I see.' Shen looked at Meng. Meng nodded back to him as an affirmation. 'Right. When we have finished here, Nash will proceed to England and close these two men down. Their deaths must be seen as pure accidents, though. Just to be clear again to both of you. We will have agents shadowing you. Your freedom is a thing of the past. Anything else?'

'Yes,' Stanfield blurted out. 'In order to intimidate the Macrae organisation into selling their company, we have abducted the wife of the president.'

Shen and Meng looked grimly at each other again. 'By god, when you want something, you don't play by the rules, do you?' Shen said. 'Get her released unharmed, right now!'

Stanfield bent down and took his cell phone out of his briefcase. He dialled the number from memory and issued instructions directly to Jack at the Bulldog and Beaver pub in London to let his captor go.

'Hello, Jack. You need to release the package immediately that you picked up. There must be no damage to the contents. Do you understand?'

'Fuck off, Hugh. I know the contents of that packet and I'm going to sample it myself. It's also my ticket out of here. The price will be high, enough for my retirement in Spain.'

'Just release the package now.'

'Fuck off!' The line went dead.

General Shen looked hard at Stanfield. 'Is everything in order?'

'Yes, General. Everything is under control.' Stanfield felt

his body temperature rising. *How the hell could Jack do that to me?* He shifted in his seat and did his best to appear normal when, clearly, he had lost control of Jack Carter.

'Good. So now we've got your act cleaned up, how close are we to buying out Macrae's?' Shen asked.

'According to our mole in Macrae's, they are remarkably close to bankruptcy. They have been unable to secure any more credit and will fail to make payroll for all their employees on the fifteenth of next month. We, that is Euro-Asian, are owed a large sum of money from them for reciprocal business we did for them three months ago. I have requested a meeting with their CFO to demand repayment of our money. During this meeting, I will bring up the subject of a partnership since they will not be able to pay us. Once we own shares in the company, we can gradually take them over. We will end up owning the company and you will have the bases that you require in Europe. They still have no idea that we are a Chinese owned company.'

Secretary Meng spoke next. 'Mr Stanfield. On behalf of our chairman, I want to be one hundred percent sure that everything you have just told us is completely truthful?'

'Yes, sir. I realize now that I should not have carried on as though I continued to own the company entirely by myself. Both you and General Shen have also been clear that I only have one chance. I'm not going to screw that up. Thank you.' Stanfield, for once in his life, meant every word of what he had just said. The only problem he had now was how to control Jack Carter. If he raped her and then ransomed her, they were all done for.

32

Chapter 32

J ames checked into the Royal Horseguards Hotel near Westminster Bridge, overlooking the River Thames. The London Eye stood proud across the other side of the river. He and Jeremy went for dinner, sitting at a quiet table in the corner, sinking into plush red velvet dining room chairs. The elegant and quiet ambience of the dining room helped to somewhat calm James' nerves. It felt like a brief respite from reality.

They clinked their wine glasses together and savoured a particularly good Stag's Leap cabernet sauvignon. 'Cheers, Jeremy! Thanks for your help today. I felt as if I was entirely on my own before our meeting.' As he sliced into his tender medium-rare filet mignon, he asked, 'So what are your next steps?'

'Well, I will be flying to Zurich tomorrow to check out the address we found this afternoon in the tax files. The quicker I can do that, the better. Of course I'll also be following up on the search warrants we have taken out on Hal Spencer. I have to agree with you, he does look like the main suspect. Our agents should be able to see his bank accounts in full once we have approval from the legal department. Regarding Nash, Interpol already has his description but, to be honest, he's bound to have changed his identity by now.'

'I'm sure you are right. However, if you can get further proof of Stanfield's activities, it should help speed things up with the Allies in shutting the company down.'

'I would like to think so, but the biggest frustration I have with my job is bureaucracy. Sometimes I want to stick a firecracker up those pompous diplomatic arses. One thing is for sure, politicians the world over all belong to the same party underneath their stated party name, and that's the GSP Party. Greed and Self-Preservation.' He took a piece of his grilled salmon and closed his eyes. 'These guys know just how to prepare their fish. It's so tender!' He savoured it for several moments and continued the conversation. 'James, I saw you made a list this afternoon on your pad for actions that you want to carry out.'

'Yes, I did. I'm thinking of restructuring the company. It's not quite the poison pill technique you would use to prevent a takeover, but, if I can pull it off, it would be close to it.'

'Sounds interesting.'

***

After dinner, James paced around his hotel bedroom. He couldn't settle. He called Martin Farley, director of Legal Affairs, at home.

'Hi, Martin. Sorry to call you so late.'

'Don't worry, James. I'm always here for you. Are you still in London?'

'Yes I am. I'm staying here tonight and going home early

tomorrow morning. I had to find out if you've had any further news on maybe recouping some of our losses on the Istanbul contract yet?'

'Not yet, but we are still in with a chance. It may be a small one, but I'm not giving up.'

'Good. Thank you. Listen, Martin, I had a brainwave this afternoon. Just between ourselves at this point. How long would it take to set up a new company?'

'You mean a completely new company or a subsidiary of Macrae's?'

'A new company. I'm thinking on my feet right now. Just trying to prevent a takeover when the cash dries up. When a company goes down, they go down fast. You can only rob Peter to pay Paul for so long and then the rug gets pulled from underneath both Peter and Paul.'

'That's for sure, James. That's why I'm trying to work through this Istanbul contract mess as soon as I can.'

James remained on his feet. 'What if we set up a separate property company? Let's say we split off all the fixed assets of Macrae's and form an independent property company. Call it "Newco" for now. Macrae's is then left with its operations and management services, but pay Newco rent every month to use their property and facilities. If Macrae's operations go down the toilet then we only lose the operations company but retain all of the fixed assets in Newco.'

'That could work. We would need detailed values of the land and buildings. I presume Macrae's would retain ownership of the operations equipment?'

'Yes, Martin, that would make sense since this is their field of expertise. The property company would only be responsible for the land, and buildings.'

'The short answer is it would take several weeks but I could start preparations right away. Let me see if I can fast-track it.'

'Go ahead, Martin. Do it, but let's keep this completely confidential between me and you. I'll let Richard know, but that's all. Also, I don't want Hal Spencer involved at this point. Understood?'

'Understood. I'll keep you posted, boss.'

James sat down at the office desk in his bedroom. *I never thought of this until now.*

He called Chris Claybourne. Chris was in a similar position to himself. His father owned a large transportation and warehousing company based in Birmingham. Chris was also in his late thirties and was effectively running the company with his father in semi-retirement. Both their fathers had done business together for years.

'Hey, Chris, James Macrae.'

'Hi, James. Good to hear from you.'

'Are you free in the next couple of days? I'd like to get together with you as soon as possible.'

'Well, I've got a dispatch meeting in the morning, but I'd be free after about ten. Would that work?'

'That would be great. I'm catching the early InterCity out of London in the morning. I can be there by 10.00 a.m.'

'What would you like to discuss? I think we are both up to date on our accounts with each other.'

'No, nothing like that. I want to float an idea for a joint business venture together.'

'Oh. I didn't expect that but, hey, let's talk. See you in the morning.'

James felt better. At least he had a plan now and hopefully he could make some headway at saving his company. He yawned.

It had been a long day, so he decided to turn in and grab a good night's sleep. He did not realize his cell phone battery was dead.

Chapter 33

'Mason? Did you say Mommy isn't there?' Mary asked her grandson quizzically. The sobbing continued on the other end of the line. 'Listen, Nana's here. Are you okay?'

'Ye-yes. I'm okay.'

'Are the girls okay?'

'Ye-yes. They are okay.'

'And you say mommy's not there?'

'No. She's gone but her car is in the garage.'

'Alright, Mason. Sit tight! I'm coming over straight away. Stay calm and look after your sisters.'

Mary and Richard Macrae jumped in their car and dashed straight over to James and Sarah's house. They knew James was in London, so something unusual must have happened. As soon as they arrived and entered the house it wasn't difficult to deduce what had taken place. The police were summoned immediately.

While Mary comforted the children, Richard Macrae spoke with the police inspector.

'Looking at the ladders, the spray foam in the alarm box and the skilled diamond cut in the window, this was not just a break and enter. This is a professional kidnapping. There's no sign of a struggle, no blood stains, no signs of a burglary; otherwise all the drawers and cupboards would be open. Burglars don't clean up after themselves. It would seem that the intruder only wanted Sarah Macrae, as the children were not harmed or even aware of anything untoward. I have the forensic team on their way over here right now.'

Within an hour, photos of Sarah were relayed to every police force in the country. Forensics could not find any fingerprints, but did find evidence of the anaesthetic used on the carpet outside the bedroom. Even though the liquid had long evaporated, it left an invisible residue that could be seen with a black light. Tyre moulds were taken from the indented grass verge outside the house. Door-to-door enquiries were made in the local rural area.

Already computer databases were sifting through likely criminals who might have done this. A search of the surrounding countryside was started.

While Mary kept her grandchildren occupied as best she could, Richard kept trying James's cell phone. There was no response. He informed the police so they could help track him down.

**

James arrived back in Birmingham from London. The train pulled into New Street station at 9.00 a.m. James had tried to charge his phone on the train, but he was unable to plug in anywhere. He drove straight to see Chris Claybourne at his transport terminal on their twenty-acre site in the Aston district, not far from the city centre. There were neatly parked dry-van trailers, flatbeds, and multi-axle heavy haul trailers. Tractors and straight trucks were all parked separately. All fifteen overhead bay doors were open in the workshop. The sound of air wrenches and other tools tried to compete with loud music blaring from the radio at the back of the shop. Mechanics strode around, whistling as they went about their business. James realized, with the bright sunshine and warm temperature, everyone's spirits were lifted. Vehicles came and went all around him, some shunting trailers, other tractors without trailers.

Chris's office door was open, but he still had four people in with him sitting round a meeting table. His secretary, Rachel, greeted him. 'Oh hi, James, haven't seen you for a while. Are you well?'

'Hey, Rachel, yes, great. How about you?'

'Very well, but you know that boss of mine is a handful, eh?' She laughed and gave him a wink.

Chris looked up and saw James. 'Hey, James. We're just finishing up. Come on in.'

James shook Chris's hand and asked. 'How are you and how is your dad doing?'

'I'm good and as for Dad, he's seventy now and is spending less and less time here. He's talking about him and Mum retiring somewhere down in the Cotswolds. They both love that part of the country and, if he wants to come back in to work at any time, it's not that far.'

'Sounds great. My dad is struggling at the moment and I think a rest would do him good, especially now. Trouble is, he just doesn't want to stop working, says it would kill him!

Having said that, he wants me to take charge now.'

'Yeah, I guess both our dads are the same. They've worked their asses off all their lives and they just can't turn off. It's like they have to learn how to relax.'

'So, Chris, why I am here? Well to tell you the truth, desperation drove me to this. Let me explain.' For the next little while, James relayed everything that had happened to his company over the last few months.

Chris listened and did not interrupt.

'God, James. This sounds like something out of a suspense movie. It's hard to believe it's happening in real life. They often say truth is stranger than fiction. So, how can I help?'

James got straight to the point. 'Here's what I want to do. Once we get Euro-Asian Freight Services off our backs, I believe we can get solvent again from our banks and possibly other lenders. If Euro-Asian Freight Services collapses, once the truth is out, we will be able to easily pick up a lot of their business. Right now, Chad Greening, our director of Sales and Marketing has launched an all-out attack on their customers. With the losses of ships Euro-Asian Freight Services has had in the last two years, Chad is selling security, uptime and goods safely delivered on time with Macrae's. We've picked up some business from them already, but, as you know, it takes at least six months before you see the returns roll into the bank.'

'Good, James. That makes sense but I don't see how can I help? I'm sure Dad would agree; we could lend you money to help tide you over. That's not an issue.'

'Here's what I'm thinking. We want to set up whoever it is that is leaking confidential information to Euro-Asian Freight. I want to feed them false information. Not sure if it would work, but it would sure throw a wrench in the works for them. What if you and I said we were amalgamating our two companies? Imagine, Macrae Shipping and Claybourne Cartage became 'Macrae-Claybourne Logistics'. As one company we would be able to offer a completely integrated transportation solution door to door for all our customers. If news of this false company partnership got back to Euro-Asian, then we would no longer be an easy target for them to take us over. We could easily say, based on share ownership, that the company now has X euros in cash, X euros in fixed assets and X billion in turnover. You are one of the biggest transportation companies in the UK with major depots and warehouses in London, Birmingham, Manchester and Glasgow, not to mention Dublin. It would be a smack in the face for Euro-Asian Freight Services.'

Chris sat back quietly in his office chair and slowly digested what he had just heard. It wasn't just what James had said of merely throwing a wrench in the works, he was thinking beyond that. He knew the importance of Just-in-Time transport. Trucks were now rolling warehouses for parts to supply manufacturing plants. They had to deliver goods to feed production lines at specific times. If they were early or late, they got fined by the customer. The days of manufacturing companies having millions of dollars tied up in stock were long gone. Competition was too fierce to allow profit margins to cover dormant warehouse inventory costs.

Finally, Chris said, 'You know, James, if you weren't fighting Euro-Asian, this would be a good idea anyway. For you and me to get together; we could provide a seamless integrated transport pipeline for both our customers door to door. As your ships unload, our trucks pick up and deliver the goods or containers straight away. Not only that, but with our new cold-store warehouses, we could corner the market for frozen and fresh produce. The fact is, if we were the same company, we would be more efficient in integration as well as reducing both of our admin overheads. We could have a central planning and logistics control room 24/7.'

'You like the idea, eh, and not just for misinformation purposes, but in reality?'

'Yes. I do, James, as a concept. Let me talk it over with Dad. You talk it over with your Dad and let's see if we can't make this happen. It would take a lot of planning and careful arithmetic, but it could just work.'

James felt much happier when he jumped into his car. He had left his cell phone charging in there. He turned it on, and it immediately lit up with a ton of missed calls and text messages.

***

Cramped in the aircraft seat on the flight from Beijing to Shanghai, Nash put both hands to his ribs when the G force pressed him back into his seat as the plane gained speed down the runway to take off. He winced.

'Are you okay, Dan?' Stanfield asked, leaning across the seat.

'Not really,' he replied, gasping for air. 'I just found out I'm not immortal after all. It's the effects of waterboarding. I'm often short of breath and my lungs feel like they want to explode.'

Stanfield waited for Nash to regain some of his composure. 'What was it like being on the receiving end?'

'You really want to know?'

'Yes, because I can't imagine what it's like.'

'Well I hope you never have to! It's pure terror. It's not just your lungs that hurt afterwards, you feel like your brain has shrunk having been starved of oxygen. Your wrists and ankles also constantly hurt from the tight bindings. Your whole body convulses in panic fighting for precious gasps of air, whatever you can take in.'

Stanfield nodded quietly. He tried to take a drink of his orange juice from the plastic cup, but had to put it down again on the folding table as his hand was shaking so much. Nash watched him and observed, 'You're not right either, are you, Hugh?

Stanfield gave a forced smile. 'I'm okay, really.'

Nash kept quiet. He knew his boss wasn't right. Whereas he had been tortured physically, he ventured to think that his boss had been tortured mentally.

Stanfield lifted his cup up with two hands and sipped his drink, then closed his eyes and put his head back on the headrest. He knew he wasn't okay. He was quietly being mentally tortured by what General Shen had told him, 'One more mistake and you are finished.' Even the Chairman and leader of the Chinese Communist Party was involved! To make matters worse, he had lied even after he had been warned. How could his life-long friend, Jack Carter, disobey his orders to release Sarah Macrae? He knew Carter was a highly dangerous criminal and that he was a rampant sexual predator having raped and beaten several women over the course of his life. Somehow he had to get a grip of the situation that he had created. It was all starting to spin outside of his control.

Stanfield opened his eyes. 'You realize, Dan, that our lives will never be our own from now on, but at least we're not rotting in some secret Chinese re-education jail somewhere. We can still enjoy fresh air and all the other delights that come with the freedom to move around. We are going to have to be good boys from now on. We just have a few loose ends to tie up first.'

'Yeah. I know. You just tell me what to do and I'll do it.'

Stanfield nodded quietly and sank back into thought. Most of all he realized that the Chinese were no longer his partners in their eyes. They were his owners. The bottom line was that, for the first time in his life, he now knew he was dispensable.

Once back in Shanghai, before they entered the Euro-Asian Freight Services office, Stanfield said, 'Dan, we need to talk privately and for all I know the office could be bugged. Let's go round the corner and get a coffee at the Spices Cafe on Dongfang Road.' They sat at a private table at the rear of the dimly lit cafe. Stanfield looked warily around them and lowered his voice further. 'From now on we need to travel separately. I will not return to the UK until after you have dealt with David Morris, the insurance adjuster. I can't afford to be there when this unfortunate accident happens. To the open world you no longer are associated with Euro-Asian Freight Services with your new European passport. I'm not sure that I can get used to your new identity as Dennis Haddleton from Nottingham, England. Anyway, I've set up an account for you so you can continue to be on the payroll, albeit through another company. I suggest you fly back to the UK via Amsterdam or Frankfurt. The sooner you deal with David Morris and Ben Mitchell, the better. Get rid of Morris first. Right now, he's our most immediate threat. Here's a new number for you to contact me. Take some petty cash as well to help cover your expenses. Pay cash wherever you can and try to avoid using that new credit card you have. I'm going to return to the UK office after you. Then I'll set up the meeting with Macrae Shipping. Be careful. You and I have stirred up a lot of shit in the last few weeks. We will be watched on specific instructions from Deng Xiaoping. It doesn't get any more serious than that and you better not forget it! Talk soon and keep yourself under the radar.'

Stanfield knew he had to deal with Carter himself. He tried multiple times over the next few hours to call him, but there was no answer. It was clear Carter was ignoring him.

34

Chapter 34

J ames called his father using his hands-free device in the car. His father had left multiple messages for James to call him immediately. There were also a host of voicemails from other numbers. James listened to his father's grave voice reporting the abduction of Sarah.

James was distraught.

'Dad, I just picked up your message! Oh my god! How could I have left her and the children all on their own? It's my fault! I should have seen how ruthless these bastards are. I can't let anything happen to her! She hasn't done anything.'

'James. I'm at your house right now with the police. The children are with Mary at our house. Go check on them first and then come here.'

James drove the Range Rover hard, straight to his parents' house to see his children. He smashed his hand repeatedly on the dashboard screaming, "*those bloody bastards! How dare they! What have we done to deserve this?*" Life wasn't fair! Why was everybody so full of greed and dishonesty that they had to go about wrecking the lives of innocent people all around them? My wife was an innocent bystander! The tears streamed down his face. Shaking his head violently, he didn't know how much more he could take.

There were several police officers outside, guarding his parents' house. One police officer stopped him in the driveway but realizing it was James Macrae, let him pass. Another police officer knocked on the front door. His mum came to the door and froze, breaking down in tears. James just stood there, shell-shocked.

'Daddy, daddy!' Mason, Mia and Olivia rushed to meet James. They hugged his legs tightly for what seemed an eternity, weeping uncontrollably. James wiped his eyes and tried to control his body from shaking. He bent down to hold then. Then, eventually, he pulled away and looked at each in turn. He said, 'Mason, Mia and Olivia. I need you all to be very grown up right now. No, Mummy is not here. She had an emergency and had to rush off very quickly. She's fine and will be back very soon. I promise you that. For now, I want you to stay with Nana and Gramps at their house.'

'But where will you be, Daddy?' asked Mason.

'I have to go to see Gramps at our own house and then I have to finish off some very important business and I will be back as soon as I can.'

'Will you bring Mummy back?' asked Mia softly.

'Yes, I will bring Mummy back,' James replied confidently. He silently wished he could be confident.

James left the children with Mary and returned to his own house to meet with his father and the police.

Richard met him at the door. 'James, thank goodness you are here now.' He gave his son a hug. James was brought up to speed with how everything had unfolded.

A burly middle-aged detective approached him. 'Mr Macrae, I am Detective Inspector Brian Garrigan. We have been briefed already by MI6 on your situation and we are treating your wife's kidnapping as a related incident to the previous attacks on your company. Have you had a phone call from anyone at all asking you for a ransom?'

James checked his phone again. He checked every message he had received, again. Many were from the police, trying to contact him. In addition to the multiple calls from Richard, there was one message from Jack Fox at MI6 to also call him back urgently. There were certainly no ransom calls.

'Okay, we are keeping several officers here to guard your house and monitor your phones. We will be tracking the source of any call. Police officers will remain at your parents' home to do the same. We have already alerted your company staff to be on guard in case there are any further threats to them. I understand that this is very upsetting for you, and I can arrange for a grief counsellor to be with you.'

'Thank you, Detective Garrigan, I will not need the services of a grief counsellor. What I do need from you though are constant updates and to know of any leads that you are following up on.'

'Here is my mobile number, Mr Macrae. Let's stay in constant touch.'

'Thank you, DI Garrigan.'

James took his father to one side. 'Dad, let's go outside for a second. I need to talk to you.' When they were both in the garden, James spoke quietly. 'Dad, are you still a member of the shooting club?'

'Yes, I am. Are you going where I think you are going with

this?' Richard asked.

'Yes, Dad. I am. Do you still have your pistol?'

'Yes, I do. It's in the gun cabinet, together with my shotguns and ammunition. Listen, I don't feel comfortable with this you know. Wouldn't you rather let the police handle it. I love you and don't want anything to happen to you.'

'Dad, I know what you are saying, but Sarah is my life. Without her, I have nothing. Everything is closing in on us fast. I have to find her before anything else happens to her.'

Richard took a few steps across the lawn and took a few moments alone. He returned to James. 'Look, here's the key to the cabinet.' He pulled out a bunch of keys from his pocket and separated one. 'I just had to ask myself what I would do in your position.'

'Thanks, Dad. Listen, I have to make a phone call now, so I'll be here for a little longer.'

'Okay, James. I'll go and check on the window company. They are replacing the broken one right now. Also, I ordered the security company to come and install an upgraded system. It will be done today, given the circumstances.'

James went towards the back garden. He stood on the lawn between the garden shed and the children's empty swings. He rang Jack Fox. The phone was immediately answered by his secretary. 'Oh yes, Mr Macrae. He's in a meeting right now but I know he is anxious to speak with you. Let me see if I can interrupt him.'

'James, Jack Fox. Listen, I'm so sorry to hear your news. We are giving the local police as much help as we can give them. Your wife's description and photo have been posted everywhere including all the news media. Between us we are making every effort to find her.'

'This is Stanfield's doing, right? I'm sure of it!'

'James, I have to believe that it is somehow related to all the previous events that have taken place, but I can tell you that Hugh Stanfield is out of the country right now. We believe he is in Shanghai. He left Heathrow over two weeks ago.'

'What about Nash? Has he surfaced again anywhere?'

'No, he has not. We are watching every entry point as we speak. But listen, I do have some news on your CFO, Hal Spencer. You may want to sit down.'

'Let me have it straight, Jack. Nothing can shock me anymore.'

'We executed the search warrants and were able to access the bank accounts of Mr Spencer. In the last six months he has been receiving a monthly sum from Coombes & Co. The total so far is nearly one hundred thousand pounds sterling.'

'Okay, but do we know who sent the funds?' James asked.

'Well, one step at a time. It was a numbered company that sent the funds to another numbered company that then deposited those same funds into Spencer's account.'

James remained silent.

Jack Fox continued. 'We could not source the origin of the funds, but one of the directors of each numbered company is a man by the name of Edmond Andreas.'

'The same name as the CFO of Euro-Asian. The one who signed off the tax returns of the company that we saw yesterday,' said James.

'That's correct, James. It is the same man. We believe the source of the funds being channelled through the numbered companies is in fact Euro-Asian. We will want to interview Mr Spencer, but not right now.'

'Why can't you do it today? I need to get that bastard out of our company right now!'

'James, slow down. Here's why. We are monitoring all his calls and that includes the burner phones he has purchased. We can eavesdrop on everything he says by monitoring all the phone masts close to him. He may be able to lead us to Sarah. I'm sure he will have heard the news by now and will try to have contact with Euro-Asian Freight.'

James became quiet. 'Yes, I see. Do you think he was involved in the break-in?'

'Not directly. It was a professional criminal that took your wife. It was someone who has maybe done this before. Our databases are churning this over. Please have faith in us, James. We are doing everything possible to locate your wife. One more thing. Jeremy is in Zurich right now. If he can uncover a direct link with Stanfield with the other business, we should be able to save your company sooner rather than later.'

'Okay, thanks, Jack. Let me know if you get anything further. What can I do?'

'Stay with your family and stay by the phone. I'm sending you the documents implicating Spencer by encrypted email right now. But listen, James, do not approach Spencer. Hopefully he may be able to lead us to Sarah.'

As he finished the call, James started to feel the blood drain from his face. He felt sick. 'How could he? How could he? Hal Spencer, our own CFO. Hal Spencer, a long-time and trusted friend of my father. Hal Spencer who repeatedly said he felt like he was one of the family. My god, he has betrayed that trust and stabbed everyone at Macrae's in the back.' In James's mind Spencer was also guilty of murder of the Macrae employees and complicit in Sarah's disappearance. It was too much to absorb. He wanted to drive to work right now and confront

Spencer, but he knew he had to keep his anger in check. Jack Fox was right. Spencer might give them a clue as to where Sarah was.

He paced the garden and wrestled some more with his thoughts. He felt icy with rage and a growing feeling of detachment. My god, what a mess! On the one hand, if I tell my dad about Spencer now, he could have a heart attack, but on the other hand he has to know.

His father was standing at the back at the house, on the stone patio, instructing the security company technician who had just arrived. 'Dad, I need to update you on the latest developments.' He paused and put his hand on his father's shoulder. 'This is going to be an exceedingly difficult conversation, but what I'm about to tell you now has to be absolutely kept confidential between you and I.'

'I see.' Richard looked at his son quizzically.

'Dad, you already know about the sabotage at work. I have shielded you as much as I can from the latest facts because I wanted to take the pressure off you while you were in hospital. The fact is that we have been sabotaged by Euro-Asian Freight and they have been assisted by one of our own board members.'

'What! I don't understand, James. Why would one of our own team want to help a competitor? This just doesn't make any sense!' Richard shook his head.

'Well, we will find out in due course why he has betrayed us, but we have to leave this person in their position right now as he might help lead us to Sarah.'

'Oh dear god. Spit it out, James. Who is it? I'm a big boy.'

'Dad, it's Hal Spencer.'

Richard's mouth opened wide as he sat quietly on one of the patio chairs and looked up at James for some time. The silence was deafening. James sat down beside him.

'No, no. You've got it all wrong, Son. It can't be. I hired him years ago and he is without doubt beyond reproach. We've been close forever and sailed through some rough times together, but we always got through it. If ever there was a rock that was solid to help this company through, it was Hal. You better have some solid proof to convince me because, right now, I simply don't believe it. He's one of the family, for god's sake!'

'Yes, he has been one of the family and that's why this is going to be hard to swallow. Quite honestly, the thought makes me sick! I can't imagine how you are feeling right now. Spencer has stabbed you in the back and he's turned the knife. He's betrayed every single employee we have and, as far as I'm concerned, he's as guilty of murder as the actual person who did it.'

'James, James.' Richard held his hands defensively in the air. 'Slow down, slow down.'

'I'm sorry, Dad, but I'm so fucking angry at him, I want to punch his goddamn head in. The man's a lying bastard!'

'Okay. I hear you, but let's take one step at a time.'

James opened up the encrypted email from Jack Fox and handed his phone to Richard. 'Here's the proof.'

Richard looked at the file slowly and reviewed the copies of the bank statements of the Jersey offshore bank account of Hal Spencer. He saw that in the last six months, Hal had received a monthly sum that amounted to nearly one hundred thousand pounds sterling. Next, he saw the copies of the numbered companies from the Company Register, and the listed directors that had transferred the money into his account. Finally, he zeroed in on the name of Edmond Andreas as a director of each of them and then saw he was also the CFO of Euro-Asian

Freight Services.

'Oh no!' Richard said quietly, almost to himself. 'How could he do this to us, James?'

'Dad, I knew you would take it hard. That's why I had to keep it from you until I was sure.' James then proceeded to tell Richard about the wording that had been surgically inserted into the customer contract in Istanbul. Even Jusuf Kahya, the Istanbul terminal manager, had claimed that these changes could only have come from the Macrae head office in Birmingham. Finally, he told his father that Spencer was draining the cash flow by paying bills within thirty days but not chasing receivables. At least James had secretly reversed that decision until the company recovered financially.

Richard sat looking down for some time. He propped his forehead up with his left hand. All the wind had been knocked out of him. Father and son sat in silence for a while, then James leaned over and gave his dad a big hug and a kiss. 'I love you, Dad, but I have to go now.'

Richard seemed to gather himself together. 'This, together with Sarah's disappearance, has been a huge shock. I still can't believe it. What do you think we should do now, James?'

'Dad, you stay here until the police have gone and then look after Mason, Mia and Olivia with Mum. I'm going to pay a visit to Edmond Andreas. I know the police want me to just stay here and wait for a call, but I can't sit here and wait for the police to do something. I need to find Sarah and rescue her. It's all I can think of – I have to do something!'

James began to feel increasingly remote, cold and isolated. It started to feel as though this was happening to someone else, another person completely outside his own being. The day had started out to be promising but had spiralled downwards at lightning speed. His despair and helplessness had morphed into an anger that was lasering in on Euro-Asian Freight. If he couldn't get hold of Stanfield or Nash right now, he was zeroing in on Andreas. Returning to his parents' house, he covertly picked up his father's pistol, two shotguns and ammunition, wrapped them in a blanket and slipped them into the trunk of his vehicle.

35

Chapter 35

S arah opened her eyes slowly. Her eyelids flickered for a few moments. She felt groggy and confused. Her mouth felt dry and, for a minute, she thought she might be sick. She tried to take in her surroundings, but could not comprehend where she was at all. This was not her bedroom and the rest of the room looked unfamiliar. She appeared to be lying in a bed that had been folded down from the wall from inside a tall cupboard. There was a dull electric light on, suspended from a high stone vaulted ceiling. Two of the walls were also constructed out of the same stone, while the other two were bricks and mortar. A pine wooden table and two chairs stood across the other side of the room. There were two doors on the far side. One was an interior wooden door while the other was a solid exterior door. A large worn patterned wool rug covered the floor of rough flagstone paving. *Where am I?* she said to herself. She tried to remember what had happened to her and then, gradually, it came back to her. The dark shadow of a man outside her bedroom, the shock and horror of it all. She remembered trying to fight him off after he had grabbed her, but had felt herself slipping out of consciousness.

She pushed back the blanket covering her and tried to get off the bed but felt giddy. Finally she sat up and waited for the faintness to pass. She stood up shakily and took a few steps, then sat on the chair and put her head in her hands. After she felt herself start to recover, she went to the door nearest to her. It opened and she peered inside. There was a shower, bathroom vanity set and toilet. She drank thirstily from the tap and started to feel a little better. Next, she went to the other door, but it was locked. A noise from the other side made her stand away from it. A man with a well-worn sot of a face entered the room. He looked like some kind of a scaly lounge lizard with his protruding purple nose.

'Who are you and where am I?'

'Never you mind who I am or where you are. It's more important that I know who you are, isn't it, Mrs Sarah Macrae?'

'I don't understand. What is going on?'

'You are my guest right now and we'll be spending some time together, at least until your husband comes up with the ransom money. After that you can go back to your perfect little life and your three beautiful children.'

'Where are my children?' she screamed with a flushed face.

'Fucked if I know. They were in bed asleep the last time I saw them.'

She ran towards him swinging punches at him anyway she could and yelled, 'You bastard! So it was you who drugged me?'

Carter stood his ground and grasped her upper arms tightly. 'Yes. But, first things first, you need to get cleaned up. I will bring you some clothes and then maybe we can start to have some fun together.' Sarah recoiled further away.

She stared at him defiantly. 'You need to get me some toiletries and Tampax. There's nothing in the bathroom.'

Carter sneered. He felt like beating her up and raping her there and then. 'You cheeky fucking bitch! Who do you think you are? I enjoy slapping women around and then you will see who is the boss!

He had to take control of himself. A beaten-up woman on the video might not look so good. He could give her a good pounding afterwards, but he wanted the money and he wanted it quickly. If he was not paid out on the first demand, then he would threaten physical violence and rape of the victim. The second video would demonstrate that he had carried out his threat. Again, if he was not paid, the final step would be murder and he meant it. He had done it before.

'Very well. I will get what you want. By the way, don't waste your breath shouting and screaming. No one knows you are here besides me and nobody will be able to hear you. You really are a beautiful woman, I can hardly wait!' He leered at her, rubbing his crotch enthusiastically, turned around and left, slamming and locking the door behind him.

**

Jeremy Hirons landed at Zurich airport on the early morning British Airways flight. The Airbus A320 taxied across two runways and pulled slowly up to the passenger ramp. Only carrying an overnight bag, he cleared Immigration quickly and descended from the airport to the train station below. It was only eleven minutes by train from the airport to the central station in Zurich, with regular trains every few minutes.

Having spent some of his professional career at the British embassy in Bern, he was very familiar with the country and its customs. On exiting the station, he took a short walk to the Hotel Krone, which he had booked before leaving England. After dropping his overnight bag with the bellman at reception, he returned straight away to the Bahnhosstrasse, Zurich's main downtown artery. With wide tree-lined sidewalks and a two-way electric tram line down the centre of the street, it was one of the most expensive real estate areas, not just in Switzerland, but in the world. Old five-storey buildings built out of traditional grey stone stood well back from the road. There were many exclusive cosmetic, fashion and jewellery stores being browsed by the early autumn visitors to the city. Jeremy walked down the street, always looking for tails, either by checking reflections in shop windows or under the pretence of inspecting something that may have been of interest to him. He wasn't expecting any interference, but after a lifetime of being employed in the underworld, old habits died hard. Moving away from the station, he was getting closer to the Paradeplatz; the old square that housed much of the financial district of the Swiss banking fraternity, including UBS bank and Credit Suisse. Above the shopfronts were a combination of exclusive apartments and offices stretching up on four floors with long, vertical windows and high ceilings.

The address he was seeking was just before the Paradeplatz. He found it in between a travel boutique and an exclusive handbag store. Jeremy entered the reception area, giving access to the floors above it. He scanned the mailboxes and then saw a polished brass plaque on the wall to the side of them. It was clear that this was not an apartment building after all, but an office complex. While the address that he turned up in the expense file of Euro-Asian's tax records had given the street address, it did not give a unit number. *Hmmmm, what to do? What to do?* he thought. Most of the companies listed were for financial services, however there was one company listed on the second floor named 'ETC – Euro Trade Services' and another on the fifth floor named 'IRC – Industrial Robotics Corp'. He decided to try both companies to start.

He took the stairs, rather than the antiquated lift with a concertina lattice metal door. All the time, he was looking for cameras. There was one in the elevator that he could see, but none on the stairway. On the second floor he entered the office of 'Euro Trade Services' through a solid oak door. A small reception area fronted several other offices. An attractive dark-haired, middle-aged lady greeted him in the traditional Swiss–German language.

'Guten morgen. Kann ich ihnen helfen?'

'Oh, good morning, 'Jeremy replied in English, knowing that his German wasn't up to much. 'I'm looking for a Mr Hugh Stanfield?' He made himself sound a little uncertain as to whether he had got the name right. 'I've been recommended to speak to him regarding my business.'

'I'm sorry but I don't recognise the name. Are you sure he works here?' the receptionist replied in perfect English.

'Well, I thought so. Don't you specialise in sourcing machine tools for specific industrial requirements?'

'No, I'm sorry. We are a group of consultants that advise clients on customs and brokerage of their goods both to the EU as well as outside of the EU.'

'Oh, I see. Not to worry. Thank you for your help. Good day.'

Outside the office, Jeremy proceeded back to the stairs through a fireproof door. Again, he checked thoroughly for any cameras. There were none. 'A trusting lot, these Swiss,' he thought, 'not like us Brits, we don't trust anyone anymore.'

On the fifth floor, he located the office of the Industrial Robotics Corp. The reception was fronted by a wide set of double doors of patterned opaque glass. Jeremy was just able to make out a solitary figure on the other side. Just as he opened the door, the girl behind the reception desk sneezed loudly.

'*Gesundheit*!' Jeremy immediately exclaimed and laughed at the same time. The young blond girl, clearly embarrassed, laughed as well.

'Oh, I'm so sorry,' she said in English. 'It's that time of year for my allergies.' She smiled warmly at Jeremy.

'Ah, so I'm not the only one.'

'What can I do for you?' The ice was broken, and she really wanted to be of assistance.

Jeremy gave her his best smile and spoke confidently, as if he knew what he was talking about. 'I need your help, please. One of my business colleagues suggested that I should talk to Hugh Stanfield. He believes that Hugh can advise me on my business. Not sure if Hugh is in right now, but, if not, I can make an appointment.'

'Oh, no problem, Mr...?'

'Lapointe, Henry Lapointe.'

'Well, Mr Lapointe. Mr Stanfield is away on business right now. May I ask what it is concerning?'

'Of course, Maja.' He had read the name plaque on the front of her desk. It read Maja Brunner – Manager of First Impressions. 'I represent a mechatronics company and need advice on increasing our export capabilities.'

'Mechatronics. You know I had never heard that name until a few months ago, but I believe it's a new term for industrial robot machines that have a combination of mechanical engineering and electronics. That's it, isn't it?'

'That's exactly it, Maja. You sound as if you have worked here a long time?'

'Oh yes, Mr Lapointe. Mr Stanfield recruited me from an agency just after I had finished my apprenticeship. I have now worked for him for four years. It's been interesting learning all about machine tools. We buy and sell new and used machines all over the world.'

Jeremy then asked, 'Do you think Mr Stanfield would be able to help me? It sounds as though he really knows the international market.'

'Yes, I believe he could, although he uses me a lot of the time to deal with some of the business. Are you interested in any particular market right now?'

'Yes I am. I would like to try and export some of our products to Saudi Arabia.' Just then the phone rang.

'Oh, please excuse me a moment.' She picked up the receiver and spoke in English. 'IRC Corporation. Good day.' There was a pause and then she answered, 'Oh hello, Mr Mueller, just let me check Mr Stanfield's diary.' She got up and went into the office behind and left the door open. Jeremy was just able to see enough of what he wanted. There was a large square skylight above the desk where Maja was checking her boss's diary. Just to the right, behind the cherry-wood desk, was a safe. The safe did not look particularly complicated. It just had an electronic keypad and handle in the door.

When Maja returned, Jeremy was reading an IRC brochure he had found in reception. He had also picked up a business card of Hugh Stanfield.

'Yes, Mr Mueller, he is free on Thursday October 6th at 2.00

p.m.' Again, there was a pause and then she continued. 'Right, I'll set up the appointment. Thank you and take care.'

'Sorry about that, Mr Lapointe. Now you mentioned Saudi Arabia?'

'Yes, I did.'

'That's interesting because we ship a lot of machine tools to Saudi. They are developing their agricultural industry, believe it or not. They are irrigating lots of different crops that include wheat, dates, fruits and vegetables, as well as developing their dairy farms. They sure have the money.'

'That sounds great. When will Mr Stanfield be back? I'll give him a call first as I have a few questions on his terms of business before I meet with him. Can I take this brochure and his card?'

'Yes, of course you can. I just checked his schedule a few moments ago. He's due back on Monday 3rd October.'

'Great, I'll call him that week. Thank you so much for your help and try not to sneeze!'

Outside the office, Jeremy checked another door at the end of the corridor. It was locked and had a sign on it, 'Zugang zum Dach' – *access to roof.* He smiled to himself on remembering the famous quote from Arnold Schwarzenegger in the *Terminator* movie, *'I'll be back,'* just before he ploughed back through the front doors of a police station in a car. Jeremy then left the building and returned to his hotel via the side streets. He found a hardware shop called 'Bauhaus', where he purchased a high-quality screwdriver set and hammer.

36

Chapter 36

Dennis Haddleton, alias Dan Nash, landed at London Heathrow, terminal two, via Frankfurt mid-morning on a Lufthansa Boeing 737 and presented his forged EU passport at Immigration. His hair was neat and tidy, matching his new identity. The passport already had a few international stamps in it and was a little dog-eared. The Immigration Officer simply checked his ID with his photo and asked if he had anything to declare. As the answer was 'no', Dennis Haddleton sailed easily through customs into the country. *God, that was easy*, he thought. If only the rest of this trip goes that easy, it will be a piece of cake.' Outside the terminal he took an Avis Car Rental shuttle bus for a short ride to their office and parking area outside the airport perimeter. He rented a Mercedes Benz C class saloon car with automatic transmission. He did not want to bother with sorting out the gears while he drove on the wrong side of the road. How come the British always did things differently? They also had those funny roundabouts. Having grabbed a UK map from Avis, he drove west along the M4 to Bristol where the head office of

Sterling-Judge Marine Insurance was located. While he had waited for the Avis agent to complete the paperwork, he called the Rodney Hotel in Bristol and booked a room for two nights. The hotel was a modest Georgian townhouse building close to David Morris's office.

Due to heavy traffic, his drive from London took him nearly three hours. Having checked into the hotel, he left the building and strolled nonchalantly down the winding road in front of the hotel towards the River Avon. Close to the river on Hotwell Road were a series of timber-framed and older brick warehouses that had clearly been converted into both offices, lofts and apartments. He walked towards the Clifton Suspension Bridge, towering over three hundred feet above. The Sterling-Judge office building was four storeys high and while the reception area was fairly modern, he could see that the structure of the offices was original, even if it had been refurbished. Looking through the ground floor windows as he walked on, he could see exposed large square pine support beams holding up the hardwood ceiling. There was an extensive use of barn board along the walls. He looked up to the top of the building and saw a large set of wooden warehouse doors on the fourth floor, complete with a protruding gantry, hook and pulley. It was obviously a left-over from the old days when goods were hoisted up on the exterior of the building from the docks to be stored in the warehouse. As he walked around the rear of the building there was a narrow service road and a loading dock that served the entire building. A plan began to evolve in his mind as to how an accident would occur to terminate the David Morris problem once and for all.

Nash was up early the following morning. He had dressed in a newly acquired suit he had bought the day before at

Marks & Spencer's, together with shirt and tie. Complete with raincoat and a briefcase, he blended in with all the other office workers on their way to the centre of Bristol. He wore a heavy-framed set of glasses to help with his deception and entered the Sterling-Judge offices, walking confidently up to the reception desk. The receptionist looked up and smiled.

'Good morning, sir. How can I help you?'

'Good morning to you too. David Morris asked me to drop off some important claim forms for him today.'

'I can take them from you and see he gets them.'

'Oh, I'm sorry, David asked that I deliver them personally to him. They are very important, and he is waiting for them.'

The phone rang, and the receptionist held up her hand and asked Nash to excuse her for a moment.

'Sterling-Judge Marine Insurance. Please hold for a moment.' She looked back at her visitor and said, 'Go ahead, his office is on the fourth floor.' She went back to her phone call.

Nash mouthed a 'thank you' and put his hand up to acknowledge her. He left the reception area and went through the rear door to the stairs and elevator. First, he checked the outside door facing him. It was the rear service entrance to the loading bay. Next to the door was an antiquated lift that was clearly used for both freight and personnel. Heavy sackcloth covered the sides of the lift to protect the surfaces when carrying heavy items such as office furniture. He noticed scraps of cardboard on the lift floor. Another door from the area led to the boiler room. He quickly entered the room and checked every piece of equipment in there and then he found what he was looking for. Several fuse boxes were installed side-by-side on the wall of the room. Nash inspected the panels carefully. As a trained technician he knew what to look for. One of the breaker panels used the older-type separate glass fuses that screwed in like a light bulb fixture. Each fuse-able link was contained within its own glass surround. He noticed several spare 15-, 20- and 30-amp fuses sitting on top of the breaker box. He left the boiler room unnoticed and ascended the stairs to the fourth floor, walked through a connecting door and along a narrow corridor. One of the offices on his left had the name of David Morris on a plaque. The top half of the door was glazed with clear glass. Inside was a man sitting at the desk typing away on a computer keyboard. A large drafting table and stool was positioned to the side of his desk. On the other side was a bank of filing cabinets, half open with papers sitting on the top of the cabinets, as well as on the floor. Nash scrutinised the man who was engrossed in what he was doing. He looked the same as his photograph on the Sterling-Judge website. It was clearly David Morris. Nash smiled to himself and returned to the boiler room. He swapped the glass fuses around, placing 30-amp fuses into the circuits marked 15 and 20 amp. He knew it was only a matter of time before the circuits overloaded heating up the lower rated 15- and 20-amp wiring. As they heated up, the insulation would catch fire easily. The older building was full of dry wood and other combustible materials. Within minutes it would turn into a blazing inferno. He jammed open the elevator door with a small piece of wood he found, hoping to use the lift shaft as a fire accelerator up to the upper floors. If he had done everything correctly then the sackcloth in the lift would catch fire and the small piece of wood would burn leaving no trace of sabotage. The fire inspectors would easily determine that overloaded circuits would have caused the fire by overheating. An accident waiting to happen in an old building such as this!

***

'Jack Fox.' He picked up the internal phone as soon as it rang.

'Good morning, Director, this is Sharon Templeton, MI6 software division. I've been assigned to monitor the pilot testing of our new facial recognition program. I was told to contact you directly if we had a match on any wanted persons.'

'Yes, Sharon. Who is it?'

'Sir, we have a match on a 'Dan Nash'.'

'Come to my office straightaway please and bring all the details and photos you can.' Less than five minutes later they were both poring over the match details.

'Wow. I have to say this is impressive. There's no doubt that this person "Dennis Haddleton", travelling on a European passport is the same person as Dan Nash, even though he has changed his hair style. I see he flew into Heathrow two days ago from Shanghai via Frankfurt. Thanks, Sharon, leave it with me. Good work!'

Jack Fox flew into action. Within less than an hour he had circulated Dennis Haddleton's details to every police force in the UK as well as Interpol. MI6 also placed checks on all credit, debit cards and banking transactions for the same name. The APB – all person bulletin – was marked TOP PRIORITY. Jack wished they could link the new software they had to all the other cameras around London, but that was not possible at this stage.

***

Jeremy Hirons waited until later that evening before he left his downtown Zurich hotel to return to the IRC office of

Hugh Stanfield. He had purposely dressed down but retained business attire, just in case he was challenged by any office security personnel. He could always claim he was working late if questioned by anyone. The wide sidewalks were busy with the evening tourists either window shopping in the various exclusive boutiques or searching for that perfect cosy little restaurant to eat dinner. Jeremy had his briefcase with him. On reaching the reception area of the office block, he sauntered straight in and up the stairs to the fifth floor. There were some late workers in some of the offices below, but the fifth floor was all quiet. He hoped that any office cleaners, if there were any, would not come until later in the night.

Jeremy had already checked the double glass reception doors of the office earlier. There was a chrome barrel lock at the top of the left and right door. On the right-hand door there was a central handle and a bolt on the bottom. He had decided he would try to access the office this way first. If that failed, he would access the roof through the door down the corridor and then drop down from the skylight above Stanfield's office. The second option was way more complicated and the risk of being spotted on the roof was much higher. He went back to the stairs again and checked there was no one there. Then he checked the antiquated elevator. That was still on the ground floor and with the metal lattice gates, he would easily be able to hear it open and close. He put on his latex gloves and extracted a Z- shaped tool from his briefcase. As wide as a hacksaw blade but smooth on each edge, he slid it through the gap in the middle of the doors at the bottom. Since the glass was opaque, he could still see the shape of the bolt on the other side of the right-hand door. He was able to use the top end of the 'Z' to hook underneath the head of the bolt. Moving the tool upwards, he then lifted the bolt out of the floor. He waited and listened carefully some more. So far so good. Next, he used a special thin shaped tool like an ice pick and was able to open the handle in the middle of the door. That meant the double doors were just held by the locks at the top. The nine-foot-high doors were proportionate to the height of the twelve-foot ceiling. Jeremy pushed the bottom of the left-hand door back and brought the bottom of the right-hand door forward. There was barely enough room to squeeze through, but he made it by laying down and inched himself forward, dragging his briefcase after him. Just as his bag was disappearing from the corridor, he heard to elevator doors being operated. Quickly, as quietly as he could, he shoved the bolt back into the floor, flicked the central handle across and dove behind the reception desk. Within seconds, he heard the office doors being checked and then watched the shadow of a person with a peak hat pass by only to hear them check the door to the roof seconds later. He waited some more and then after what seemed like minutes, he heard the elevator go downwards.

Jeremy crawled his way across the floor and opened the door of Stanfield's office. Residual light from the city shone faintly down through the skylight. He did not need to use his flashlight. He inspected the safe which he had spotted earlier in the day, but there was no identification of the manufacturer anywhere. An electronic keypad on the door with a rotating handle on the left presented him with a choice. He could either use his MI6-supplied digital counter or what he called a Birmingham screwdriver, in other words, a lump hammer. He chose the magnetised digital counter that he attached to the door. Pressing the ON button, green LED lights sped through a series of letters and numbers. It took about two minutes to complete but it provided the combination for the lock. Removing the magnetic counter, Jeremy punched in the combination and was able to access the safe without any damage to the exterior.

Inside were several ledgers, some cash of different foreign denominations and a three-and-a half-inch floppy computer disc. He checked the ledgers one by one. They all appeared to record what appeared to be genuine transactions of machine tools to various customers and destinations, however at the bottom of the pile was a ledger of shorthand descriptions and numbers. Jeremy recognised the types of serial numbers used. They were known to him as military arms reference numbers. US dollar amounts were listed in three columns to the right side of the descriptions and serial numbers – Buy, Sell, Net Profit. The fourth column listed bank account numbers in several Swiss banks. Jeremy grabbed the ledger and the floppy disk and placed them in his briefcase. Next, he returned the other contents to their original position in the safe, including all the cash. He closed the safe door and made sure it was locked.

Jeremy waited several minutes behind the reception desk just to check there were no security or office cleaning personnel on the floor. He listed intently and could not see any shadows through the opaque glass doors. Satisfied that there were none, he left by the same way he came in, ensuring that the reception doors were locked as before. He exited the building safely via the staircase and returned to his hotel. At 11.00 a.m. the next morning, he was on a Swissair Airbus A340 on his way back to London Heathrow.

37

Chapter 37

James Macrae gunned the powerful 5.0 litre V8 engine of his Range Rover down the slip road of the M40 and filtered through the traffic flowing south east towards Oxford and London. The early afternoon weather was starting to deteriorate, and a dense drizzle impaired his vision. The roads were becoming slick with a combination of smooth tarmac, rubber and oil. The traffic in front of him slowed down as the conditions worsened. James became frustrated as his windshield was coated with a layer of grease thrown up by the wheels of the vehicles around him. He moved into the outside lane and, feeling confident in the stability of his four-wheel drive vehicle, pressured the cars in front of him; pushing them to either drive faster or move over to the slower lanes. He constantly flashed his headlights on main beam at the rear of the cars holding him up. The intimidated cars moved over but some were either oblivious to him breathing down their necks or just pig-headed. James dismissed them, overtaking on the inside. He didn't care about speeding or safety; he wanted to find his wife. He emptied the windshield washer bottle in a very short time and was eventually forced to pull into the Oxford services area where he filled both the washer bottle and fuel tank. He needed to get to the Euro-Asian Freight office before they went home. As far as he was concerned, Edmond Andreas was his focus right now.

The traffic became heavier as he approached London where he took M25 south and then the M4 east. The traffic became agonisingly slow. He had set his destination on his GPS for One Canada Square, Canary Wharf. When the traffic slowed, he got off the motorway and navigated around the hold-ups using the side streets. With every stop light, junction or traffic island he became angrier, cursing at everybody and everything. If his windows hadn't been tinted so dark, onlookers might have thought he was having a mental break-down. When a delivery truck stopped in a high street in Whitechapel blocking both lanes of traffic, he felt his head might burst. To try to calm himself down, he turned the radio on. Magic Radio was playing the full version of the Rolling Stones, 'Can't You Hear Me Knocking'. Keith Richard's deep bluesy style only helped to build up his resentment and aggression. Finally, he pulled into the underground car park at his destination, took a parking ticket at the entry barrier and raced to find the nearest vacant spot. He backed into a space and flipped open the trunk. He put on his light raincoat, picked up the Browning 9mm and inserted a fifteen-round magazine. He slid the pistol into a large inside pocket and dashed towards the exit sign, taking an elevator to the ground floor of the office block. The main entrance of Britain's second tallest building was a combination of glass, stainless steel and marble. The glare from the lights was intense. James scanned the information board listing every tenant in the building. He saw the Euro-Asian Freight office was located on the forty-eighth floor. As he made his way to the group of elevators, he felt like a salmon swimming upstream as a tidal wave of office workers met him head on, leaving the building to make their way home. James took an express elevator to the forty-eighth floor. As the doors opened, he turned right in the corridor and saw a set of floor-to-ceiling glass doors fronting the entrance to the Euro-Asian offices. The receptionist looked up just as she was putting on her coat and grabbing her handbag. She was in a hurry.

'Hi,' said James. 'I hope I'm not too late. I'm meeting with Edmond Andreas. He's expecting me.'

'Okay, just go down the corridor and towards the end you'll find his office on the left.' She dashed out of the office.

'Great, thank you!'

James moved swiftly and quietly down the carpet-tiled corridor and walked straight into a small office that Andreas's secretary presumably sat in. It was empty. James closed the door behind him. There was an open door to the left. A person with a white shirt and blue tie sat at a desk calculating figures. He was a middle-aged balding man with round gold-rimmed spectacles. James entered the office confidently and again closed the door behind him, striding towards the man.

'Edmond?'

'Yes? Who are you?'

'James Macrae. I'm pleased to meet you.'

Edmond Andreas stood up behind his desk and stared directly at James. He appeared to try to speak, but no words were forthcoming. With a smiling gesture, James stretched out his right hand to shake hands. Edmond leaned forward and offered his right hand in return. He tried to compose himself with a reciprocal forced smile. At the same time that they shook

243

hands, James, being left-handed, smashed Andreas square in the face with a solid blow. Andreas's head flew back, and he collapsed in a heap behind the desk, blood spraying across his papers on top of his desk. His glasses had gone spiralling up in the air and landed beside him on the office floor. James went behind the desk, trod on his glasses, and grabbed Andreas by the throat in a vicious pincer grip. A pair of wide eyes stared back at him in sheer terror.

'I, I c-can't breathe!'

'No, and you won't be breathing much longer if you don't tell me where my wife is!'

'I, I don't know!' he wheezed.

'Bullshit! Where is she?'

Andreas was breathing hard and started to swallow his own blood. He coughed, 'I don't know anything. Why are you asking me? Let me go! Please!'

'You don't know anything, eh? Well let me help you. Your employee Dan Nash has murdered and injured my employees and you are also paying my CFO under the table so don't fucking tell me you don't know anything! I'm losing my patience! Where's my wife?' James screeched, baring his teeth. He grabbed a ball-point pen off the desk and stabbed it into Andreas's ear. A scream of pain erupted from his mouth, spraying out a mixture of blood and spit. Fluid started oozing out of his ear.

'Oh god! Oh god! Help me.'

'No one's going to help you. One more time. Where is...'

'It must be Stanfield. It must be!'

James shoved Andreas's head to the other side and was just about to stab him in the other ear.

Andreas was now crying. 'Wait! Wait! Please, please. I'm

begging you!'

'Why. Why should I wait?' James held the pen up in front of him.

'Look, I honestly don't know where she is, but Stanfield has a friend who sometimes does some dirty work for him.'

'Who is it? Where is he?' James shouted and started to poke the pen into his ear again moving it up and down.

Andreas was now shaking and stammered. 'It's a man by the name of Jack Carter. He has a pub in the City called the Beaver and something.'

'Are you telling me the truth, because I will kill you here and now if you are not.'

'Yes, yes but I can't say she is there. I don't know!'

James stabbed Andreas again in the ear. Andreas passed out.

James saw a private bathroom at the side of the office and cleaned himself up. He left the office quietly without rushing and returned to his SUV. Once outside the underground car park, he pulled over to the side and Googled 'the beaver pub city of london'. Immediately, the name Bulldog and Beaver popped up.

'Godammit! That's the pub that Jeremy Hirons mentioned when we pulled out Euro-Asian's tax files! He had wondered why that pub would be used to cater for a company like that. A friend of Stanfield's, eh?'

James used his GPS to locate the pub and then drove about four miles through the back streets of London, sometimes frustrated by the one-way systems. He couldn't access Artillery Passage, but found a narrow street around the back. There was a loading bay behind a large building. He backed in there and parked to the side of it. It was starting to get dark. Walking around the block he entered the narrow alleyway of

Artillery Passage and casually strolled down it. He walked past the front of the pub underneath its swinging sign depicting a Bulldog and Beaver. He could hear the chatter and clinking of glassware from inside the pub. Rather than just enter the pub straightaway, he decided to circle the block on foot. It was clear there must be another entrance somewhere, as it would be impossible to make beer deliveries through the front of the pub. He turned right on another small alleyway and then found himself at the other end of the narrow side street he had parked on. He tried to estimate where the rear of the pub was and saw a set of tall warehouse doors containing a small wicket gate. Just to the side of the warehouse entrance was a set of sturdy hardwood trap doors with thick metal hinges set horizontally in the ground. This would be where the draymen would roll down the barrels of beer into the pub cellar. He tried the wicket door, but it was locked.

James returned to the front of the pub and entered the bar. He was hit by a thick cloud of blue cigarette smoke trying to escape through the door. The plaster on the walls and ceiling between the wood beams was a dull yellow. The walls were covered in polished horse brasses and old black and white framed photographs of London. Beer-soaked round wooden tables with black wrought-iron legs were surrounded mostly by men sitting on stools drinking and talking animatedly. A few patrons stood drinking at the bar, chatting with the barman. James went up to the bar and ordered a pint of Bank's bitter. The barman looked like his skin had absorbed abnormal quantities of both alcohol and smoke from both sides over a long period of time. His nose had a blueish tinge. James slid a ten-pound note across the bar and said, 'Have one yourself.'

'Cheers, mate. Haven't seen you in here before.'

'No, I'm just passing through. Just here on business. I love this part of London.'

'Yeah, it's pretty unique. Nowhere else like it in the world!'

The barman got called away by another patron. James turned his back on the bar and started to drink his beer, taking in all the features of the small bar. To the right side of the bar was a door marked 'private'. Another door across the far side was the entrance to the toilets. A second barman came into the bar through the 'private' door and immediately struck up a conversation with a man and woman sitting down nearby. They all laughed and carried on talking as the barman collected empty glasses from their table. James quietly moved away from the bar, leaving his beer there. He slipped through the door marked 'private'. Inside was a narrow corridor that led to the back of the pub, presumably to the warehouse. Another door opened into a kitchen. James peered through the porthole door and saw two chefs preparing food on a long wooden table. Across the way was a set of narrow stairs. James ascended them as quietly as he could, but the stairs were wooden and uneven. One of them near the top creaked loudly. He carried on regardless, checking out two empty bedrooms and a bathroom. He decided this would not be a good place to hide a hostage. It would have been too easy to draw attention to yourself either by screaming through a locked door or window. James descended the stairs and ran into one of the chefs bringing out a plate of French fries and salad.

'Hey! What are you doing back 'ere?'

'Where are the washrooms, mate?'

'You have to use the door on the other side of the bar. This is private.'

'Oh, sorry. I'll do that.' James went out into the bar again and walked into the toilets. He stood next to an older man in an old grey check sportscoat and cloth cap as they peed into their separate urinals.

'How it going?' James asked.

'Not great these days, takes me forever to have a gypsy's kiss.' The old man remarked.

'Shit, this is a bad place to be in with a problem like that and all those different beers on tap,' James commented.

'Tell me about it! I've been coming 'ere for fifty years and I think I've drunk every one in this place.'

'Wow, Jack must have a big cellar to keep all those barrels on tap!'

'Yeah. Sometimes I think he spends more time in that cellar than he does in the bar. Always says he has to keep his pipes clean. That's the secret of a good pint, you know.'

James zipped himself up, went back out into the bar and picked up his pint.

'You've been gone a long time,' said the barman who had served him. He had a funny expression on his face that James couldn't quite make out.

'I know. Just talking to some bloke in the washrooms who says it takes him forever to pee!' James said laughing. The barman seemed to relax.

'Oh, you mean old Tom?'

'I don't know his name. Look, there he is now.' He waved to him. The barman carried on pulling pints.

James left the pub not wanting to try his hand again so soon. Somehow he had to find a way into the basement. He picked up his Range Rover and found a Travelodge hotel nearby. He would return to the pub in the morning when he hoped it would be quieter.

After a restless night and very little sleep, he returned to the pub. He left his vehicle in the hotel car park. Wearing his light raincoat with the Browning pistol in the inside pocket, he walked back to the rear of the pub. Both warehouse doors were open, and James could see an older guy standing at the entrance. A Fuller's brewery delivery truck stood outside in the street. Two men were carefully rolling barrels of beer down the ramp into the cellar through the set of open trap doors. James loitered around for a few minutes, pretending to be on his phone. After a few minutes they loaded several empty beer barrels back onto the truck and drove off. James squinted down into the dim cellar. In between the two rails that the barrels were rolled down there was a set of wooden steps. He peered further into the dark room and decided to go down the steps. The air was stale and musty. His eyes began to adjust to the subdued light in the cellar and he could pick out groups of wooden and aluminium beer barrels. Some were standing on wooden pallets attached to sets of transparent plastic pipes going up through the ceiling to the bar. He heard a loud click and quickly darted behind some of the wooden barrels stacked in one of the corners of the cellar. Peering carefully around them, he saw the barman with the yellow parchment skin, that he had met last night. He was coming out of what appeared to be a large wooden cupboard placed on the far wall of the cellar. The man walked past him and closed the two trap doors locking them tight. Next, he walked to a set of stairs on the other side of the cellar and left the room. James heard him shout, 'Okay, Banjo, you can close the warehouse doors now.'

A gruff reply came back. 'Okay, guv.'

James was alone. He waited and listened. It was quiet. Slowly he advanced to the cupboard and opened the door as quietly as he could. The cupboard was partially filled with draymen's aprons hanging on a central rail. Several pairs of wellington boots stood upright on the floor. James was baffled. The barman could not have just been inside the cupboard all that time when he came down from the street and peered around. James stepped inside and swept the aprons aside. He felt around the back panel of the cupboard. It all felt smooth.

James came back out of the cupboard again and searched the whole cellar. All the walls were built out of solid stone. Next he checked the stairs going up to the main hallway in the pub. He listened at the door, but there was nothing unusual. He went back to the cupboard again for a further inspection. He placed both of his hands flat on the back panel and worked in a grid-like pattern. Close to the centre of the panel at the top he felt a small knob. He pressed it and half of the rear panel swung open away from him. He did not see a small-gauge black wire with a sensor attached to the top lip of the door.

Jack Carter felt his phone vibrate in his pocket. The alarm in his cellar cupboard had just been triggered.

38

Chapter 38

Hugh Stanfield strode from one side of his Shanghai office to the other. He punched Jack Carter's number into his phone yet again. It rang and rang. He left yet another message.

'Jack, where are you? For God's sake, call me back. Whatever you do, do not touch the goods. They need to be kept safe and intact!'

He had tried relentlessly to contact Jack Carter, without success. He also knew it was only a matter of time before General Shen caught up with him after finding out that Macrae's wife had not been released unharmed. Carter had gone rogue and was now operating under his own set of rules. Stanfield's original plan had been to return to the UK after Nash had dealt with David Morris. That way he could deny any knowledge of Morris's death. With the loss of control of Carter, Stanfield had no choice but to return to London as fast as he could and prevent Carter from making a catastrophic mistake. He landed at Heathrow in the late afternoon, the same day Jeremy Hirons was returning from Zurich. Jeremy had not yet had time to report to MI6 on his conclusive proof of Stanfield's illegal arms smuggling. It was a stroke of luck for Stanfield although he didn't know it. He passed through Immigration and Customs unchallenged.

***

Dan Nash hung around his hotel, waiting patiently for some sign of a fire. He listened for sirens, he looked for smoke, he smelled the air. Nothing. The day was on the cool side with a light breeze coming from the west. It channelled up the Avon Gorge, bringing with it a faint smell of fish and algae. Should he go back and check out the boiler room again to see if anyone had discovered and rectified what he had so carefully planned? He decided to be patient. Revisiting the scene of the crime might cause him a problem. He changed out of his suit and tie into more comfortable casual clothes. He walked around the area trying to regain some of the fitness he had possessed before the terrible ordeal of the waterboarding. His chest still felt tight and there were times when it was difficult to breathe.

David Morris was near to completing his extensive report on the insurance fraud committed by Euro-Asian Freight. His office was strewn with papers. Once completed, he would email copies to the International Maritime Organization (IMO), a division of the United Nations, to which all shipping nations belong. It was addressed to the Head, Global Maritime Crime Programme. David's boss, Peter Owens was copied on the report. He had wanted David to send the report off as soon as possible. David had included his complete findings, calculations, photographs and metallurgy analysis concerning each one of the company's vessels that he had inspected. He had also compared point-by-point each one of Ben Mitchell's findings when he had signed off on the safety certifications of these vessels. The separate reports were diametrically opposed. David was lighting the fuse to a major bomb. It would bring down Euro-Asian Freight and Ben Mitchell, together with his employer, Blue Water Maritime Bureau of Shipping. He expected criminal proceedings to follow that would include murder charges. As the afternoon wore on, the sun dropped lower in the western sky, casting a shadow within the Avon Gorge. The air became chilly. Several of the office personnel started to feel cold in the Sterling-Judge offices. They turned up the electric base board heaters. In the office kitchen, someone was boiling an electric kettle and warming some leftovers in the microwave. A single electrical socket with an adapter provided power to both appliances. A couple of copying machines were churning out large insurance policies. By 5 o'clock many of the office personnel had left for the day. David Morris was still there. Come hell or high water, he was going to get this report off before he went home.

Unseen to the naked eye, the lower-gauge wires emerging from the fuse box in the boiler room were already warm due to the increasing electricity overload. They were getting hotter all the time. The insulation casing started to melt and smell. Finally, they could take no more. The wiring flamed along its entire length in a spontaneous combustion fire that took over the old wooden framed building in seconds. Flames erupted from the boiler room and quickly spread up the lift shaft in a blazing upthrust. The lower floors of the entire office block were already a fierce inferno. David Morris had just finished his report and was about to press the Send button when a huge tongue of fire burst through his office door spreading out evil fingers of flames in all directions.

Dan Nash smelled the smoke first. He was walking close to the floating harbour, an attractive area for tourists to visit with its waterfront, marina, artisan shops, bars and cafes. The westerly wind was blowing up the gorge and the sky was already hazy. Nash smiled. Finally! He walked quickly back to his hotel to collect the rest of his belongings. He could see the heavy plume of dense black and white smoke erupting up in front of him from the Sterling-Judge office building lower down. Fire trucks surrounded the area in a futile attempt to quell the fire. A large truck with a swivel extendable ladder was directed at the front of the crumbling structure. As he approached the Rodney Hotel, he saw a heavy police presence surrounding the entire building. An armed policeman stood by his Avis car. It was clear to Nash that he was the target. 'Damn, how the hell do they know I'm here? I'm Dennis Haddleton!' He had to think quick. If they knew his new identity then, of course, he could easily be traced using the credit card transactions at Avis and the hotel, neither establishment accepting cash. He backtracked away from the hotel and walked towards the city centre of Bristol. He was wearing casual clothes but decided to buy an ordinary-looking anorak, woollen hat and rucksack as soon as he could find a suitable shop. Walking past a department store, he saw his face on a TV screen in the window. Nash deliberately messed his hair up and ducked inside. Within a short time, he had chosen all the items he needed including an additional luminous-green safety jacket, white hard hat and work gloves. This was his favourite disguise as nobody ever questioned workmen going about their business. He paid cash at a central cashier point. The girl there was busy chewing gum and chatting with another assistant. She couldn't have cared less who she was serving. Nash went back into the changing rooms and put on his new clothes, stuffing the hard hat, gloves and luminous jacket into the rucksack.

Once outside the store, he hailed a taxi and asked the driver to take him to the nearest motorway service area. He knew it wasn't far because he had passed it on his way into the city the day before. He was dropped off at the Gordano service area on the M5 where he called Hugh Stanfield on his disposable phone.

The call was answered. 'Hugh? It's Dan Nash.' Nash could hear loud noises at the end of the phone and the voice of airline arrivals announcing the carousel numbers to find the passenger's luggage.

'Dan, why aren't you using your new name? Where the hell are you?'

'Look, Hugh, I'm in Bristol and I'm in trouble. They know who Haddleton is and my picture is all over the news. I need to lie low till you can get me a new identity.'

'Okay, let's think this thing through.' The line went quiet for a few moments. 'Were you able to take care of the other business?'

'You will probably see something on the news very shortly. It seems there was an accidental fire somewhere near here!' said Nash, laughing.

'Good work. Okay. I need you to get to London as fast as you can. I need your help to tidy up some loose ends here. Call me as soon as you have arrived in the city.'

Nash already knew how he would get to another destination. Using the trains, buses and airports was a 'no-no'. Hitching a ride on a truck was much more anonymous.

255

***

As the rear panel of the cupboard swung away from him, James found himself in a small dark room. He used the light on his phone to inspect where he was. The walls were all solid stone, the same as in the main cellar. *What would this room be used for*, he wondered? A soiled rug lay on the floor. James rolled it back. There was a trap door in the floor. He went back and checked the open rear panel of the cupboard, and, seeing a handle on the other side, it meant it could be opened easily from the small room. He closed the panel back into place and opened the trap door. He flicked on a nearby light switch illuminating the set of narrow stone steps leading down below. James held back for a few moments. All was quiet so he descended, following the spiralling worn stone steps into the large underground room with the vaulted ceiling. He was surprised by the enormity of the great hall with its vast colonnades and wide-spanning arches and domes. He stood on the mosaic floor and rather than marvel at where he had found himself, he looked for any sign or clue that might lead him to Sarah. In the partial light he saw the door to a smaller room constructed out of modern brick. Moving closer to it, he listened some more but all was still. He saw two sliding bolts on the door and smoothly slid them back. Within the room a body was lying on a bed in a foetal position. He was not sure who it was or if they were alive. James moved closer to the body and saw his wife. Her face was dirty and smeared and her hair was all straggly. She looked like a washed-out crumbled specimen of a human being.

'Sarah, Sarah, my love! Wake up! Wake up!' He took her head and hugged her tight and then took off his raincoat and lay it on top of her. Her eyes opened slowly and looked at him for a while. It took her a few minutes to realize it was James. Her eyes widened and she found the strength in her arms to hug him weakly back.

'Thank God I've found you! Listen, I have to get you out of here. Do you think you can stand?'

Speaking very quietly, she murmured, 'Let me try, James.'

He helped her unfold herself and to stretch her legs off the bed and stand on the floor. She was a bit wobbly, but managed to stand up. James stood in front of her, coaxing her to step forward. He didn't see or hear the cricket bat come down over the back of his head. He collapsed to the floor.

Chapter 39

Hugh Stanfield went straight from Heathrow to see Jack Carter at the Bulldog and Beaver pub. Even if Jack wasn't there, at least he knew where James Macrae's wife would be hidden. He took a cab straight there. The ride was agonizingly slow. Roadworks, roadworks and more roadworks. This year seemed worse than ever for traffic congestion. With the slowdown in the economy, many governments were funnelling tax dollars into repairing the infrastructure in their economies to help keep their work forces employed. The UK government had done the same.

Stanfield became fidgety. 'Can't you find a way round these bloody roadworks, mate?' he asked the cabbie.

'This is it, me old china. Just have to be patient. Used to drive me bonkers, this lot, but what can you do? It's not like the old days, is it? Too many cars on the bleedin' road. That's what it is. The place is full of these cheap little fart-boxes driving all over the sodding place. Fucks us cabbies up good and proper it does!'

Stanfield sighed and resigned himself to stare at the fare

meter clicking upwards every few moments. He thought of calling General Shen and reporting that he had everything under control, but decided against it. Once he was at the pub, he would release Sarah Macrae and take care of Jack Carter himself. If Dan Nash could make it in time, he could help.

***

Dan Nash walked around the trucks parked at the service area. Drivers were either stopping to use the facilities or taking their mandatory breaks from driving by resting in their sleeper cabs. He stopped a few drivers and asked them where they were going. Some refused to pick him up because it was against company policy, others weren't going where he wanted to go. Finally, he saw a driver coming back to his tractor and trailer from the cafeteria.

'You wouldn't be going to London by any chance, would you?' asked Nash.

'I am, but I can't pick up hitch-hikers. Sorry,' replied the driver.

'Well, I'm a truck driver myself. An owner-operator and I've had to leave my truck in Bristol. It's broken down. Won't be fixed for at least five days. I need to get home.'

'Look I'm sorry to hear that, but the company forbids it.'

'Please help me. I'm desperate. Look, I can make it worth your while with a bit of cash,' pleaded Nash.

The driver of the truck hesitated. Nothing like earning a few pounds on the side. 'Look I could get fired for this. Give me thirty quid in readies. Get in the cab quick and stay inside the sleeper till we get there!'

Nash got into the ERF tractor and stayed sitting on the rear bed, out of sight.

'Thanks, mate. I really appreciate it.' He handed over thirty pounds to the driver. 'My name's Pete, by the way.'

'I'm Bill. Listen, I'm carrying a trailer load of aircraft parts to Heathrow. I can drop you off at the Heston services. Safer to drop you off there.'

'Cheers. Thank you. I can get back driving a company truck myself then while my own truck is down.'

The trip took them about two and half hours.

***

'So, you two little love birds are back together again, are you? How sweet!' Jack Carter pushed Sarah back onto the bed. He went through James' pockets but found nothing except his phone. He took it and slipped it into his own trouser pocket. 'Okay, my dear little Sarah, you are going to get yourself cleaned up. I've brought you clothes but you haven't even showered and put them on. Now get in there and do it while I decide what to do with your gallant husband. Sarah went slowly into the bathroom as Carter sneered and waved the cricket bat at her. James started to come to and felt the lump on the back of his head. He managed to gradually ease himself up off the floor and sat shakily on the bed. Carter stood back still with the bat in his right hand. He produced a knife in the other hand.

'Ah, Mr Macrae. Welcome back. I doubt that you have bought any ransom money for your wife, but today must be my lucky day. The value of my hostages has suddenly increased. You are going to demand five million euros for your safety. I'm sure your father can raise that sum very quickly.'

James held his head and looked up at Carter. 'You bastard! I'm going to kill you!'

'Ha!' Carter retorted. Look at you, you're finished and once more I'm going to shag your wife rotten. You can watch if you like. I've been wanting to slip her a crippler from the word go. She's just cleaning herself up.'

James moved his hands behind him, propping himself up on the bed. As his stream of consciousness began to return, he realized that he had his hand on his own coat. He felt the outline of the Browning pistol. 'Okay, Carter, I'll get what you want. Give me my phone and I'll call my father. We'll get you your money once you've released us both without further harm.'

'Good. I knew you would see sense. Let's get on with it then. I will give you an offshore bank account number and once the funds are in place, you will be freed.' Carter looked down, slid the knife back in its sheath and tried to pull the phone out his pocket. Trying to prise the phone out of his pocket gave James just enough time. He grabbed the pistol behind him and pointed it at Carter's head. The gun fired leaving a perfectly circular red hole in the middle of Carter's forehead. Carter's eyes went empty and his jaw dropped down into a sickly and wide gawping shape. The sound of the shot was still reverberating around the amphitheatre sometime after Carter had collapsed onto the worn-out rug beneath him.

James rescued Sarah from the shower. All she had done was put on a sweater and full-length pants. She clearly wasn't fully aware of what was happening. It was as though she had detached herself from her real being. James helped her into her shoes and put his coat around her. All she could say meekly was, 'Thank you, thank you. I never thought I would see you again.'

'Come on, Sarah, we have to go. We don't have much time,' he said, grabbing his phone off the floor.

He led her by the hand and with the Browning in his other hand they left the room. Sarah was in a state of shock; she felt cold. Her eyes did not take into account the dead body of Carter or the Roman ruins she now found herself going through. James helped her up through the open trap door and through the cupboard into the beer cellar. James waited a few moments, Sarah clinging onto him and shaking uncontrollably. The sound of the shot had clearly not been heard up here. He thought they might escape through the warehouse but decided against it, preferring to exit up through the drayman's ramp. The one door was heavy, but James managed to swing it upward giving them enough room to squeeze through into the street. James and Sarah moved as fast as they could towards his hotel along the narrow street. There was no time to talk; James was intent on getting as far away from the pub as they could. He didn't see the man peering from the open wicket door as they turned the corner out of sight. 'Banjo', Stanfield's warehouse guard quickly went back into the premises and grabbed his sawn-off shotgun. He went after them. James managed to get Sarah back into his vehicle at his nearby hotel. He was just going round the back of the trunk to his own side when Banjo appeared close to the exit of the parking garage. James flicked the trunk lid open and grabbed the shotgun. Rather than acknowledging the stranger with the sawn-off gun, he fired his own shotgun and gave the man both barrels in the chest. A thick mixture of blood, tissue, organs and bone fragments spewed out of his torso. The man's feet left the ground, and his bloody body flew backwards. James fired up the Range Rover and with the tyres screaming left the parking garage, taking the horizontal wooden parking barrier with it. He drove to the nearest hospital and pulled up in front of the emergency entrance.

Two paramedics saw him pull up and brought out a stretcher after James frantically beckoned them. They placed Sarah onto it and wheeled her into the hospital, while James shouted instructions to the duty nurse to call the police immediately. While she did that, he used his phone to call MI6.

James managed to get through to Jack Fox's secretary. His heart rate was racing as he paced back and forth, waiting for her to put him through. Finally, he got hold of the director.

'Jack. It's James Macrae. Listen, I've got Sarah. We are at London Bridge Hospital. Two things. We need a heavy police guard here and you need to visit the Bulldog and Beaver pub right now. I've killed a couple of people rescuing Sarah.'

'Got it. Stay where you are. I'll have my department work with the police both at the hospital and at the pub. Stay out of sight.'

James went to where his wife was taken but was asked to wait outside the emergency room until they called him. Police cars arrived, lights and sirens flashing. At the same time, two MI6 agents arrived. The agents and a police inspector huddled with James in a private office and absorbed all the details he told them. The MI6 agents also briefed the police about James's previous meeting with their director and Jeremy Hirons. Afterwards, James waited patiently in emergency, out of sight of the reception and waiting room. Two policemen were now guarding the doorway to where Sarah was being examined. One of the doctors came out of the room and spoke to James.

'Mr Macrae. You wife is in a state of severe shock. We've sedated her for the moment. Physically she appears to be unharmed although it's clear she has been heavily subjected to some kind of an anaesthetic. There are no signs of sexual or other physical abuse. She will need a lot of rest and we will need to keep an eye on her mental health. We will move her to a private and secure room shortly. I understand there will be a police guard at all times.'

'Yes, that is correct. Thank you, doctor. I appreciate it. What can I do?'

'Nothing for the moment. Just let her rest. She knows you have rescued her, and she knows she is safe. She just needs time right now to recover from the shock and the ordeal that she has been through. Obviously, we know about the kidnapping of your wife. The story has been all over the news. I can assure you that we will give Sarah the best care possible to help bring her back to a safe, healthy and happy life.'

The MI6 agent came over to James. 'Mr Macrae, we will want you to make a statement as soon as you are able. Currently we are carrying out a sweep of the pub and the warehouse. We have also cordoned off the hotel carpark as a crime scene. I know our director will want to speak to you as soon as possible, however he is involved in government meetings for the next few hours.'

James went back out to his vehicle. Someone had moved it into the adjoining car park. He sat in the driver's seat and looked out through the cracked windshield at the damaged hood. He called his parents to let them know the news.

'Hi, Mum, it's James. Good news! Sarah is safe! I'm at London Bridge Hospital with her right now. She's in a state of shock but first reports are good. She does not appear to have been physically harmed. She's sedated right now but I just wanted to get the news to you straight away. How are Mason, Mia and Olivia?'

'Thank god, James. We've been so worried. Pass on our love to Sarah. Both of you have been in our prayers. The children have been asking lots of questions and we've kept them away from any news. We've tried to keep them occupied as much as we can. It seemed the best plan to keep their minds busy.'

'That's good! I'll be back when I can, but I want to stay close to Sarah so I can help her recover as soon as possible. I'll give you and Dad and the children a call later today.'

'Okay, James. Thank God you are both safe.'

James sat in silence for a while. The palms of his hands felt sweaty on the leather steering wheel. Now his wife had been rescued and was safe for the time being, his mind went back to the one man who had caused all this chaos and tragedy. Hugh Stanfield. It was time for a reckoning.

40

Chapter 40

Hugh Stanfield's cab pulled up on Middlesex Street in the old City after a frustrating journey. He asked the driver to take his suitcase to his office after giving him the address. The trip between the airport and here had been a joke. Trouble was, he had no other choice. Stanfield walked through the narrow streets towards Artillery Passage. He was astonished to see that the whole passageway had been cordoned off by the police. He surreptitiously walked by to the narrow lane behind the pub. There were more police there, combined with ambulances and the tactical squad. The whole area was awash with security personnel. He didn't know if it was related to a bombing or otherwise.

'Holy shit! What the hell's been going on?' He decided it was too risky to announce that he knew Jack Carter, the landlord of the pub, to try to gain access to the cordoned-off zone. Instead, he chose to distance himself from anything to do with the area. He slipped away quietly and hailed a cab from a nearby street, hightailing it back to his office. He called Dan Nash from the cab. 'Dan, where are you?'

'Just got dropped off at Heston services.'

'Okay, get a cab and meet me at the office as soon as you can.'

'Got it, boss. See you in a bit.'

Nash called a cab and got picked up. He decided it was a better idea to travel by cab as opposed to using the underground tube train. Less people to recognize him. He was beginning to get hot in his new anorak and hat and momentarily took them off to lose heat in the rear seat. He did not see the driver looking at him in his mirror. The driver didn't make any attempt at a conversation and neither did Nash. As soon as the cab entered onto the M4 eastbound, the driver flicked a switch on his dashboard below the steering column. An orange light came on at the rear of the cab. Unknown to Nash, this was a distress signal to the outside world that the driver was in trouble. The cab carried on driving normally. After about ten minutes a code came up on the cabbie's screen. It looked innocent enough. The driver punched in his own code and carried on driving. Nash had closed his eyes in the back seat. It had been a helluva day.

Back at central control of the black cabs, one of the controllers had received a call from a private motorist that there was an orange light on at the rear of a black cab travelling along the M4 eastbound. He gave the number of the cab to the operator. The operator immediately sent a coded message to the driver. The code simply asked for another coded reply in return, identifying the type of danger the driver was in. The driver had punched in the code for 'terrorist'. Along with all his colleagues, he had spent many hours being trained by the Metropolitan police to look out for terrorists. It was a programme that had been started at the time of the IRA bombings across the UK. The central operator called a special number at Scotland Yard and reported the type of distress signal and position of the cab. Within minutes, the flying squad was in action. Heavily armed police complete with Colt M4 carbines and Glock 22's spread across all the exits of the motorway. The driver of the cab carried on as normal, saying nothing. Four unmarked squad cars came up behind him. He recognized what was happening and moved from the inside lane to the centre lane. The four squad cars immediately split up. One came up on his inside, another came in front of him and another stayed next to him in the outside lane. He was neatly boxed in. Brake lights came on and all cars screeched to a halt. The police were out of their vehicles in seconds, pointing a heavy artillery at the cab. Nash's eyes widened as he realized what had happened. He had been taken completely unawares. His mind went quickly into gear. If he had a weapon, he could have taken the driver hostage. As it was, he was unarmed. He decided to yield, it was hopeless. He got out of the cab with his hands up in the air. It had been a textbook take down and he had fallen for it. The best he could hope for was a good legal defence from his employer, or so he thought.

41

Chapter 41

James continued to sit in his car stewing over Stanfield. Yes, he had rescued his wife, but the main architect of all the murder and carnage still hadn't been touched by the authorities. Stanfield had blood and guilt written all over him. He was nothing but a cold manipulating monster. The time of reckoning was now. Right now. He hit the cracker and powerful V8 engine roared to life. James dropped it into gear and set off eastwards across London under a darkening sky towards Stanfield's office. He crossed the River Thames using the Limehouse Link tunnel and emerged on the northern side of the river. He drove eastwards again back to Canary Wharf and parked in the same underground car park that he had used the day before. So much had happened in such a short time. He had rescued his wife and, in his mind, justifiably killed two men in the process. He had become immune to the violence. They had pushed him and dished out more than he could bear. Now he was going to make the main culprit pay with his life.

It was well after 6.00 p.m., but James figured it would be a good starting point to try to find Stanfield. Andreas had told him he was returning from Shanghai so there was a good possibility he might find him here. There were fewer office workers around this time as he took the express elevator back up to the forty-eighth floor. The glass reception doors were still open. He walked along the corridor past Andreas's office. It was empty. Further along there was a corner office with an ornate rosewood door. That would have to be Stanfield's office. He moved quietly over the carpeted floor and gently rotated the brass door handle. The large door opened quietly. James took out the Browning pistol from his raincoat and softly entered the vacant outer office. He waited a few moments and then silently closed the door behind him.

Placing his ear against the inter-connecting door, he could hear a man's voice talking in what sounded like Mandarin. James didn't know if Stanfield was fluent in the language or not, although he figured there was a good chance, since he knew Stanfield had lived there for many years. The conversation ended and all was quiet. James's adrenaline was running high and rising again. Almost remotely, he quietly opened the door and faced Stanfield sitting at his desk. He pointed the gun at him.

Stanfield dropped his pen and pushed his office chair back from his desk. He took a few moments to weigh up the situation. 'Mr Macrae, I presume? I say that as you resemble your photograph on your website. I don't think we have ever met, but I know your father of course. We have met a few times at various shipping conferences. What is the reason for the gun? I'm surprised. Why would you think you would need that?' Stanfield stood up.

James was surprised by the how cool Stanfield appeared to be.

'What a stupid question, you slippery little fucker! Do you think I'm stupid? First you kill and maim my employees, next you bribe my CFO and then you kidnap my wife all with the blessing of the Chinese government to take my business over and gain my ports. And if you think that's not enough you have been caught smuggling arms.'

'James. All this is preposterous. Where on earth did you dream all this up from. I run a very successful and reputable business. Have done for years. This is highly irregular and, more to the point, I have always respected your father and the business you run. Now, please, put down the gun and let's talk like gentlemen.'

'You really are delusional! I have enough proof to put you behind bars for the rest of your life. Mr Edmond Andreas has told me a great deal about you. Let's not forget Dan Nash or Jack Carter either.'

Stanfield's face started to go pale. He raised his hands to his sides in a futile gesture. He said nothing.

James raised his voice. 'Did you think that you could keep sabotaging my company, kill my employees and abduct my wife and nothing would happen?'

Stanfield remained silent.

'Well, did you?' James yelled. 'Time to pay up, Stanfield!'

Just then the office door behind James opened. A man in a collar and tie said, 'Is everything alright, Mr Stanfield?'

The distraction gave Stanfield enough time to streak across the office, push the man out of the way and dart out of the door. James was taken off guard. He ran after Stanfield and just saw him leave the inner corridor and take the fire escape stair well. He charged after him through the single blue exit door. He heard heavy footsteps above him and followed as fast as he could. As he got close to level fifty, he heard a door open and then slam shut. James followed Stanfield through the door. A painted sign on the wall said 'Access to Roof' with an arrow pointing up at forty-five degrees. He followed another set of stairs upwards past a group of fire extinguishers and sprinkler valves. Yet another fireproof door took him through to a floor full of horizontal and vertical thick metal pipes of several dimensions all coupled together with large water tanks. The floor consisted of stone slabs. Huge pumps and stand-by generators were also installed across the vast length and breadth of the whole tower office block. James had to climb over the pipes and duck his head in the maze of plumbing. It was a noisy area. This was the heart of the building. As he looked up, he saw a set of anti-slip metal stairs leading up to the roof door. He climbed them cautiously. The door opened inwards as he tugged it slowly towards him. He found himself in a dark area covered with more plumbing and electrical hardware. Looking up, he briefly saw a flash of light high up above him. Using the light on his phone, James saw a white metal catwalk and ladder rising vertically above him. The ladder had round metal safety loops to prevent climbers from falling backwards. Rung by rung, using a three-point hold, he climbed the ladder and gradually opened the door at the top onto the roof. The chill wind was fierce, the force of which took his breath away, and whistled in his ears. He found himself on a narrow balcony with a waist-high railing surrounding the top of the office pyramid, nearly 800 feet above the ground. He gripped the railing tightly. The lights of London shone brightly hundreds of feet below contrasting with the darkness of the night sky above. Stanfield appeared suddenly out of the darkness and lunged at him hard. James was thrown backwards onto the floor of the balcony. All he could see for the moment were the flashing red aviation lights attached to the top of the building. He tried to take the gun out of his coat pocket, but Stanfield kicked him hard on his chest. James grabbed hold of the side of the rail and pulled himself up with one hand, his other hand shielding the barrage of blows from Stanfield. James had a height and strength advantage, but the restricted space helped even the playing field. Stanfield came at James again trying to punch him both in the face and body. James stepped back but then came forward at Stanfield, launching a flurry of vicious blows. One caught Stanfield on his jaw and steadied him up. James took advantage and smashed his fists into Stanfield's face time and time again. He broke his nose and his jaw and then grabbed him by his shirt collar and belt of his trousers to throw him off the tower. Stanfield could only make grunting noises at this stage. He was unable to speak, blood pouring from his battered face.

A voice boomed from behind him as he felt a strong hand on his shoulder. 'Stop, James! Stop! For God's sake stop!'

James turned his head to see Jeremy Hirons pleading with him to stop. More police were behind Jeremy and others came from the opposite direction around the balcony from the other side.

'We'll take it from here. It's okay, James. You can let go now. It's all over.'

***

Per-Olof Lindquist sat in his armchair and stared at the report in front of him. He had read it first on his computer, when it dropped into his mailbox at his office on the Albert

Embankment facing the river Thames in Lambeth. He was shaken by what he had read and printed out hard copies to take home with him to study it further. As Head of the Global Maritime Crime Programme of the International Maritime Organization (IMO), a division of the United Nations, he was responsible for safety and legal matters. This was the most damning report he had ever seen. He called the phone number of the writer, David Morris but the call was redirected to another number.

'This is Peter Owens, Sterling-Judge Marine Insurance.'

'Oh, I'm sorry. I wanted to speak with a Mr David Morris. This is Per-Olof Lindquist, Head of the Global Maritime Crime Programme.'

'Mr Lindquist. I'm David's boss. I'm afraid David is in hospital right now. He is undergoing surgery for first-degree burns. I'm sorry to tell you that we believe this has been the result of an attempt on his life to silence him and prevent publication of the report that was sent to you just before he was injured. The police have established arson and the alleged perpetrator is already in custody.'

'Oh dear. I'm so sorry to hear that. Will Mr Morris be alright?'

'We believe so, although there will be a long period of recovery. I can help you with the report though.'

They talked for a while and afterwards, Per-Olof said 'Okay. I'm satisfied with the authenticity of the report and its findings. I'm passing this straight onto Scotland Yard. Euro-Asian Freight needs to be shut down immediately and Mr Ben Mitchell needs to be arrested and charged. Thank you, Mr Owens. I'll be back in touch and oh, tell Mr Morris, he's done a great job not just for your company but for the good of the whole global shipping industry. We need to make an example out of this horrendous crime.'

**

The officer in charge stepped forward in front of Jeremy Hirons. 'Hugh Stanfield. You're being arrested for murder and kidnapping. You do not have to say anything, but it may harm your defence if you do not mention when questioned, something which you later rely on in court, and anything you do say may be given in evidence'

Stanfield was taken away in handcuffs. Back down at street level, Jeremy sat down with James in the reception of the office tower. The building had been cordoned off completely.

'Holy shit, James. You don't take prisoners, do you?' It was more of a statement than a question.

James was highly agitated. He tried to sit still but couldn't, no matter how hard he tried. 'Well, what did you think was going to happen? Stanfield attacks my wife, my family and my business. Did you expect me not to fight back?'

'Well Stanfield's actions sure triggered a reaction from you that we didn't see coming. At least not to that extent! Having said that I can't blame you. Your speed and effectiveness took us all by surprise! Listen, we need to go back to MI6 HQ. We are going to have to massage how we report what's happened. Jack Fox is holding a meeting right now and will explain. I'll come back with you in your car. I can drive.'

'Okay, but let me check on Sarah first.' James rang the hospital, authenticated who he was and found out from the duty nurse that Sarah was comfortable and still sleeping.

'Let's go.'

42

Chapter 42

J eremy and James arrived at the brightly lit MI6 offices on Westminster Bridge Road in Lambeth. In spite of the time, the whole office was buzzing with personnel. Jeremy took James into a large conference room close to the Director's office. Large white boards mounted on the walls of the oblong meeting room were covered with arrows and flow charts between the photographs of Stanfield, Nash, Andreas, Carter, Spencer, Mitchell, Baig and what looked like a Chinese General. Company names included Macrae Shipping Group, Euro-Asian Freight Services, Blue Water Classification Society, Sterling-Judge Insurance, IRC-Industrial Robotics Corp and numerous arms manufacturers. There was also a box entitled 'Government of the People's Republic of China'. In addition, there were names of several ships: *Endeavour, Wayfarer, Wenzhou* and *Solstice.* Lists of people's names were underneath each vessel. Other names of persons included were, James Macrae, Sarah Macrae, David Morris, Sultan Dastagir and the Macrae personnel that had died due to the direct acts of sabotage at their various European terminals.

Several people were already sitting round the conference table working away independently. Jack Fox was at the head of the table. He stood up when Jeremy and James entered the room and immediately said to them, 'Let's go to my office.'

Once in the office he got straight down to business. 'Okay, let's all sit down and work out our story. Firstly, let me say how glad I am that you were able to find your wife. In fact, we weren't far behind you, but you beat us there! Now, in conjunction with the foreign secretary, we have issued a "D" notice to the press on this matter. The reason is two-fold. One, we do not want to publicise Chinese involvement at this stage and secondly, we don't want word getting out about the arms smuggling. This is because we can arrest more of Stanfield's arms accomplices and contacts. That said, we are saying that the death of Jack Carter and his henchman, 'Banjo' as he is called, are the result of a gangland dispute. Regarding Andreas, we arrested him at his home earlier on today. He was off sick from work and was found in bed in considerable pain. He claimed he had fallen badly on his head and injured himself. You wouldn't happen to know anything about this would you, James?'

'No, I can't say that I do.'

Jack Fox and Jeremy both grinned at each other. James remained sitting with a straight face.

'No. I didn't think you would,' Jack replied. 'Andreas will never say it was you as that could implicate him with Macrae Shipping. So, what does all this mean? Well, it means we can keep you, James, free from any attempt at criminal prosecution, silly as it sounds, but often defence arguments try to say that methods used to get to the truth were illegal. Now I understand that Stanfield is in rough shape. Clearly, he was resisting arrest. Any questions?'

'I hear you, Jack, but what about my earlier statements to the police and your agents that I gave at the hospital? I told them the truth.'

'Don't worry about that. Between us, you were justified in what you did but, of course, I could never say that! Thank goodness it all turned out well and that you and your wife were not hurt or killed. Now let's get back to the conference room. We still have a lot of work to do to ensure these guys are all put away for a very long time.'

One by one, Jack Fox introduced all of the attendees in the conference room, which included his own staff, a number of Crown prosecutors, as well as representatives from MI5, Scotland Yard and Sterling-Judge Insurance.

Jack Fox explained to James, 'Our objective today is to pool all the information and intelligence that we have gathered on this complex series of crimes. In this case there is not one single crime, but a whole series of related crimes that are woven together into a web of intrigue and terror. We have gathered all the evidence from several different sources that spans the entire globe. As you know, there are a multitude of suspects involved, from a multitude of different companies in a multitude of different countries spread worldwide.'

He paused. 'We have some of the suspects in custody already, Edmond Andreas, Dan Nash and now Hugh Stanfield.'

James interjected. 'Did I hear you correctly? You said you had Dan Nash in custody?'

'Yes, James, you heard me correctly. He was arrested this afternoon on the M4 motorway after committing arson at the Sterling-Judge Insurance Company in Bristol. He was on his way to meet Stanfield at his office at Canary Wharf.'

'Now that is good news! I thought he might still come after Sarah and myself.'

Jack Fox continued. 'Their arrests are being kept secret for the time being. None of these men will be granted bail. They are all a flight risk. That leaves us with two suspects still at large, Hal Spencer and Ben Mitchell. I can assure you that these suspects are both under our surveillance.'

He continued, 'Crown prosecutors and advisers are working on possible charges that include, First Degree Murder, Second Degree Murder, Conspiracy to commit Murder, Fraud, Terrorism, Kidnapping, Blackmail, Tax Evasion and Illegal Arms Dealing. It is one of the biggest dirty laundry lists anyone has seen in a long time. The plan is for charges to be brought against each of the defendants by the UK legal system first. The European and US governments will have their shot at Stanfield for breaking arms embargoes later. It is difficult to imagine that Stanfield will ever see the light of day again.'

Fox directed James to look at the white boards on the wall. 'The motives for the crimes have been divided into two categories. The first motive for some of the crimes was to build and expand the Euro-Asian Freight Services Company by any means available and as quickly as possible. They included insurance fraud, falsified safety and maintenance requirements and murder. The murder being related to the sinking of the vessel *Endeavour* in the South Atlantic Ocean.'

He pointed to the adjoining white board. 'The second motive for crimes committed was to take ownership of the Macrae terminals in Valencia, Genoa, Piraeus and Istanbul using terror, intimidation, fraud, murder and subversion. The Chinese connection and ownership of Euro-Asian Freight Services was inextricably linked to this motive. Evidence

279

has been produced that conclusively proves that the Chinese Government was the owner of Euro-Asian Freight Services. While you had uncovered some of the evidence yourself, a secret MI6 agent from the British Hong Kong office had infiltrated the Shanghai branch of Euro-Asian Freight Services and had secured documents showing the intent of the Chinese to take over these strategically important ports. From our intelligence sources, we already know that one of their top Generals reporting to Deng Xiaoping, a General Shen, has had meetings with both Stanfield and Nash in Beijing. We believe he now heads-up Euro-Asian Freight Services.'

Fox continued, 'The prosecution against Nash has decided to join together the count of murder that will include Sultan Dastagir, the Macrae employees that died because of the sabotage he caused, and the entire crew of *Endeavour*.'

A secretary poked her head round the door. 'Excuse me, Mr Fox, there is an urgent call for you. I think you need to take it.'

Jack Fox left the room. Several minutes later he returned.

'Listen up, everybody.' Heads all turned to face him. 'I've just been told that the UN in conjunction with our own government has suspended all activities of Euro-Asian Freight after receiving documentary evidence of fraud and safety violations. Now that is good news!'

James sat down on the nearest chair. It seemed that nothing was happening when he cried 'wolf' about sabotage and murder of his company and now events were unfolding at breakneck speed. It was almost too much to absorb. He put his head in his hands, closed his eyes and let out a loud sigh of relief.

Jack Fox came over and touched James on the shoulder. 'The warrant to arrest another accomplice of Stanfield and Andreas,

Ben Mitchell, has already been issued. He will be arrested very soon at his house in Virginia Water and charged with conspiracy to commit murder, fraud and tax evasion. Spencer has no idea of any of these events. We plan to confront him tomorrow.'

'No. I want to confront Spencer myself before you. I think you owe me that.'

'I hear you, James.' He thought for a moment. 'Alright, I recognize why you want to do that, but I want Jeremy with you. There must be no rough stuff here. Do you understand?'

'Yes, I do,' James conceded.

Jack Fox continued. 'Our aim is to charge Spencer with tax evasion and additional charges that include "Conspiracy to Commit Murder".'

'Excellent. I can't wait to be in the same room as him,' James exclaimed. Jack Fox looked at Jeremy Hirons and raised his eyebrows.

43

Chapter 43

Hal Spencer waited patiently for Edmond Andreas to answer the phone. He had tried multiple times over the last day to reach him. It was not possible to leave another message as his mailbox was now full. Spencer was bursting to tell him that Macrae's was now perilously close to bankruptcy, and he believed it was now time for both Stanfield and Andreas to swoop in, take over the company and save the day. He knew that he had made the right decision to leave Macrae's and join Euro-Asian Freight. With James as Chairman and probably CEO as well, he knew he could never accept that. How he despised James, the dearly beloved prodigal son, when he believed he should have been CEO. Family businesses were all the same. At least he had a new future ahead of him and a huge signing bonus as well! He had found Edmond Andreas to be a man of his word. Everything Edmond had promised him had come to fruition. He would be able to start his new job almost immediately and looked forward to moving down to London. Spencer's wife had been ecstatic when he had told her of his new offer. She couldn't wait to sell their house in Solihull and move down to the exclusive apartment that had been provided for them in Kensington. How wonderful to be at the central hub of London, so close to Kensington Palace and Hyde Park. She would be able to shop in Knightsbridge and visit all the fine restaurants, galleries and live theatre in the west end.

Spencer knew that Macrae's could not possibly pay the outstanding debt owed to Euro-Asian Freight. He had carefully manipulated the Macrae cash flow in order to prevent that. Andreas and Spencer had set it up for Stanfield to propose a share ownership in Macrae's in lieu of the debt. If James refused, then Euro-Asian Freight Services would demand immediate payment which, in turn, would force Macrae's into bankruptcy. James would have no alternative but to accept and, of course, Spencer would be there to help guide him to the necessary takeover. He knew Richard Macrae would listen to his counsel, but James simply wasn't up to the task, so Stanfield, Andreas and Spencer would have to help him.

***

James left MI6 headquarters and returned to the hospital. After checking on Sarah, he drove back to his own home in Worcestershire. The house was cold and empty on his return, the children still staying at his parents' house. He showered and tried to grab some sleep. He would meet up with Jeremy Hirons at the Macrae Shipping office in the morning.

Low grey clouds filled the autumn sky. The chilling north-easterly wind had brought a low-pressure system into the region, filled with precipitation. Fallen brown and yellow leaves lay stuck in uneven mounds to the pavements and roads. The air was heavy and smelled of decaying foliage. Gas street basin looked as foreboding as ever, the canal water appearing to be black in colour, punctuated by tied up empty tourist barges. Rain poured down in torrents over the top of the spouting and drainpipes that couldn't handle the volume of water. The towpath was deserted. James thought it was the perfect day for what was about to happen. He turned around from the boardroom window and looked directly at Hal Spencer, who had all his papers laid out in front of him on the boardroom table.

'Just give me a few minutes, Hal. I've asked a Mergers and Acquisitions consultant to join us for this meeting.'

'Oh? I thought you just wanted me to update you on our financial position and make my recommendations to you.'

'Yes, I do, but it will be good if this consultant can just listen. He may be able to help us, given our precarious position.' There was a knock on the door and Jeremy Hirons walked in.

'Hal, I would like to meet Jeremy Hirons, a M & A consultant. He's just going to listen and get updated on our situation.'

'Okay, James,' said Hal Spencer looking a little perplexed. 'Mr Hirons, pleased to meet you.' They shook hands and Jeremy sat across from Spencer.

'So, tell me about our cash position, Hal,' James said as he sat down.

'Well, James, it's not good. I'm having great difficulty securing further funding. At the moment, I'm estimating the current value of all our assets. The banks have requested an update.' James thought, *I bet you are, and I bet you are devaluing them steeply for a fire sale with your sneaky murdering friends.*

Spencer continued. 'We have four weeks of cash reserves to

last us before we become insolvent. To make matters worse, Euro-Asian Freight want to call in their outstanding debt, however they would prefer to discuss it with us, face-to-face, before they turn it over to a debt collector.'

James, sitting at the head of the boardroom table, placed both of his hands face down on the table and looked at Spencer directly. Spencer looked down at his papers preferring not to stare directly back at James.

'What do you think we should do, Hal? Clearly we can't afford to pay them back.'

Spencer looked back up at James. 'I was thinking,' he said, 'What if, what if?' Spencer pretended to marshal his thoughts together. 'What if Euro-Asian Freight Services took a share of the Macrae Company in return for the payment of the debt and withdrew their option of bankrupting the company and putting us out of business altogether?' He continued, 'Yes, I like this idea the more I think about it. Both companies are in the same business and serve somewhat complementary niche segments within the shipping industry and what's more, you would have a base on China's mainland to add to your European bases.' Spencer made it look as though Macrae's would benefit far better than Euro-Asian Freight Services out of the merger.

James looked up from the table. His face was white and blank. He placed his left arm on the table and rested his head on his right hand and looked sadly at Spencer. 'That would mean sharing the ownership of this company, which my family has resisted for generations. I'm afraid I'm too much of a Macrae to let that happen.'

Spencer smirked. 'Alright then, James. I have another suggestion. How about this for a solution? Euro-Asian Freight Services buys Macrae Shipping lock, stock and barrel. That way you would not have to share ownership with partners outside the family and you would be rich enough to retire in comfort for the rest of your life.'

James shook his head sadly from side to side. 'I just don't know what to do right now. I've never been in this position before.'

Spencer sniffed, as though he could smell blood. Feeling bolder, he sat up in his chair, shuffled his papers once more and adjusted his glasses. 'I'll tell you what I think, James. I don't think you have any choice in the matter. I have told you repeatedly that we cannot make payroll on the fifteenth of the month and then Macrae's will fold anyway. You should consider an offer of a complete takeover. It would take a whole load of weight off your shoulders. You've had a rough time of late.'

James's demeanour changed dramatically. He felt the hot blood rising up through the collar of his shirt and his face starting to swell. He got up from his chair and stood up to his full height. 'Oh, you do, do you?'

'Yes, James, I do.'

James's face became redder and filled with venom as he spat the words out. 'Well! Now I will tell you what I think. Firstly, we are not going to go bankrupt! We will not be paying the debt to Euro-Asian Freight not now, not ever. Macrae's has turned the corner, in spite of you, Mr CFO!' Pointing directly at Spencer, he jabbed the air forcibly. 'You are finished! Do you understand me, you are finished!'

'But, but, I don't understand, James. I've always had your back and supported your family for years! Selling out is the only solution we have.'

'Really, is that what you think? Well, is it?'

'Of course it is! Where is this all coming from?' Spencer shouted back.

'Well, Mr Chief Financial Officer, does feeding confidential information back to your friends at Euro-Asian Freight Services to sabotage and murder your own company's innocent employees; altering the contract in Istanbul; taking bribes of one hundred thousand pounds sterling; promising you would contact other banks for more credit lines when you did no such thing; accelerating our payables contrary to my orders, mean you've had my back covered? Well does it?'

Hal Spencer started to go pale and shake. His jaw fell slightly, making his cheeks appear hollow. How could this stupid little prick know all this? He stood up and spouted out feebly, 'I did no such thing!'

Jeremy Hirons moved his chair slightly back from the table but remained sitting silently.

'Sit down, Spencer!' James screamed at the top of his voice. 'You better listen carefully. Your collusion with Andreas and Stanfield is clear. You think you've softened me up do you? Well now you are going to find out how hard and ruthless I can be. It's my turn now. Outside that door, the police are waiting to arrest you right now! My colleague here is also from MI6.'

Spencer got back up from his seat again and shouted into James's face, 'This is utter rubbish. I've never heard of anything so ridiculous. You better grow up quickly, Son, if you want to play with the big boys. I'm going to sue you for defamation of character!'

'Go ahead, you treacherous bastard, be my guest!' James smiled and tilted his head.

Spencer strode to the door and opened it, ready to storm out of the room. Unfortunately, Jeremy Hirons and another burly plain clothes man stood in his way. They were backed up by two other armed policemen.

Spencer stood there in disbelief, mouth wide open in shocked silence.

'Allow me to introduce myself. I am Special Agent Jeremy Hirons, MI6 and this is Chief Superintendent Fred Kennedy, Scotland Yard Flying Squad.' Superintendent Kennedy then formally cautioned Spencer read out a list of charges and made the arrest. Spencer was handcuffed with his hands behind his back.

James felt his anger boil up inside him like an attack of vitriolic bile. He clenched his right fist and was about to hurl an almighty punch, straight into the face of Spencer. Jeremy grabbed his arm and stopped him. 'Don't, James. It's not worth it. He's going to suffer more than you will ever realize.'

It was still raining heavily when Spencer was taken away in a police van.

44

Chapter 44

J ames stood in front of all the gathered Macrae employees. There was a perceptible air of uncertainty present throughout the whole building. No one knew what had been going on for the past few days and then to see Hal Spencer escorted out of the building was a shock of seismic proportions. All they knew was that James's wife had been abducted and released. Published news details of the event had been scarce. Blank, sullen looks stared back at James.

James cleared his throat. He put on his most contagious smile.

'Good morning, everybody! I finally have some excellent news for you all.' He paused and saw the beginnings of relief start to permeate throughout room.

'Firstly, you are all aware that Sarah was kidnapped. I'm happy to report that she is safe and well. She was unharmed. All being well, I'm hoping to bring her home tonight. Also, Richard is making a good recovery and is now back up and running.' Clapping started and carried on.

'Thank you, everyone. It's been a huge relief for all the

family. Secondly, you all know that the company has been on the brink of disaster. Well, I can now tell you categorically that the company will be safe, and everyone's job is secure. While I'm unable to give you the full details of what has happened, I can tell you that one of our main competitors, Euro-Asian Freight has had all their assets frozen by both the British and European governments. In addition, the criminals who launched the sabotage attacks on our company are now behind bars. I'm sorry to say that our own CFO was one of them. You will probably start to see this emerge on the news in the coming days.'

A loud gasp went through the whole company.

'Yes, it's tragic that one of our own would sink to these depths. Mirza Baig from the Istanbul terminal is also awaiting trial. Lastly, I want to thank all of you who have fought so hard to help keep us going through these dark times. We have a lot of work to do and some exciting plans for the future. So, relax everyone. Take time to look around you and appreciate everyone here. We've come through a lot together and I will be forever thankful. Thank you.'

James went back to his office and was joined by Rob Bisset, Director of Operations. Rob reported that he had managed, with Lynda Ferreira's help, to get all the terminals settled down after the chaos they had endured. All branches of the company were now operating normally, and income was steadily increasing after the vast losses they had incurred. Rob then imparted some news that was very troubling. 'James, I received a call yesterday from Jusuf Kahya from the Istanbul terminal. Jusuf informed me that Mirza Baig hung himself in his Turkish prison awaiting trial for his part in the contract fraud.'

'Oh my god, Rob. That truly is distressing news,' replied James. 'While he was guilty of fraud, no one would ever have wished that as an end for him. What a despicable and sordid business this has all turned out to be. The sooner these criminals are finally punished, the better.'

Rob further reported that Hal Spencer had been spreading gloom and despondency about the company finances to everyone. He had been nicknamed 'the Prince of Darkness'.

Chad Greening, director of Sales and Marketing, reported that they had secured more business from some of Euro-Asian's customers. It was apparent that these customers had been affected by the loss of *Endeavour* and *Solstice*. Both disasters had directly affected the customers' operations and they were prepared to pay a higher premium for a better level of service than they had received from Euro-Asian Freight. James began to feel a lot better. It had been a miserable time of late, but now, they were starting to turn the corner.

Afterwards, James met with Martin Farley, director of Legal Affairs. 'Hi, Martin, good to see you. First things first. Any further developments on retrieving some of the money we lost on the Istanbul contract debacle?'

'Yes, there is,' answered Martin. 'Looks like we can get back approximately four million dollars. I had kept this news for myself and had not told Hal Spencer, as you requested. It will certainly help our cash flow, coupled with Chad's new business that he has managed to bring in.'

'When will you get confirmation and the money?'

'There should be a wire transfer of funds from the customer's bank directly to ours next week.'

'Sounds good, Martin. Now how about Newco? How is that going?'

'Well, I have registered a new company already called 'McRae Holdings LLC'. I drafted the articles of association myself so that they will be fairly flexible in the coming years. The company can own real estate, be able to rent and lease property and buy and sell real estate both here and abroad. Of course, it will take longer to split the existing assets of Macrae's up and restructure the company but at least we have the wheels in motion.'

'Excellent. I also asked Chris Claybourne to call you. Did he tell you what we are proposing to do together?'

'Yes, we met up at Chris's office the day before yesterday. I didn't want to have the meeting here. Chris had spoken with his father and he approved of the proposed partnership between the two companies in principle, subject to the fine print. We spent some time on what the company could look like. I told him about your idea to spin off the land to a separate company and make Macrae's just an operating company. He liked that idea and said Claybourne Cartage could do the same. Then, with monthly rent being paid out to each property company by Macrae-Claybourne Logistics, you could both concentrate purely on the operations side. The real estate companies would independently gain in value and would be there as a stable foundation for generations to come. Obviously, you would be able to draw dividends from them.'

'Wow! You guys have been busy while I've been gone. Thank you, Martin. I'm so proud of you and the rest of the team.

After Martin had left their meeting, James called in Laura from Accounting.

'Hi, Laura.'

'How are you holding up, James?' She said nothing about his damaged fingers and bruises.

'Oh, I'm hanging in there. Everyone here has been wonderful in their thoughts and prayers for us. We are extremely grateful, Laura.'

'You just need to know that we are all here for you. Everyone loves this company. It's our family too you know.'

'I know. Thank you. Now, how are payables and receivables going?'

'Well, since our last conversation, I have dragged out all of our payables except for property and payroll taxes and the quarterly VAT payments. We also stepped up chasing our receivables so at least we've slowed the bleeding down. Mr Spencer has constantly been asking for updates but we've all just told him in accounting that we've posted the payment cheques and they are in the post to the recipients. I know he keeps his cash flow forecast up to date, so he's certainly deducted these cheques already off his forecast. At least you and I know we have a bit more time to bring our liquidity back in line.'

'Laura, thank you for your tremendous support. You don't know what it means to me. I have to say that I have never felt so alone before. So many problems, so many heartaches. To know that you are all behind me gives me so much more confidence. Listen, I know you recently passed your Chartered Accountant qualification status by studying so hard these past years, so I have a proposal. I want to make you Director of Finance. What do you say?'

Laura cried and hugged him.

Martin Farley was then asked to join them. 'Martin, can you tell our new Director of Finance our plans to merge with Claybourne Cartage and split the fixed assets with operations.'

James, Martin and Laura spent the next three hours going

over the details. Chris Claybourne joined them later that afternoon, and they and worked on a mutual 'Letter of Intent', together with a proposed Business Plan.

During the meeting, James excused himself and took a call from Henry Harrison, Chairman of MidCom Commercial Bank.

'Hello, James, Henry here. I promised you at our last meeting that I would do all I could to extend the line of credit that we have with your company.'

'Yes, Henry, you did. Thank you also for being so honest in terms of imparting the industry rumours at the time. This helped us probably more than you realized. I know Richard and you are close, and I sincerely hope we can continue that close relationship, not just on a business basis, but also personally.'

'I would like that too, James. Listen, can I come and see you tomorrow with a couple of my managers, say at 3.00 p.m?'

'Yes, Henry, that would be fine. I hope you have good news for us?'

'We do. Look forward to seeing you tomorrow.'

'Oh, before you go, I have some news for you. Hal Spencer is no longer with us. He was arrested here this morning. No news has leaked out yet, but I'm sure it won't be long before you hear about it.'

'Oh my goodness, James. This is a shock! Does this also mean that you know who has been responsible for the sabotage and murders?'

'Yes, it does. It was Euro-Asian Freight Services,' James replied.

'I'm shocked by the news but sincerely glad that you have got to the bottom of this mess. You need to know that the MidCom Commercial Bank is squarely behind you. I'm glad that all our managers voted to stick with you through this. After all, what is the good of having a partner if they run off when you need them the most.'

Henry Harrison went back to his group of bank managers. 'Gentlemen, we certainly made the right decision to continue supporting Macrae Shipping when they were in difficulty. Hal Spencer has been arrested and it seems Euro-Asian Freight Services was the company trying to sink them. Thank goodness we didn't take on Euro-Asian's account when they recently approached us.'

Once James had caught up at work, he needed to get to London, having received a call that it was now okay for Sarah to leave the hospital. He raced as fast as he could and arrived at the hospital in record time. Sarah fell into his arms. They remained clutching each other for ages both crying tears of happiness.

'I love you so much, Sarah Macrae. Thank god you are safe!'

'I love you too, James, but let's go home now. I want to be together with our children and be a family again.'

'Mason, Mia and Olivia want to be woken up when you are back. They are so excited.'

On the way home, Sarah leaned across the front seat with her head on James's shoulder.

'You know what, Sarah, I think we should take a holiday and go back to Wales for a couple of weeks with the children. We still have the cottage, even if it is a bit small for all of us, but who cares. It will be good to get some fresh air in the mountains and be altogether again.'

'I'd like that, James. I think we all deserve it.'

They talked of everything they would like to do going forward. Neither of them wanted to dwell on the past. At least Sarah was being positive about their future. James believed it was a major step in a full recovery from the mental trauma she had been subjected to.

***

The following day, James received a phone call from the Chairman of the National Industrial Bank.

'Oh hello, James. It's some time since our meeting. We've always had a special relationship with your company. In fact, I would like to come and visit with you as soon as it is convenient. I believe we can do a lot of business together in the coming years.'

'What special relationship was that?' said James curtly.

'Oh, my dear boy, your father and I were like brothers. We have always been here for you. You know that.'

You patronising prick, thought James. James then replied coldly, 'Well that certainly wasn't my understanding from our last meeting. In fact, I understood that you had no faith in us to turn our company around and were cancelling our line of credit at the end of this month. I suppose that now you have seen the news, all is forgiven, eh?'

The chairman replied, 'Well, I wouldn't put it quite like that. Let's get together, say on Friday, and we can extend the most favourable terms to you. I would like to do it personally. What do you say?'

'I would say, Mr Chairman, that it's not appropriate! Good day!'

The chairman was left still holding the phone with no one on the other end. He placed the phone back in the cradle and sank his head onto the desk. *My God*, he thought, *I've not only lost Macrae's business now but Euro-Asian's as well. I'm finished!*

What will the shareholders say?

45

Chapter 45

The judge looked down from his high bench in the Old Bailey at the twelve jurors to his right dwarfed by the tall dark oak panelling surrounding the court. The trial at the Central Criminal Court, just off Newgate Street, London of Stanfield, Nash, Andreas, Spencer and Mitchell had taken over four weeks to complete.

The judge had decided to combine the cases of the multiple defendants as their charges involved the same set of circumstances. One case could be resolved more efficiently, as they would not need to go through the jury selection process multiple times, and the witnesses would need to testify only once.

The chief prosecutor stood and paused dramatically in front of the ladies and gentlemen making up the jury. He placed his hands on his lapels either side of his black legal gown and looked at them truly troubled.

'Ladies and gentlemen of the jury. You have been presented with a series of the most monstrous and heinous crimes ever committed in the history of this country. Combined, these men have murdered a total of forty-eight innocent men and women. Their respective relations are now left alone and bereft somewhere in the distant world. For some of those relations, I can't imagine what it must be like to not have a proper burial and closure to their loved ones' tragic and untimely deaths. For others, all they will have for the rest of their lives, will be haunting nightmares of their loved one's bodies left to decay and rot in the depths of the cold, dark ocean currents of the world.'

The prosecutor paused and walked to the other end of the jury box. 'But that is not all. What about the other victims who were permanently crippled by these horrendous acts of sabotage? What about those poor souls that lost limbs, or suffered a broken back, who will now spend the rest of their lives in wheelchairs and can never walk, let alone work again. What about poor Mr Morris who suffered massive first-degree burns that were caused by the villainous acts of these men before you? Make no mistake, each of these five men have much in common. They have all been proven liars, they have all been greedy and they are all murderers. Of course, the charge of the degree of murder will vary with each of them and I'm sure the judge will direct you accordingly. One thing is clear however, they are all co-conspirators to murder, fraud and embezzlement.' He continued, 'Over these past weeks, you have heard an abundance of testimony from expert witnesses from within the shipping industry. These people are renowned for their expertise and honesty. You have also heard from an array of witnesses, including close friends of Sultan Dastagir and eyewitnesses to the torching of the Sterling-Judge Insurance offices. I could go on, but the bottom line is this. Forty-eight innocent people have been murdered, thirteen people have been crippled for life and countless others have been defrauded of millions of pounds by these despicable reprobates. You have no choice but to declare each of these men guilty. You must do your duty. I rest my case, your Honour.'

The chief defence lawyer stood up and addressed the jury. 'This is, indeed, a sad case but each of these defendants that you find in front of you are innocent of these crimes. Yes, innocent. I repeat innocent. Now you will ask me why? So, I will tell you. You can only convict someone of a crime if you are one hundred percent sure they are guilty. You cannot convict someone if you have a reasonable doubt in your own mind that they have actually committed a crime.' She waited to see that each juror had weighed her comments carefully and continued, 'The tragedy of the loss of lives on the vessel *Endeavour* is real but no one can say for sure what caused that ship to sink. The wreck of the ship is lost. There's a reasonable doubt. Let me give you another, there could be a reasonable doubt on the terrible accidents that happened at all the Macrae terminals as well as the Sterling-Judge offices. And, when it comes to the kidnapping of Sarah Macrae, neither Mr Stanfield nor Mr Nash were anywhere near the scene of the crime. They were both in Shanghai.'

She then returned to her desk and returned to the front of the jury stand with a piece of paper in her hand and continued, 'In the case of Sultan Dastagir, we don't know he was murdered for threatening to say that his ship was unseaworthy. This, again, could have been a tragic accident. Now let's look at Mr Harold Spencer. What's wrong with taking a signing bonus? We all change jobs from time to time, we are free agents. No one ever said Mr Spencer would have to work for Macrae Shipping for the rest of his life, now did they?' As for Mr Stanfield, he says he did not know anything about these supposed crimes. In fact, it is also clear that Mr Edmond Andreas had no part in these crimes. As for Mr Benjamin Mitchell, yes, he exaggerated a little, but no one can ever say he was involved in a conspiracy to murder. That would be ludicrous! So, I ask you to acquit each of the defendants and declare them innocent. Thank you, your Honour.'

The judge took some time in issuing his legal directions to the jury members before they could decide the fate of the defendants.

Outside the court, James was aghast. 'That was just bullshit the defence coughed up at the end. How could anyone believe those bastards are innocent.' James said to Jeremy Hirons.

Jeremy replied, 'You know what, I see this type of defence every day. It's not unusual. Defence lawyers are renowned for this. All they do is throw doubt into the jurors' minds and they've won their case. Just remember too, that there were a lot of other facts in this case that the defence glossed over when it was convenient. When you tie the motives into this case, then I would suggest that there is a strong possibility that a guilty verdict will be given. Having said that, I've been wrong before.'

***

It was late the following day when the jury returned. They had been deliberating for well over twelve hours.

The judge addressed the jury spokesperson.

'Ladies and gentlemen of the jury. Have you reached a verdict?'

The spokesperson for the jury replied, 'We have, your Honour.'

As the judge read each of the multiple charges against each defendant, the answer came back the same on every count. 'Guilty, your Honour.'

Stanfield and Nash were jailed for life with no chance of a conditional release, Andreas, Spencer and Mitchell each got fifteen years with no chance of a conditional release. 'In addition,' the judge continued, 'I am authorised by the government to use the assets of Euro-Asian Freight Services. These assets will be used to pay damages and to cover all legal costs. Messrs. Nash, Andreas, Spencer and Mitchell, you will also have all your assets forfeited. I can say that this is the worst case in my whole career that I have ever witnessed, and I will see to it that none of you will ever see a penny for your despicable and monstrous crimes. Take them down!'

James looked up into the public gallery and saw Hal Spencer's wife burst into tears.

Later, around the corner in the Viaduct Tavern on Newgate Street, James and Jeremy high-fived each other over a couple of pints of beer. 'Okay, James, one more meeting and then you can go home to your beautiful family. We need to go and see Jack Fox at the office.'

Once in the meeting room, Jack addressed James directly. 'James, you are probably wondering why there was absolutely no mention of any Chinese connection to any of the accused. Am I right?'

James responded, 'Yes I did wonder.'

'Well, it was abundantly clear from all the evidence that was gathered that this is only the beginning of the silent Chinese expansion, and we need all the help we can get to help stop

Chinese domination using hybrid warfare. We have no doubt that they will come back at you again, although, with the combination of Macrae Shipping and Claybourne Cartage, it will be more difficult for them to undermine you yet again. Deng Xiaoping or his successors will not stop here and when Hong Kong eventually reverts to Chinese rule, they will become even stronger. The British Government has made it a top priority to repel Chinese advances wherever they pop up. Of course, every communication we will have with them will be on the utmost friendly terms. For the sake of trade relations and keeping our enemies close to us we are following our usual cordial protocols.'

'Ah, we wondered why there was a cloak of secrecy regarding China. I suppose you issued a "D" notice to all news outlets to prevent publication of these developments.' James queried.

'That we did,' Jack said. 'Also, you will have noticed that there was no mention of illegal arms dealing and the breaking of European and US embargoes.'

'Again, yes,' replied James.

'Well, the answer to that is simple. Mr Stanfield and Nash will find themselves facing the European Court on these charges at a later date. The US has agreed to bring their charges forward at the same time. What this means is that these two gentlemen will never see the light of day again. It also means that their contacts in Saudi Arabia will be shut down.'

Finally, Jack said, 'Thanks to you, James, we have a huge debt of gratitude.'

James hopped back into his car. The world had slowly lifted off his shoulders. He connected his iPhone into his car's audio system and played B B King's 'I'm Moving On'.

Or was he?

The End

AFTERWORD

Finally, if you enjoyed reading the James Macrae Thriller Series, please take a few moments and let others know by leaving a review on Amazon, Goodreads, Google or other retailer websites. Reviews are tremendously helpful for authors. Believe me, we all appreciate it!

If you would like to contact with me directly, please visit my website. You can also join my mailing list for the latest news, updates and advance reader copies.

https://www.richarddross.com

Thank you for sharing your time with me.

With Best Regards,

Richard

About the Author

About the Author

Richard's career has been in the heavy transportation industry, spanning three continents. Born in England, he has also lived in the Middle East and now lives in Canada.

As a former president and general manager of several major international companies, he has been a leader and mentor in the industry. No stranger to writing, he has written many articles for trade magazines and government councils and now, with his James Macrae series of thrillers, Richard has branched out into the world of dramatic fiction. ;

His love of history, current affairs, as well as industry experience are all interweaved in his writing.

Favorite pastime: Camping in the Canadian wilderness, campfire and a scotch.

Other pastimes: Writing, golf (can be embarrassing!)

Favorite song: 'You belong to the city' by Glenn Frey

Favorite Movie: Shirley Valentine

Other Interests: Future technology

Join my mailing list on the website for news and advanced reader copies, when available:

https://www.richarddross.com

Appendix

History of The Macrae Shipping Company

James Macrae's great grandfather, Stuart came south to Birmingham from Inver, a small coastal village north of Inverness, Scotland to find work. Birmingham, being the birthplace of the industrial revolution, was drawing people in from all over the United Kingdom looking for work. He was a blacksmith by trade and managed to start a farrier and blacksmith's business. Once he had saved some money, Stuart observed that the horse-drawn barge business of transporting manufactured goods by canal to the outside world offered better returns.

Now married, he had a son, Donald. As the number of barges increased, more overheads were needed. A bigger office was opened next to Gas Street Basin. This was the hub of the spoked wheel of canals that led to the outside world. Donald, being young and ambitious saw the value of buying bigger cargo vessels that could take the barge cargo from the UK seaports to the overseas markets. They were able to expand their business into ocean going cargo ships by consolidating different cargoes going to the same regions in the world. This development served the company well in later years, as the barge business shrank with the expansion of the iii railways.

As the years went by and Stuart had passed away, Don continued to drive the business forward. By this time, he was married and had two children, Richard and Olivia. Stricken with bone cancer in her early forties, Olivia passed away leaving Richard as the sole heir to the business. When Richard eventually took over the business from his father, he immediately saw another profit opportunity to invest in several strategic ports in the Mediterranean. The company bought into the ports of Valencia, Spain; Genoa, Italy; Piraeus, Greece and Istanbul, Turkey. By controlling these strategic ports, Macrae Shipping could influence docking fees as well as loading and unloading rates of their competitor shipping lines. That, in turn affected general freight rates that could be charged. Macrae Shipping became very profitable during this period.

Richard, now gray haired and in his mid-sixties was tiring, but still held tightly to the reins of the company. He retained a sharp brain but was starting to lose his drive. James, his son started to take more responsibility in the business.

You can connect with me on:

⊕ https://www.richarddross.com

⨍ https://www.facebook.com/RichardDRoss.Author

Subscribe to my newsletter:

✉ https://www.richarddross.com

Also by Richard D Ross

The James Macrae Thriller – Book 2
  Eye of the Hybrid Storm

Eye of the Hybrid Storm

James Macrae – CEO of his family's international shipping business, loving father and husband – is about to launch a new company venture. As he and his new business partner cut the ribbon, he is yet to realise that enemies of old are still out there. Watching. Waiting.

Sabotage and industrial espionage soon threaten not only the very existence of his company, but his family – once again. He has to take matters into his own hands to find his hidden enemy before it is too late.

James must fight his way deep into the web of his ruthless enemy to prevent further destruction before their sinister plans can be fully realised.

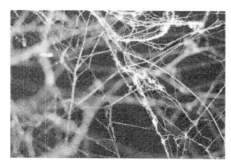

The Cobweb Enigma
A James Macrae Thriller Book 3

Coming Soon!

Printed in Great Britain
by Amazon